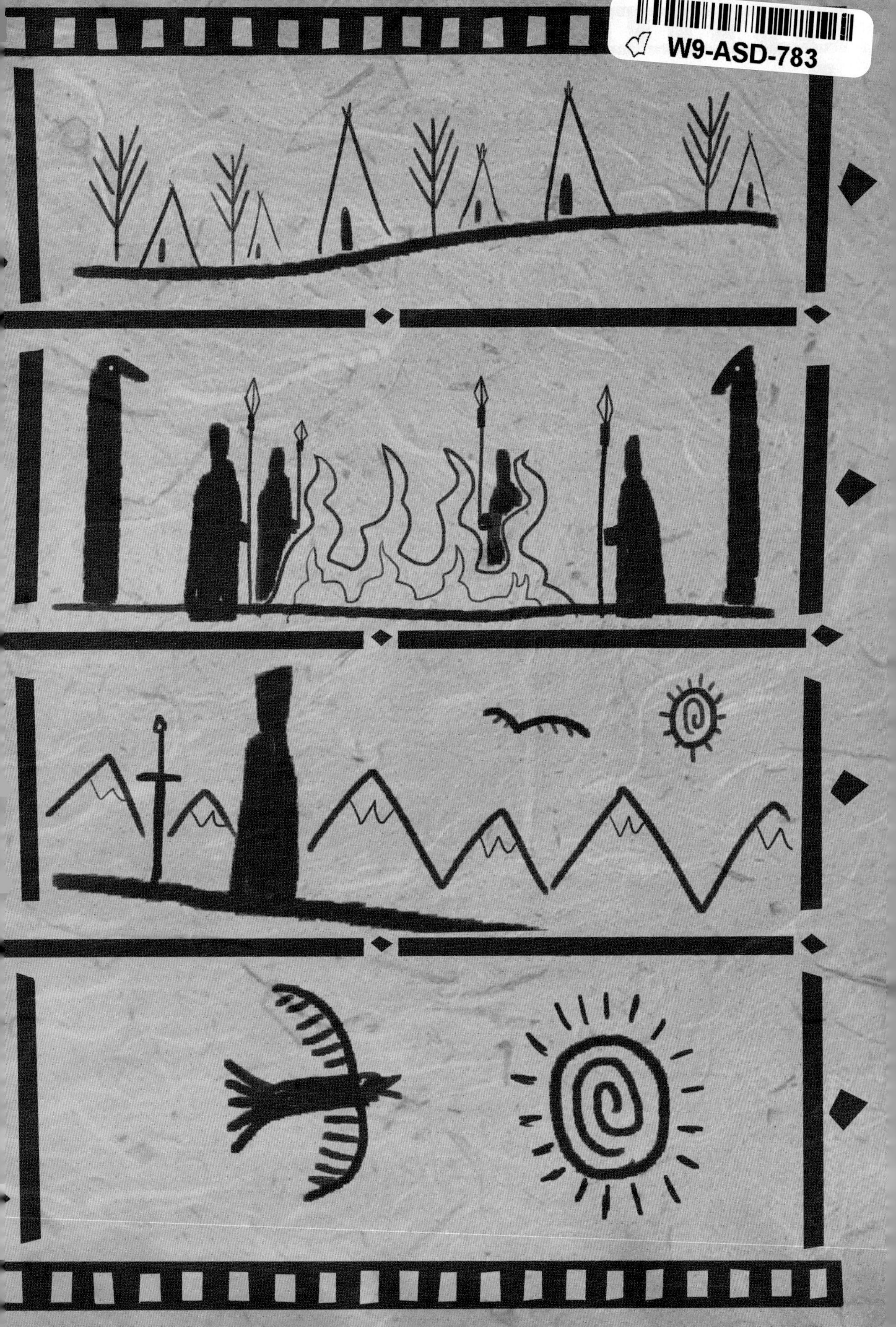

the FLOWER of the WITCH ™

story and art by
ENRICO ORLANDI

translated by
JAMIE RICHARDS

DARK HORSE BOOKS

president and publisher **MIKE RICHARDSON**

editor **KATII O'BRIEN**   assistant editor **JENNY BLENK**

designer **SKYLER WEISSENFLUH**   digital art technician **ALLYSON HALLER**

Neil Hankerson Executive Vice President • **Tom Weddle** Chief Financial Officer • **Randy Stradley** Vice President of Publishing • **Nick McWhorter** Chief Business Development Officer • **Dale LaFountain Chief** Information Officer **Matt Parkinson** Vice President of Marketing • **Vanessa Todd-Holmes** Vice President of Production and Scheduling **Mark Bernardi** Vice President of Book Trade and Digital Sales • **Ken Lizzi** General Counsel • **Dave Marshall** Editor in Chief • **Davey Estrada** Editorial Director • **Chris Warner** Senior Books Editor • **Cary Grazzini** Director of Specialty Projects • **Lia Ribacchi** Art Director • **Matt Dryer** Director of Digital Art and Prepress • **Michael Gombos** Senior Director of Licensed Publications • **Kari Yadro** Director of Custom Programs • **Kari Torson** Director of International Licensing • **Sean Brice** Director of Trade Sales

DarkHorse.com • Facebook.com/DarkHorseComics • Twitter.com/DarkHorseComics
Originally published in Italy by Tunué (www.tunue.com)

Published by Dark Horse Books
A division of Dark Horse Comics LLC
10956 SE Main Street
Milwaukie, OR 97222

Comic Shop Locator Service • comicshoplocator.com

First edition: September 2020
EBook ISBN 978-1-50671-643-5
ISBN 978-1-50671-642-8

1 3 5 7 9 10 8 6 4 2

Printed in China

Library of Congress Cataloging-in-Publication Data

Names: Orlandi, Enrico, author, artist. | Richards, Jamie, translator.
Title: The flower of the witch / story and art by Enrico Orlandi ;
   translated by Jamie Richards.
Other titles: Il Flore della Strega. Italian
Description: First edition. | Milwaukie, OR : Dark Horse Books, 2020. |
   Audience: Grades 4-6 | Summary: "Defeating monsters and saving
   princesses has not been enough, and now he must find the fabled flower
   of the witch. But in his quest, Tami inadvertently sparks a feud between
   the villagers who shelter him and the demon Yabra! And when the conflict
   comes to a head, Tami will have to choose between proving himself as a
   man and protecting the villagers he has come to love."-- Provided by
   publisher.
Identifiers: LCCN 2020004863 (print) | LCCN 2020004864 (ebook) | ISBN
   9781506716428 (paperback) | ISBN 9781506716435 (ebook)
Subjects: LCSH: Graphic novels. | CYAC: Graphic novels. | Fantasy. | Quests
   (Expeditions)--Fiction. | Coming of age--Fiction. | Identity--Fiction.
Classification: LCC PZ7.7.O75 Flo 2020 (print) | LCC PZ7.7.O75 (ebook) |
   DDC 741.5/973--dc23
LC record available at https://lccn.loc.gov/2020004863
LC ebook record available at https://lccn.loc.gov/2020004864

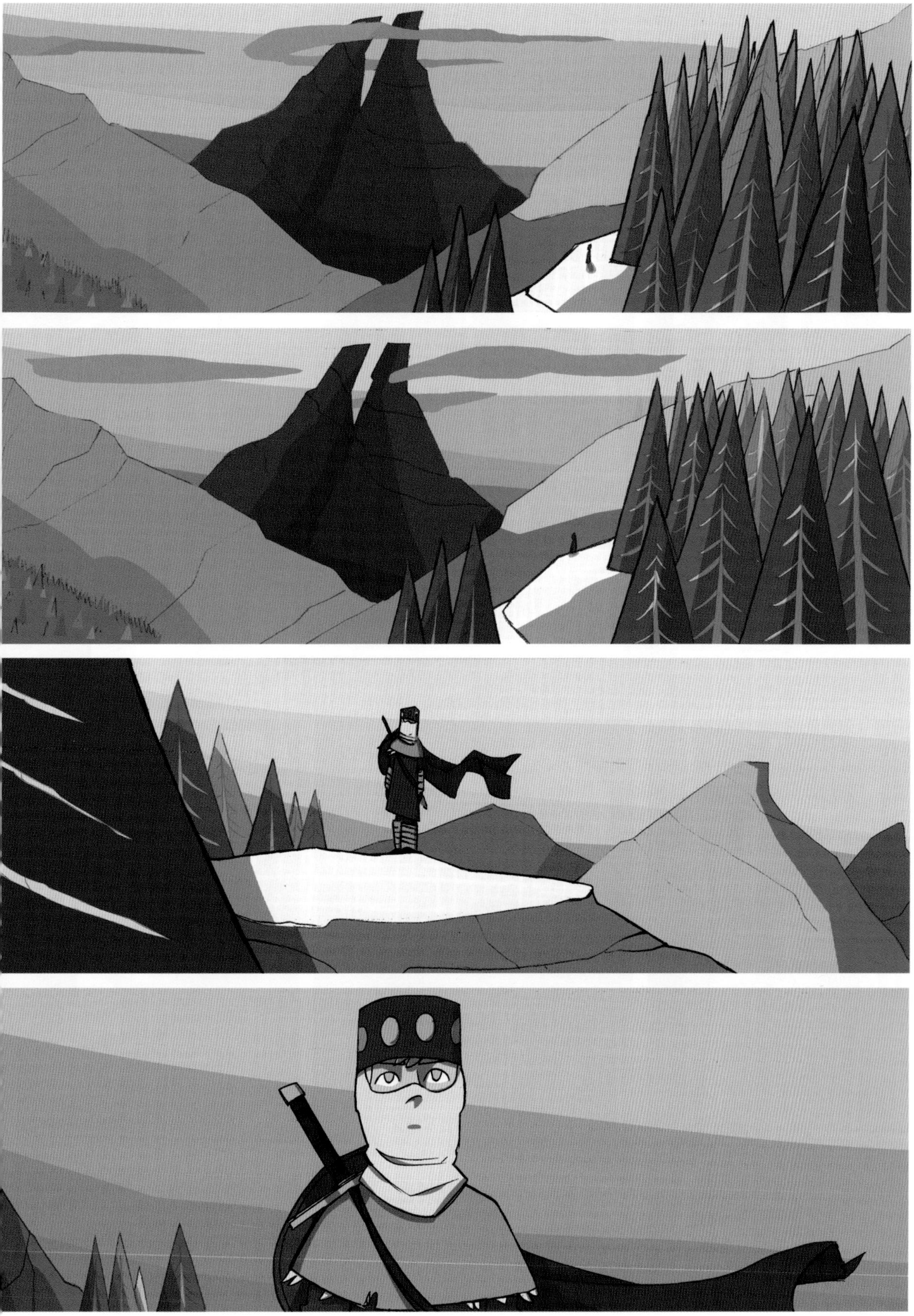

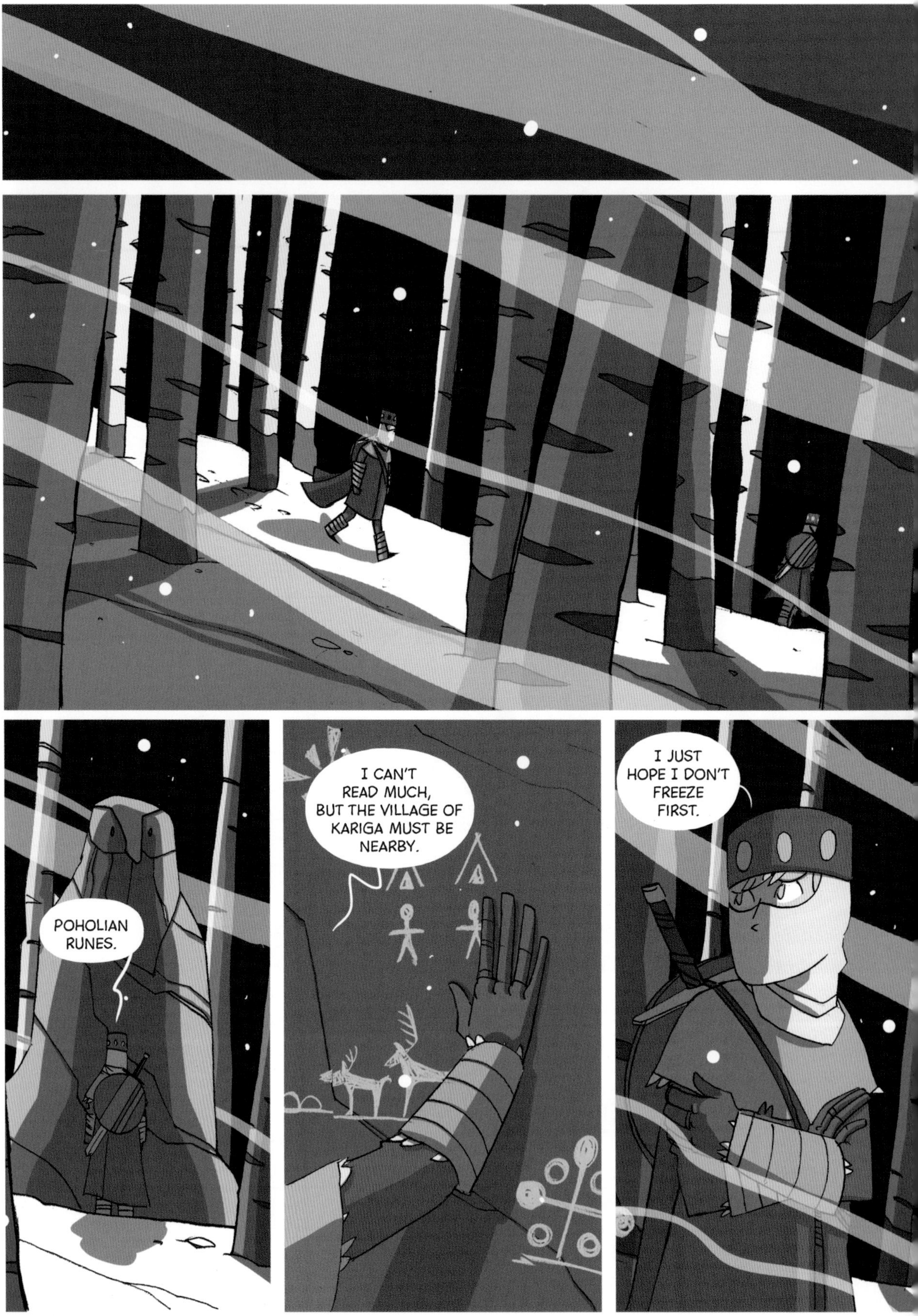
POHOLIAN RUNES.
I CAN'T READ MUCH, BUT THE VILLAGE OF KARIGA MUST BE NEARBY.
I JUST HOPE I DON'T FREEZE FIRST.

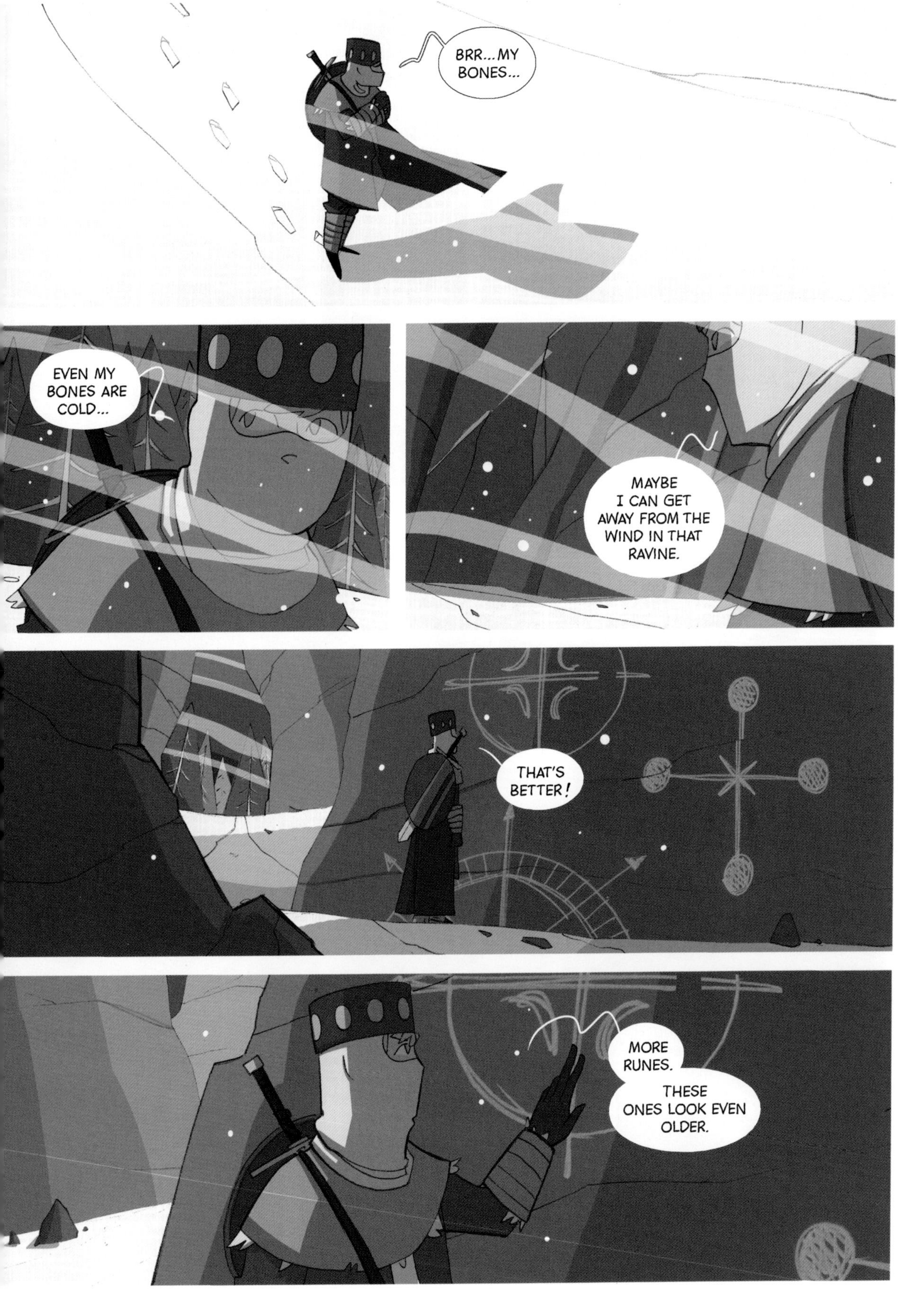
BRR... MY BONES...
EVEN MY BONES ARE COLD...
MAYBE I CAN GET AWAY FROM THE WIND IN THAT RAVINE.
THAT'S BETTER!
MORE RUNES.
THESE ONES LOOK EVEN OLDER.

THEY'RE EVERY-WHERE...

"BORDER."

"DO NOT PASS."

"RUN."

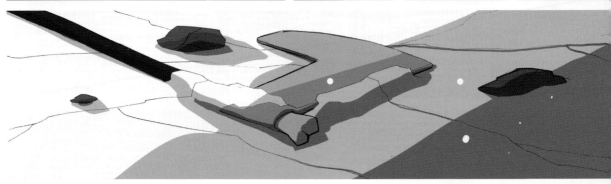

CLOSE. THAT ONE MEANS "FLEE."

I WROTE IT MYSELF, WHEN I STILL HAD HANDS.

THE WHEEL OF FATE HAS SPUN BADLY FOR YOU.

THE DEMON *RUTU* STALKS THIS RAVINE, AND PREYS ON ANY WHO ENTER.

IT WAS MY LOT, AND SEEMS IT WILL BE YOURS, TOO.

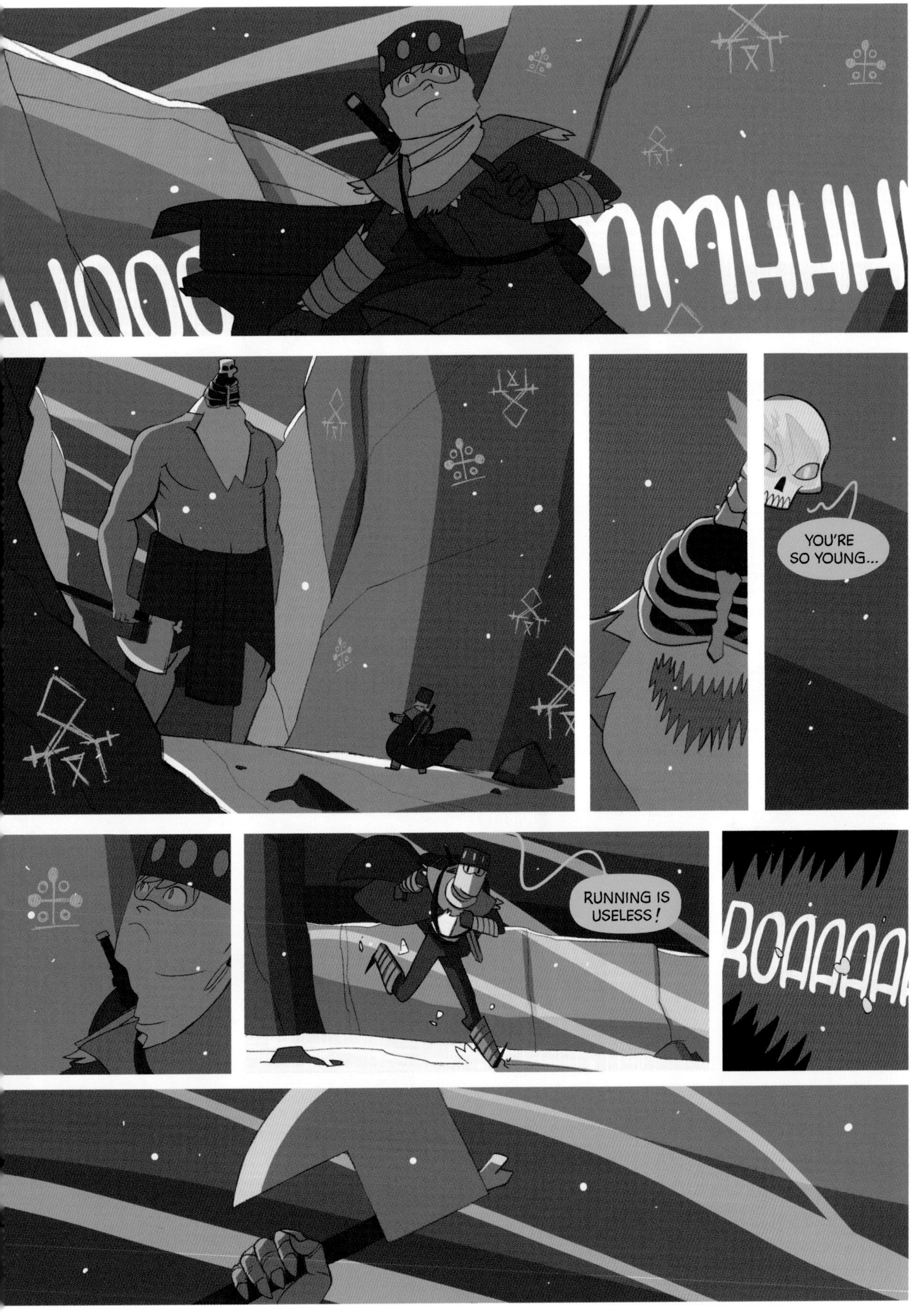
WOOO
NMHHHH
YOU'RE SO YOUNG...
RUNNING IS USELESS!
ROAAAAA

IF I CAN'T RUN...

ALL RIGHT...

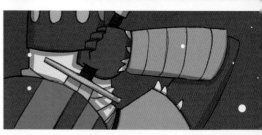

...THEN I'LL FIGHT!

DODGE RIGHT!

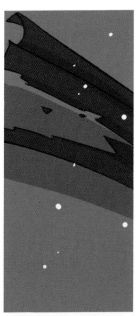

ᚾᚠᚺᛗ
ᚦᚢᚷᛉᛁ

WHY HELP ME?

DON'T YOU SERVE RUTU?

YES. BUT BEFORE THAT, I WAS HIS VICTIM JUST LIKE YOU.

HE INSULTS ME BY USING ME AS A MOUTH-PIECE.

AND A HAT.

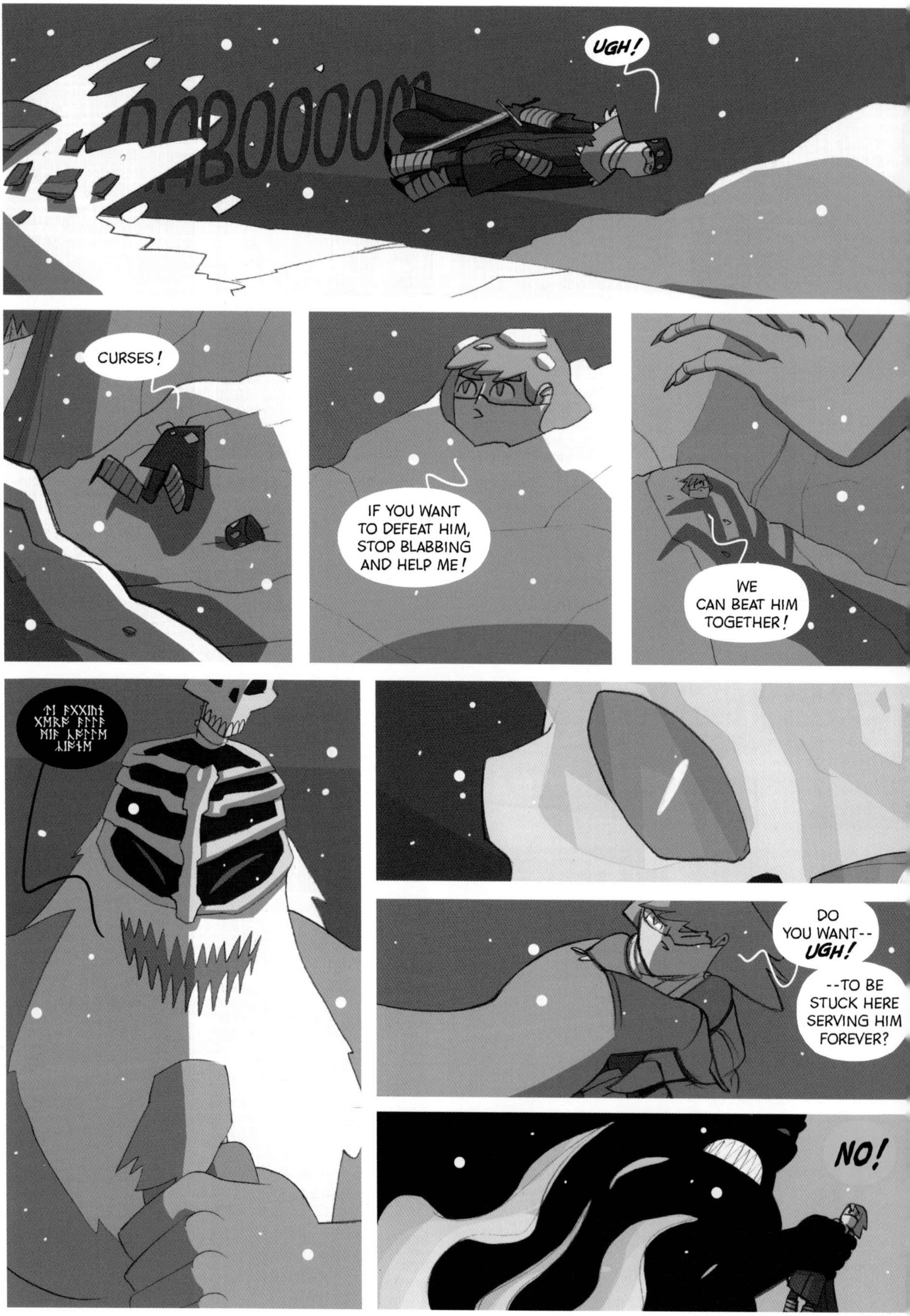

UGH!
CURSES!
IF YOU WANT TO DEFEAT HIM, STOP BLABBING AND HELP ME!
WE CAN BEAT HIM TOGETHER!
DO YOU WANT-- UGH!
--TO BE STUCK HERE SERVING HIM FOREVER?
NO!

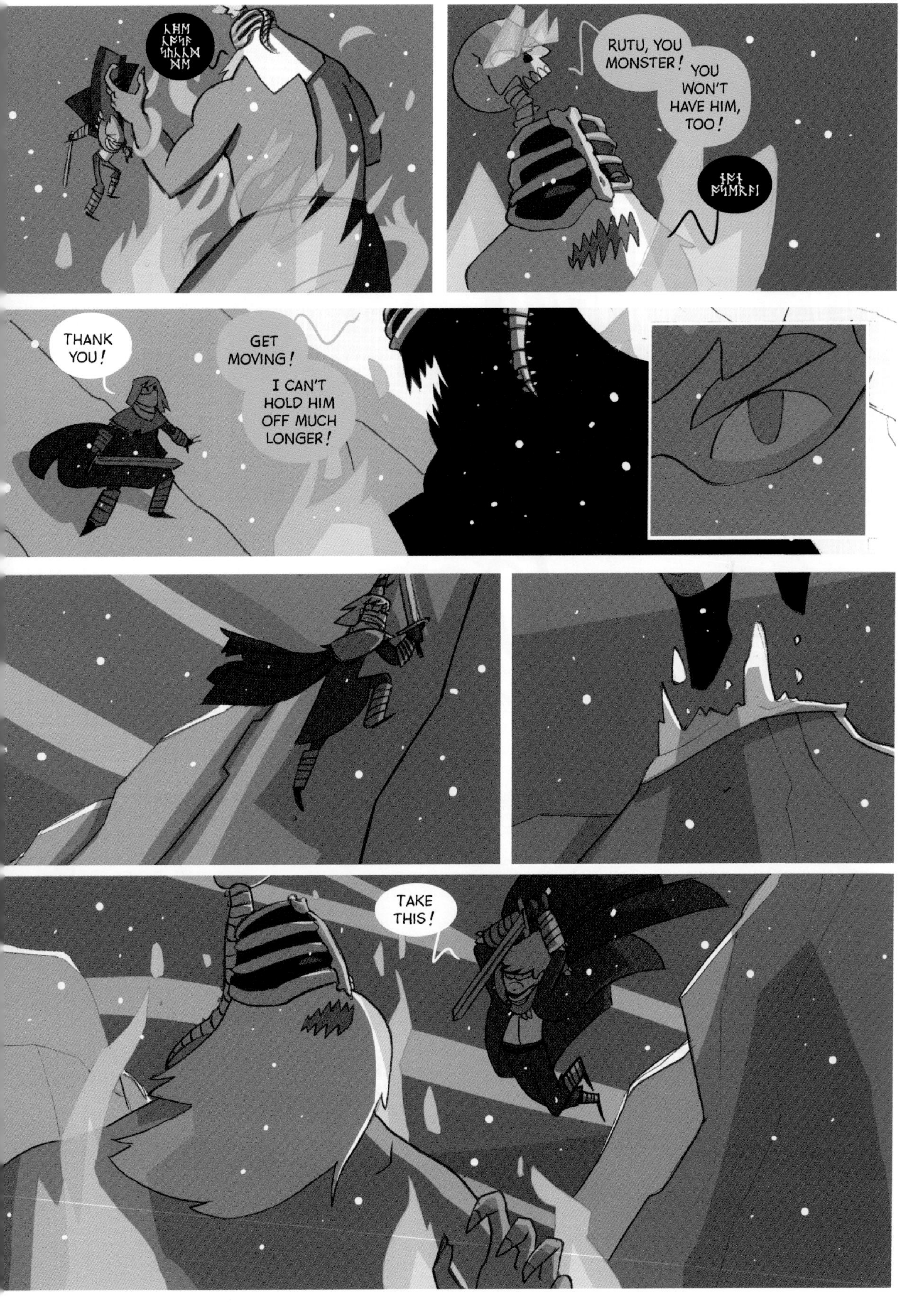

RUTU, YOU MONSTER!
YOU WON'T HAVE HIM, TOO!
THANK YOU!
GET MOVING!
I CAN'T HOLD HIM OFF MUCH LONGER!
TAKE THIS!

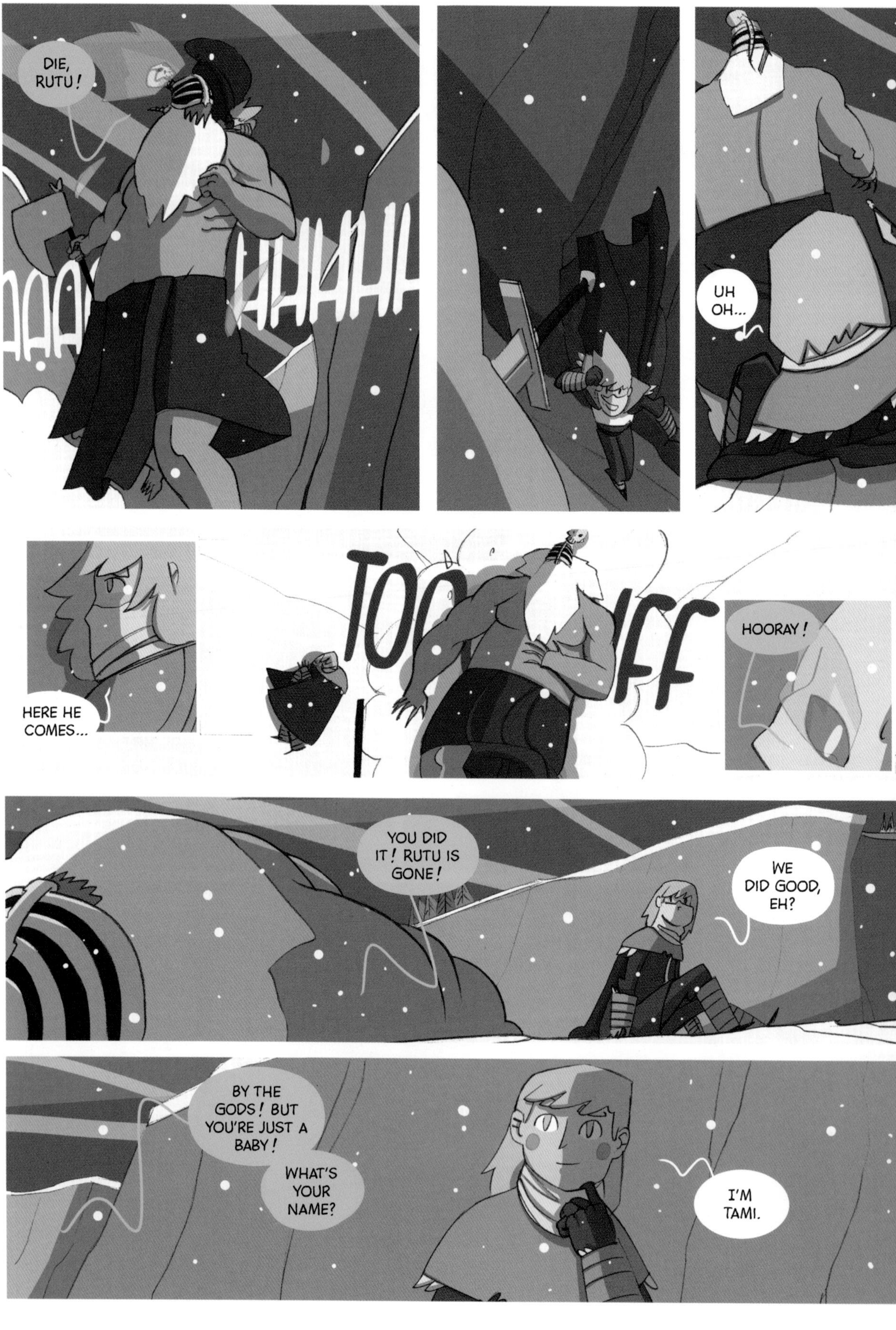
DIE, RUTU!
AAAAHHHHHH
UH OH...
HERE HE COMES...
HOORAY!
YOU DID IT! RUTU IS GONE!
WE DID GOOD, EH?
BY THE GODS! BUT YOU'RE JUST A BABY!
WHAT'S YOUR NAME?
I'M TAMI.

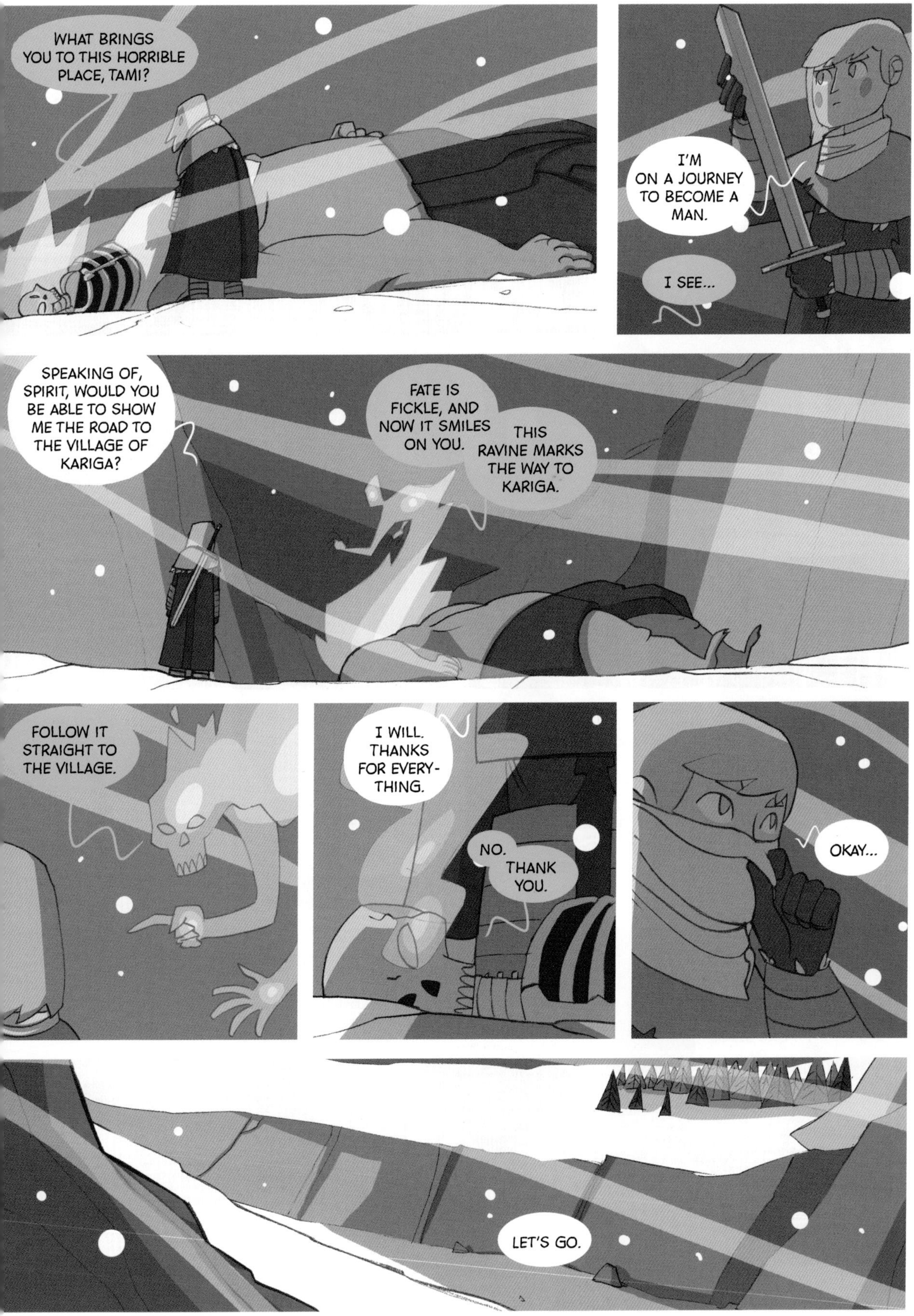
WHAT BRINGS YOU TO THIS HORRIBLE PLACE, TAMI?
I'M ON A JOURNEY TO BECOME A MAN.
I SEE...
SPEAKING OF, SPIRIT, WOULD YOU BE ABLE TO SHOW ME THE ROAD TO THE VILLAGE OF KARIGA?
FATE IS FICKLE, AND NOW IT SMILES ON YOU.
THIS RAVINE MARKS THE WAY TO KARIGA.
FOLLOW IT STRAIGHT TO THE VILLAGE.
I WILL. THANKS FOR EVERYTHING.
NO. THANK YOU.
OKAY...
LET'S GO.

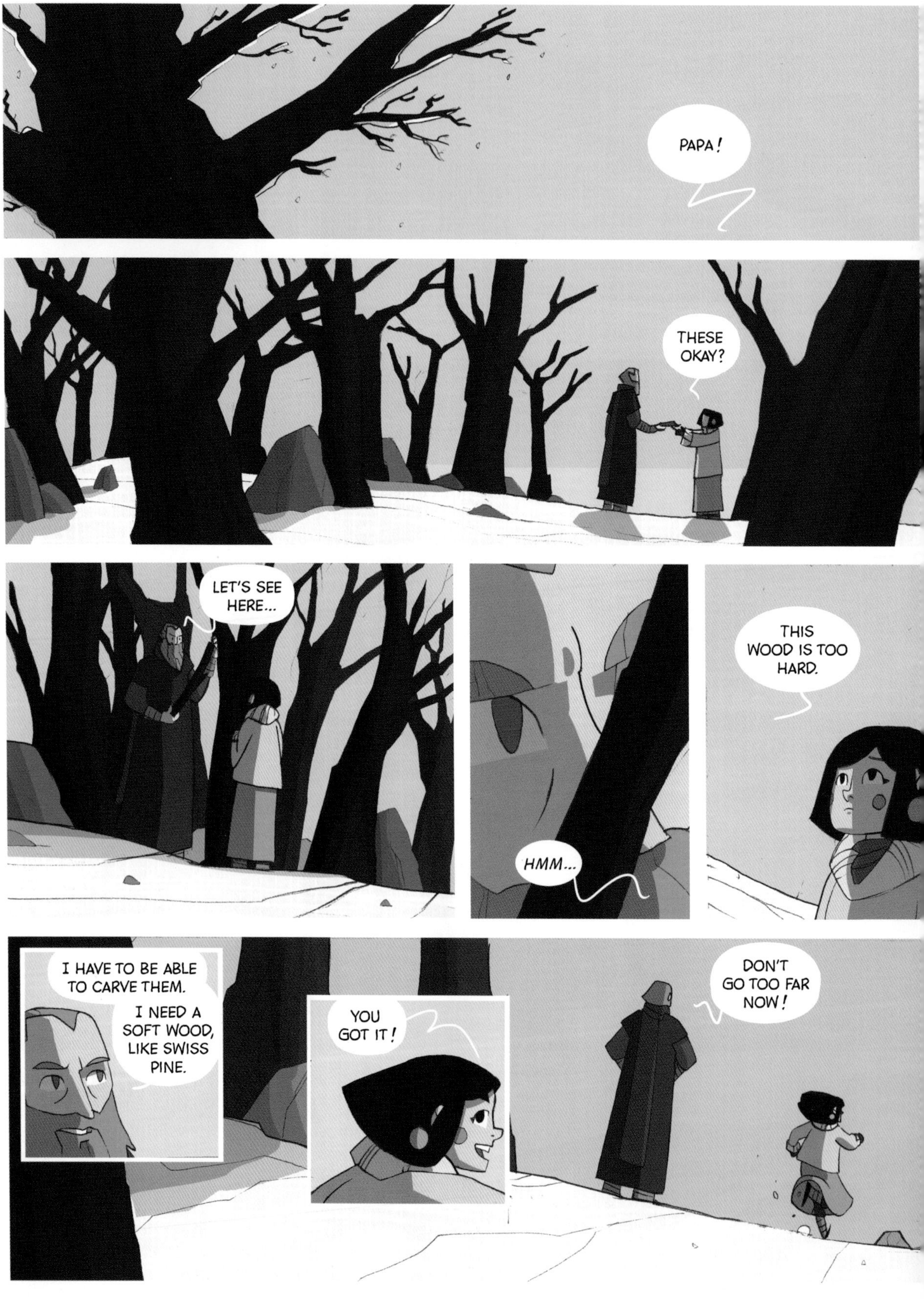
PAPA!
THESE OKAY?
LET'S SEE HERE...
HMM...
THIS WOOD IS TOO HARD.
I HAVE TO BE ABLE TO CARVE THEM.
I NEED A SOFT WOOD, LIKE SWISS PINE.
YOU GOT IT!
DON'T GO TOO FAR NOW!

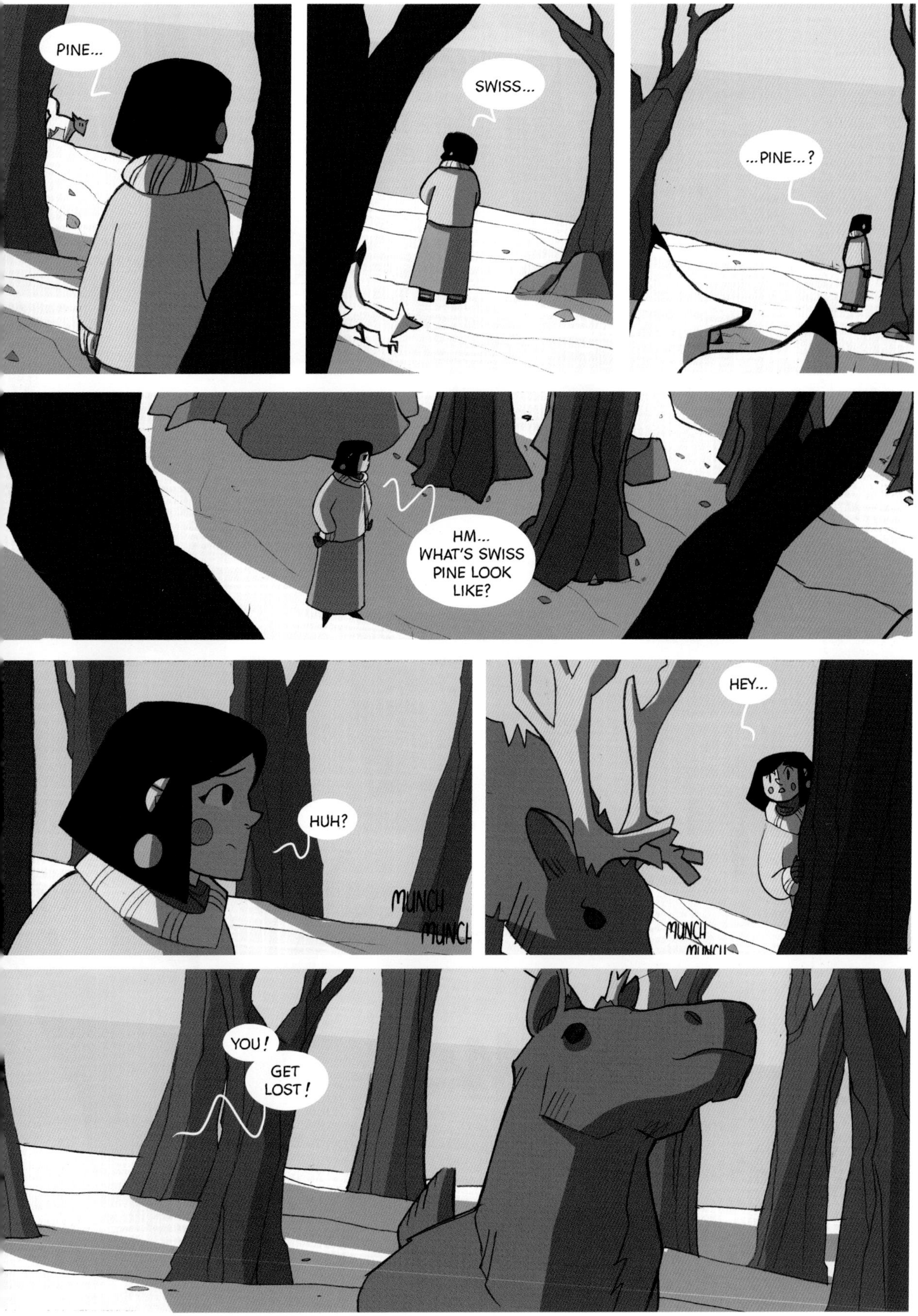
PINE...
SWISS...
...PINE...?
HM... WHAT'S SWISS PINE LOOK LIKE?
HUH?
MUNCH MUNCH
HEY...
MUNCH MUNCH
YOU!
GET LOST!

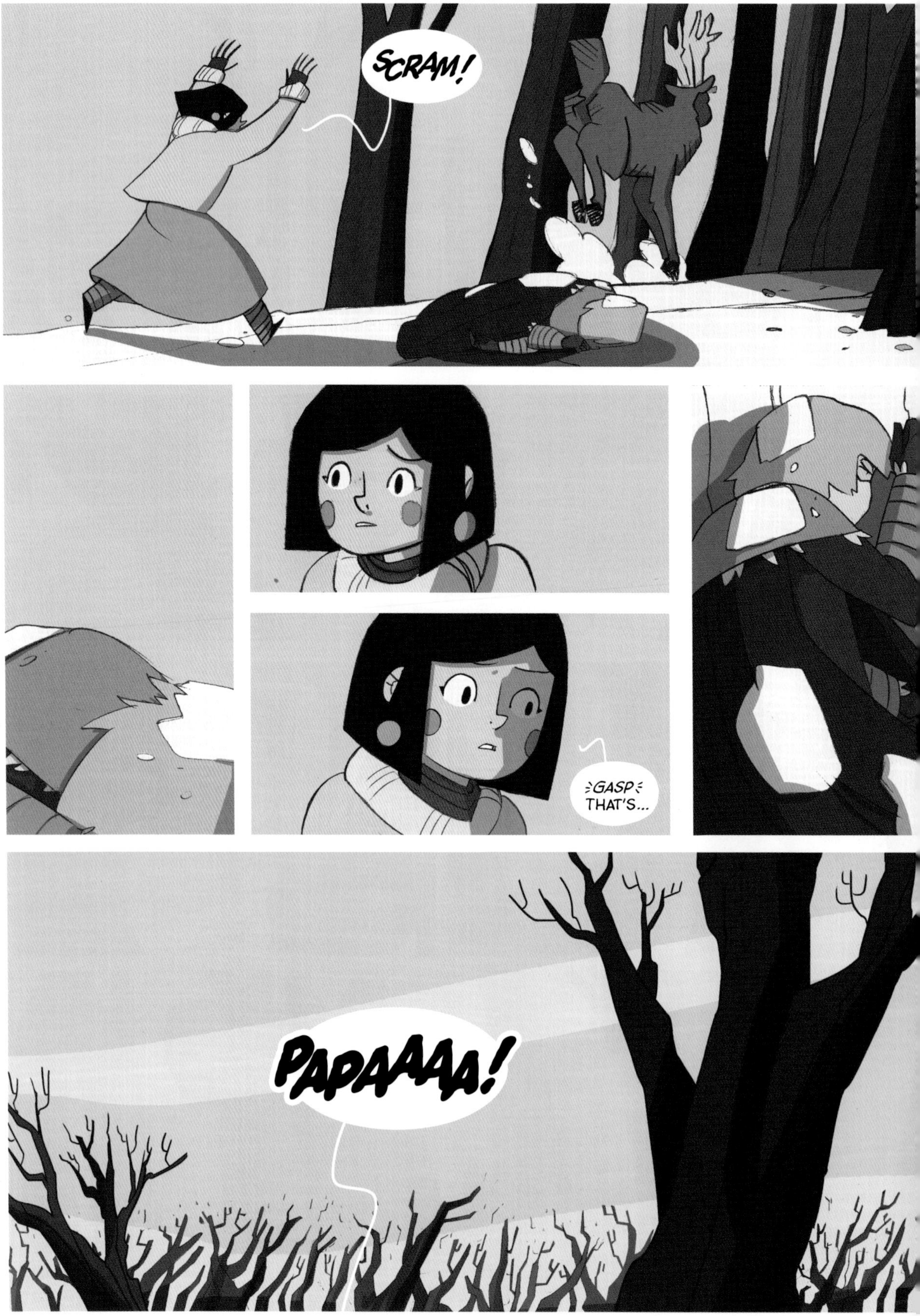
SCRAM!
GASP THAT'S...
PAPAAAA!

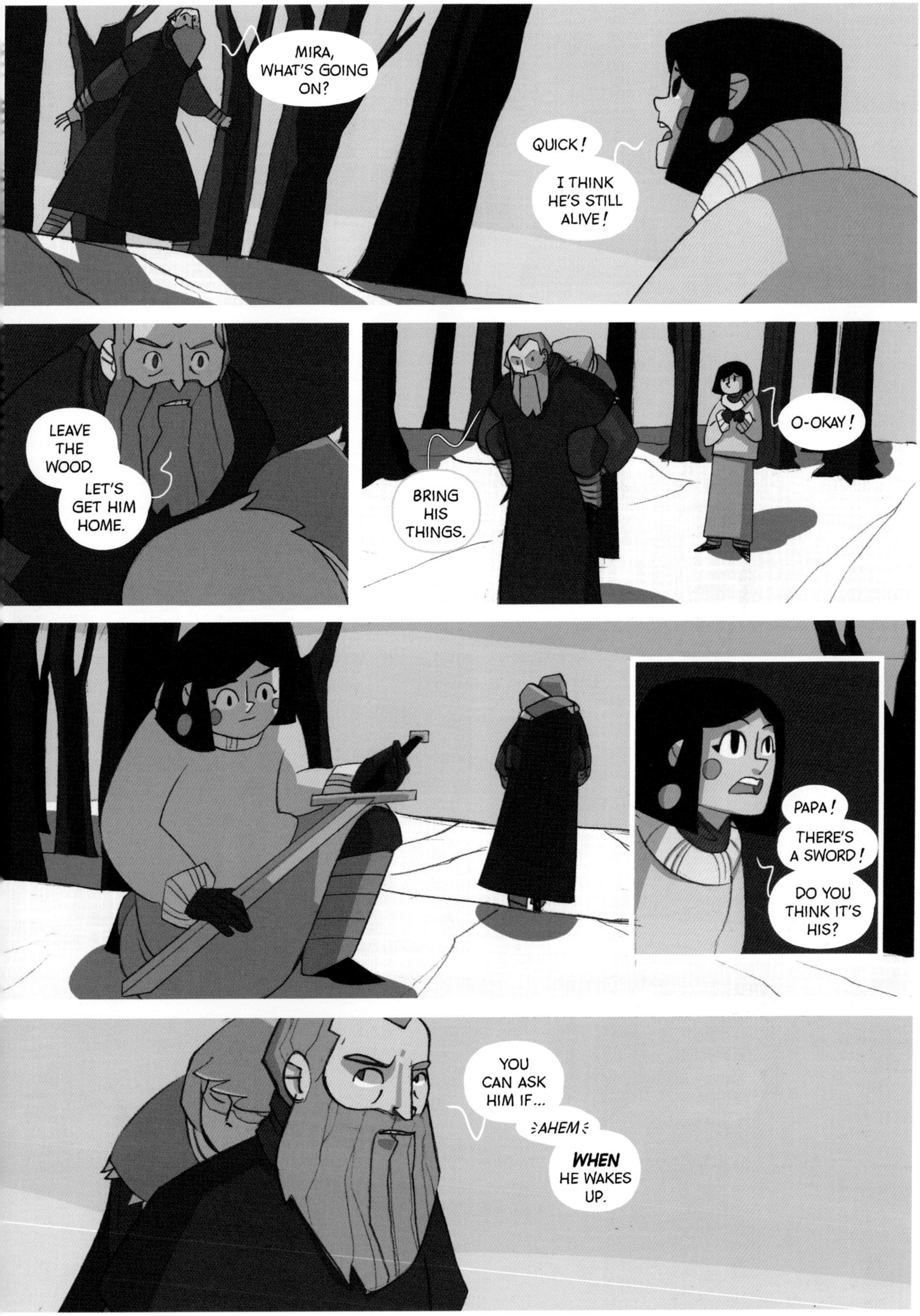
MIRA, WHAT'S GOING ON?
QUICK!
I THINK HE'S STILL ALIVE!
LEAVE THE WOOD.
LET'S GET HIM HOME.
BRING HIS THINGS.
O-OKAY!
PAPA!
THERE'S A SWORD!
DO YOU THINK IT'S HIS?
YOU CAN ASK HIM IF...
AHEM
WHEN HE WAKES UP.

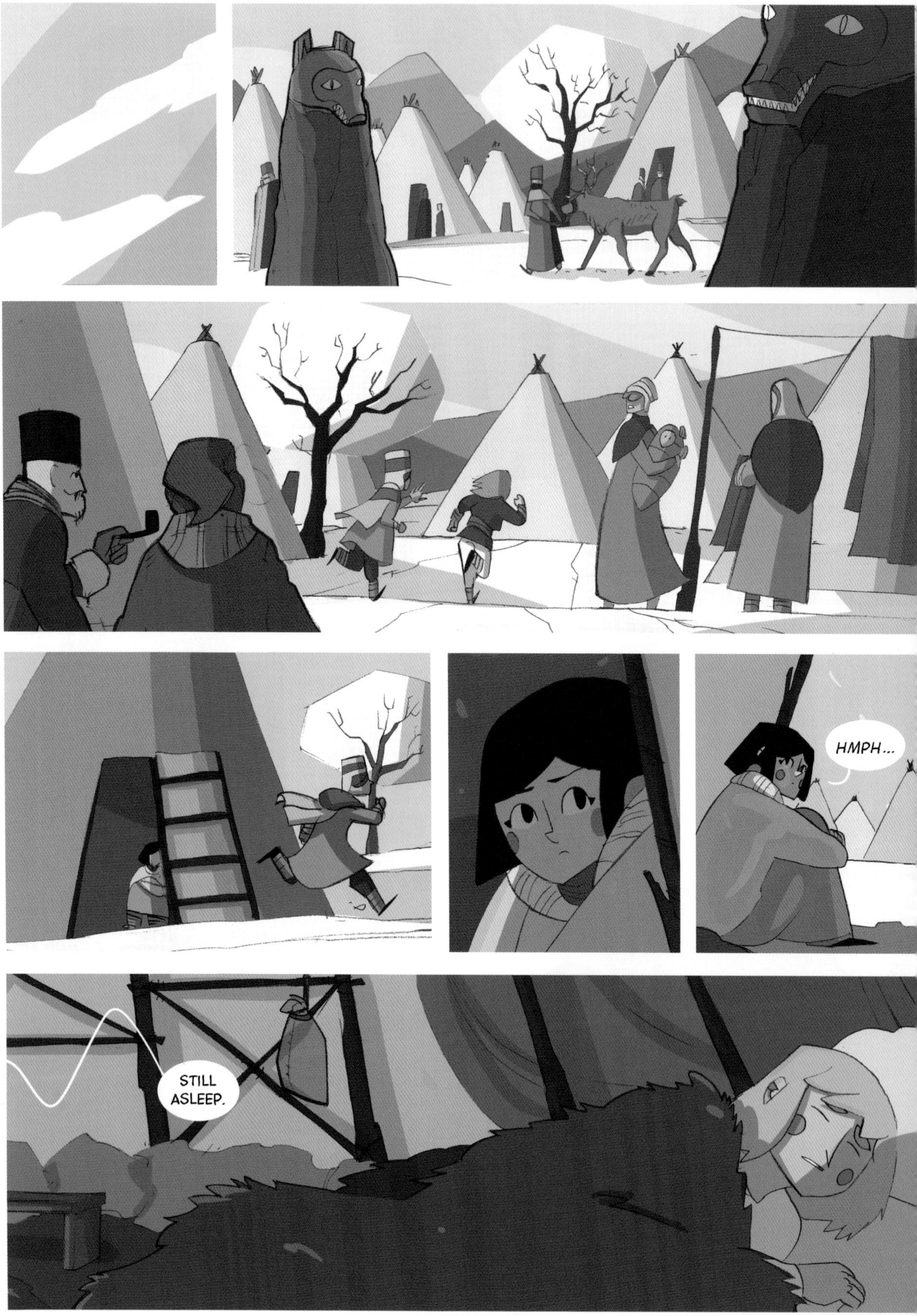
HMPH...
STILL ASLEEP.

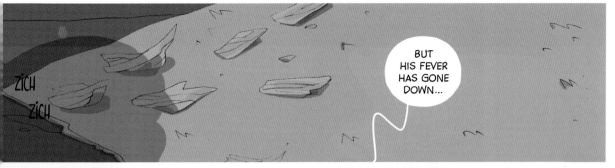

ZICH

ZICH

BUT HIS FEVER HAS GONE DOWN...

ZICH ZICH

ZICH ZICH

THAT'S IT!

IF HE WON'T WAKE UP ON HIS OWN, I'LL DO IT *FOR* HIM!

UNH...

HUH?

WH... WHERE?

FINALLY!

WH-WHO?

DON'T MOVE! I'LL GO GET PAPA AND MAMA!

WHAT?

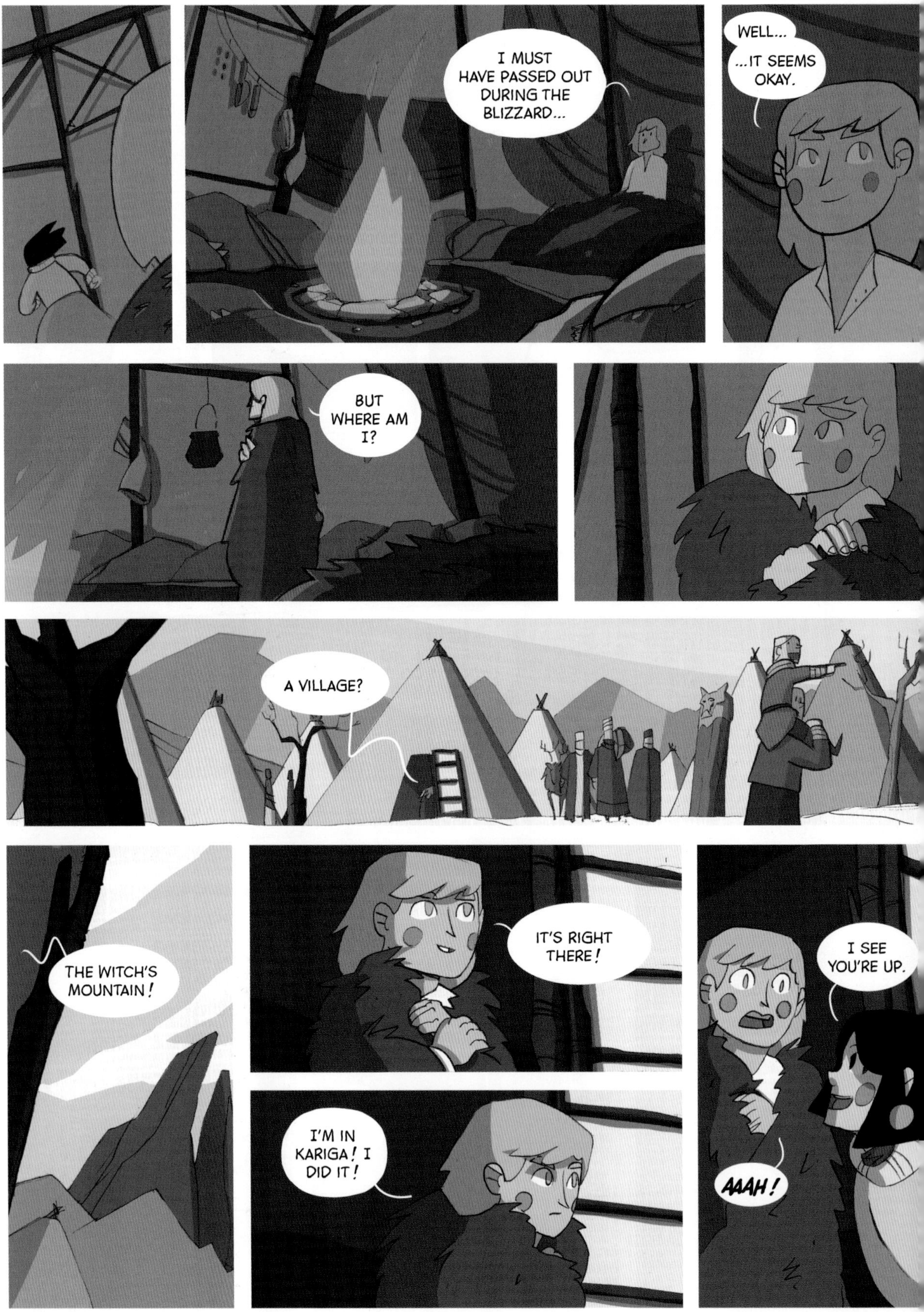
I MUST HAVE PASSED OUT DURING THE BLIZZARD...
WELL...
...IT SEEMS OKAY.
BUT WHERE AM I?
A VILLAGE?
THE WITCH'S MOUNTAIN!
IT'S RIGHT THERE!
I'M IN KARIGA! I DID IT!
I SEE YOU'RE UP.
AAAH!

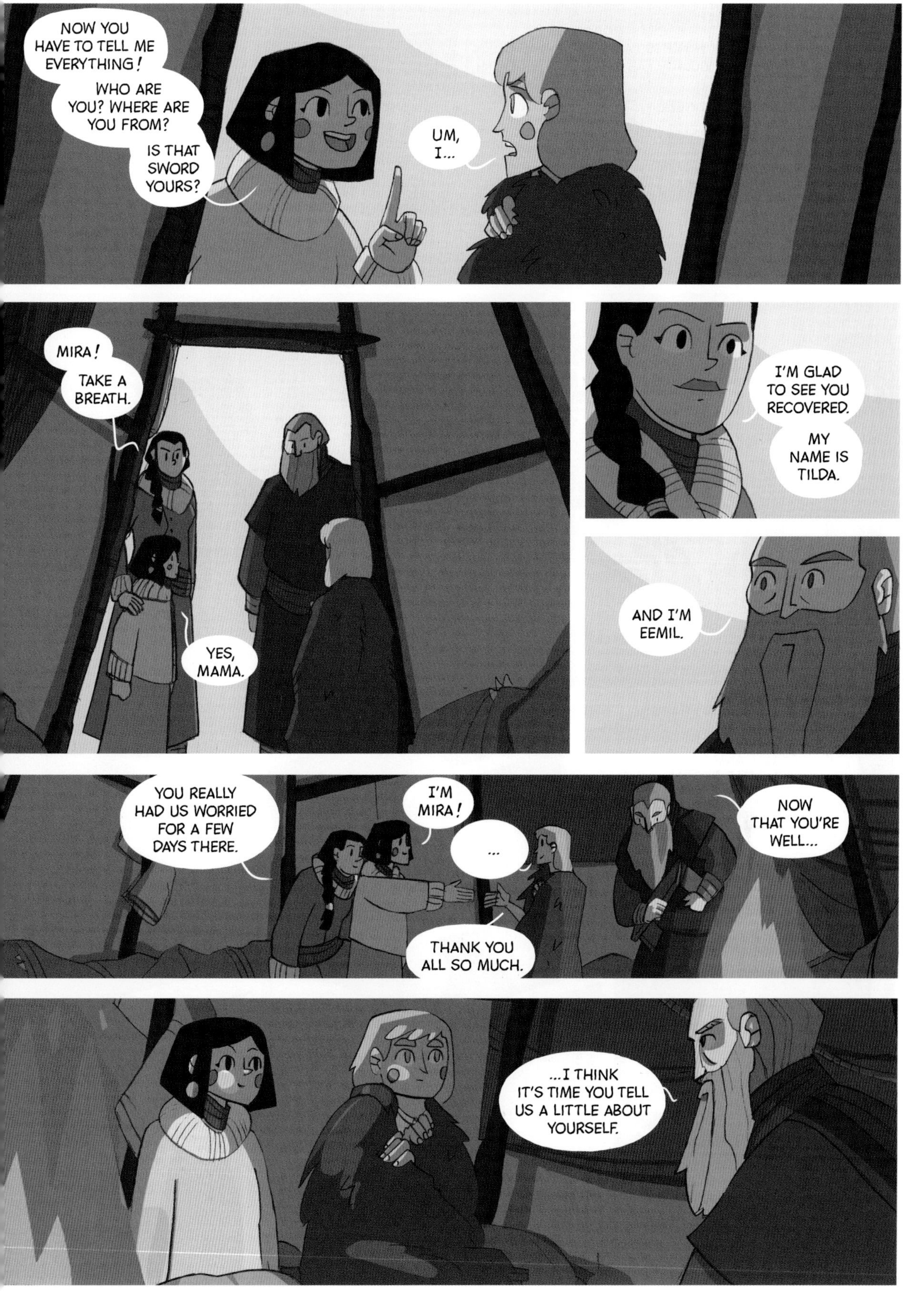
NOW YOU HAVE TO TELL ME EVERYTHING!
WHO ARE YOU? WHERE ARE YOU FROM?
IS THAT SWORD YOURS?
UM, I...
MIRA!
TAKE A BREATH.
YES, MAMA.
I'M GLAD TO SEE YOU RECOVERED.
MY NAME IS TILDA.
AND I'M EEMIL.
YOU REALLY HAD US WORRIED FOR A FEW DAYS THERE.
I'M MIRA!
...
THANK YOU ALL SO MUCH.
NOW THAT YOU'RE WELL...
...I THINK IT'S TIME YOU TELL US A LITTLE ABOUT YOURSELF.

"MY NAME IS TAMI, AND I WAS BORN IN A VILLAGE FAR AWAY, IN THE SOUTH."

"IN MY VILLAGE, WHEN A BOY REACHES TEN YEARS OF AGE, HE HAS TO LEAVE HOME ON A JOURNEY."

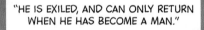

"HE IS EXILED, AND CAN ONLY RETURN WHEN HE HAS BECOME A MAN."

WHAT ABOUT GIRLS?

UM, WELL, THEY HAVE ANOTHER TRIAL THEY HAVE TO GO THROUGH.

TO PROVE THEMSELVES WOMEN.

"WHERE WAS I? OH, YES..."

"THE WORST PART ISN'T THE HUNGER..."

"...OR THE COLD..."

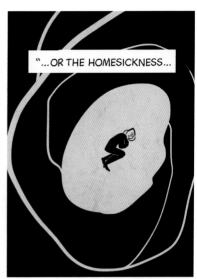

"...OR THE HOMESICKNESS..."

"THE HARDEST PART IS THAT WE ARE NEVER TOLD *HOW* TO BECOME MEN."

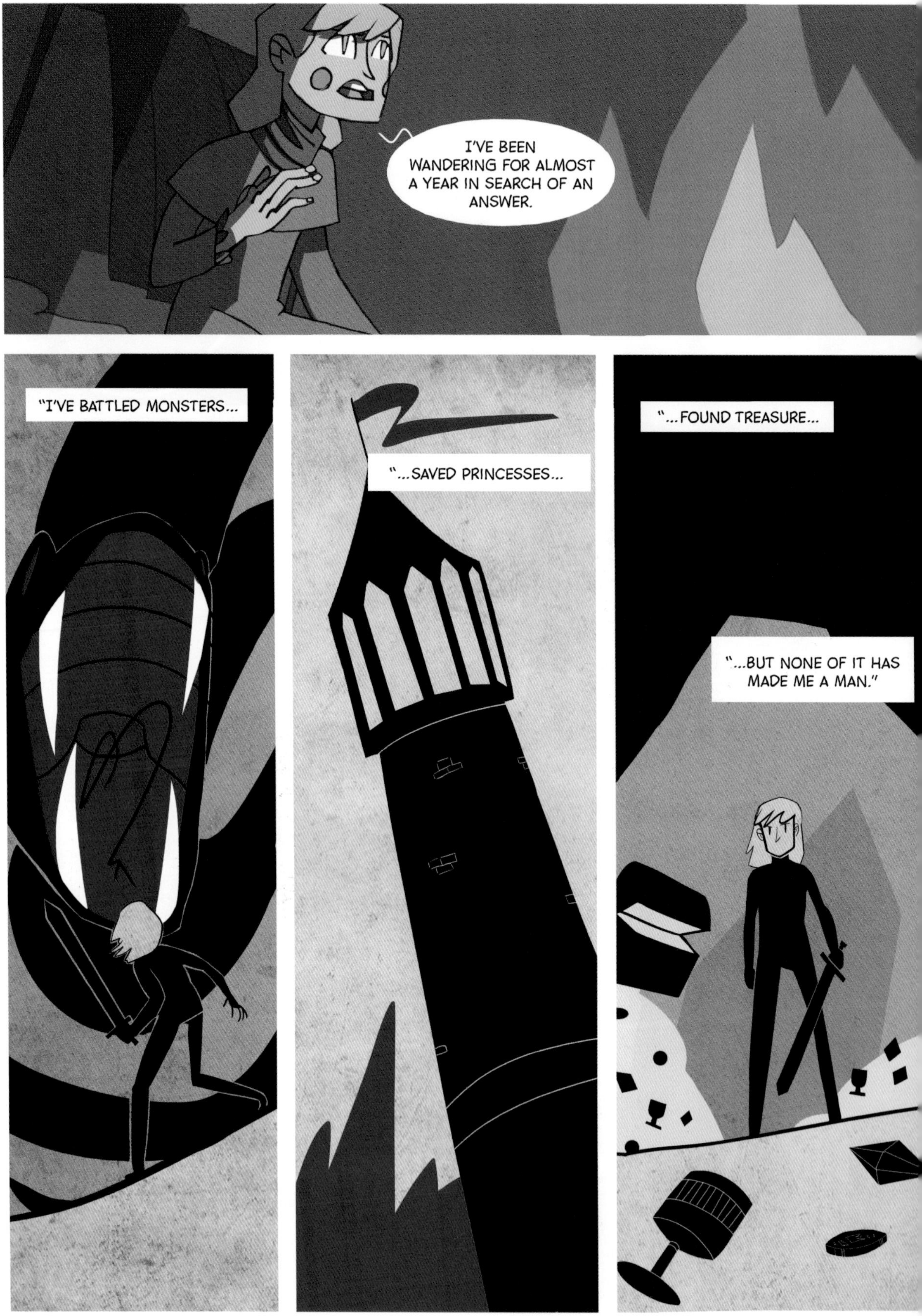
I'VE BEEN WANDERING FOR ALMOST A YEAR IN SEARCH OF AN ANSWER.
"I'VE BATTLED MONSTERS...
"...SAVED PRINCESSES...
"...FOUND TREASURE...
"...BUT NONE OF IT HAS MADE ME A MAN."

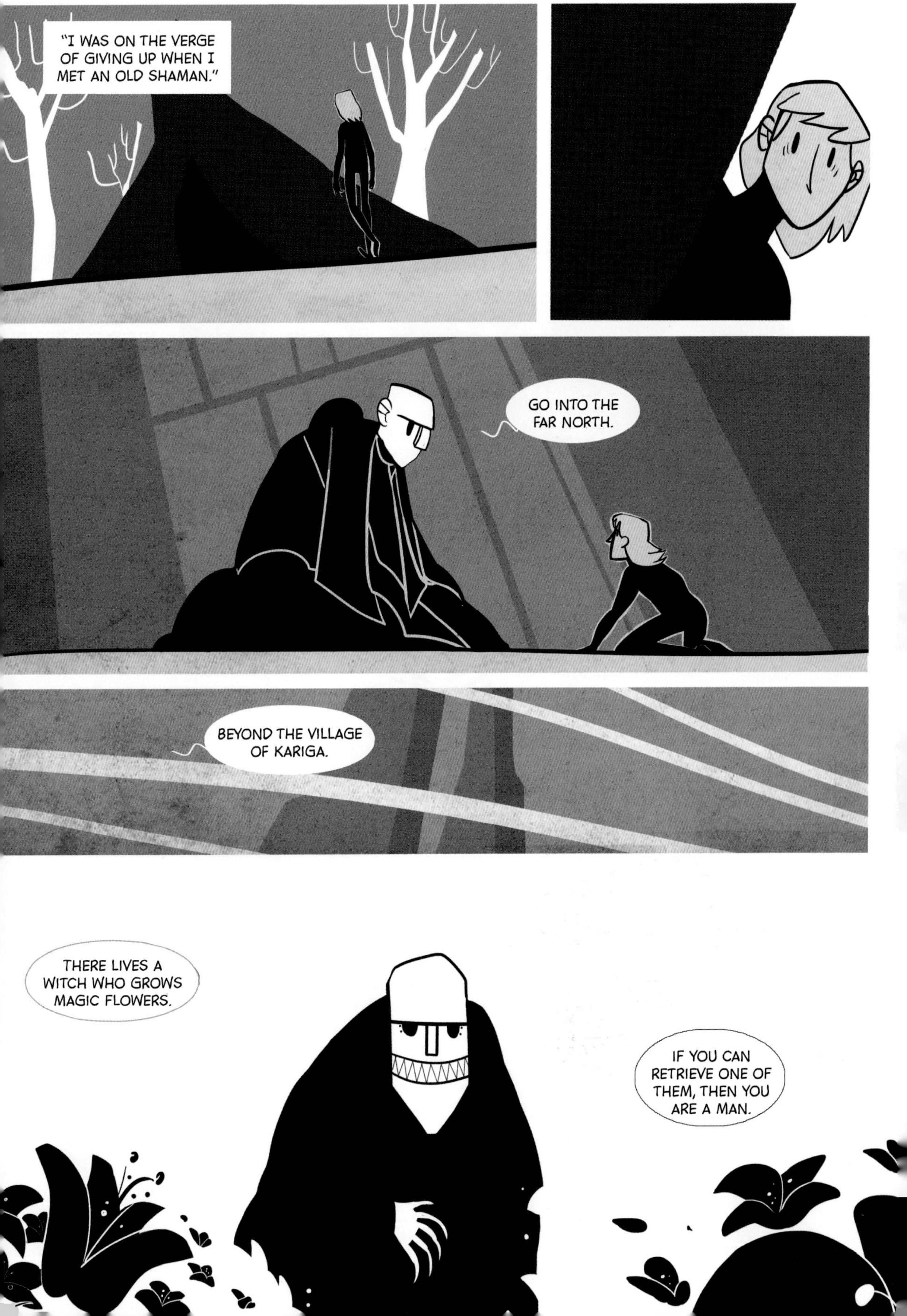
"I WAS ON THE VERGE OF GIVING UP WHEN I MET AN OLD SHAMAN."
GO INTO THE FAR NORTH.
BEYOND THE VILLAGE OF KARIGA.
THERE LIVES A WITCH WHO GROWS MAGIC FLOWERS.
IF YOU CAN RETRIEVE ONE OF THEM, THEN YOU ARE A MAN.

THAT'S WHY I'M HERE.

I REALLY DON'T UNDERSTAND HOW THEY CAN EXPECT SO MUCH FROM A CHILD.

I... WELL...

IT HAS MADE ME STRONG.

YOU MAY BE STRONG, BUT YOU SHOULDN'T HAVE HAD TO ENDURE A BLIZZARD.

ESPECIALLY SO FAR TO THE NORTH...

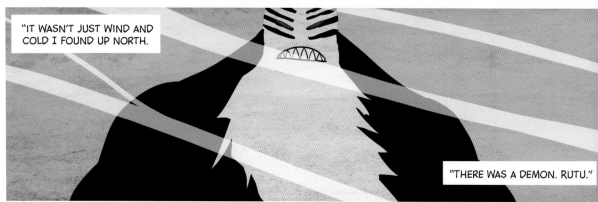

"IT WASN'T JUST WIND AND COLD I FOUND UP NORTH.

"THERE WAS A DEMON. RUTU."

YOU ACTUALLY SAW RUTU?

NO ONE HAS EVER ESCAPED HIM.

I DIDN'T ESCAPE.

I DEFEATED HIM.

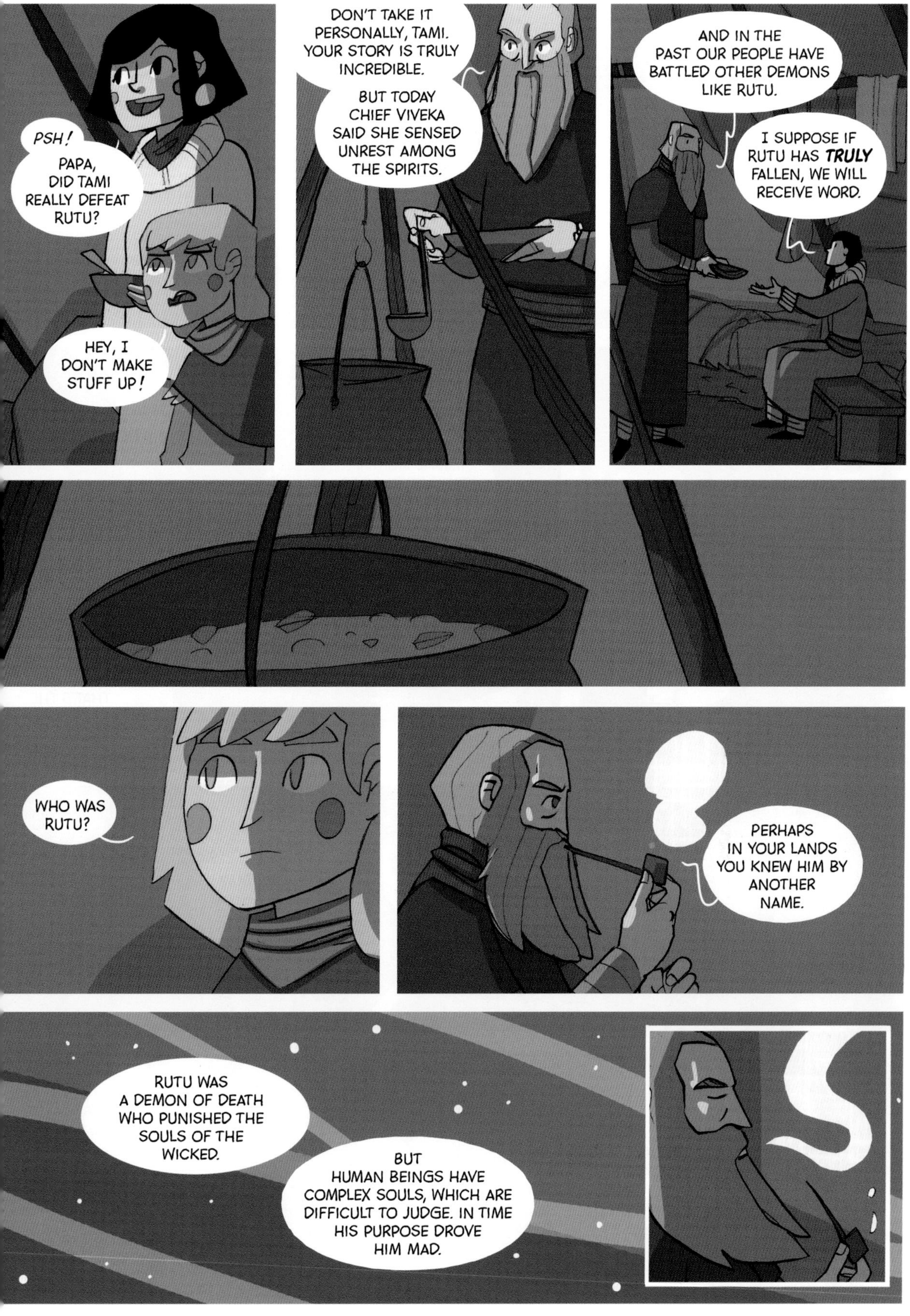
PSH!
PAPA, DID TAMI REALLY DEFEAT RUTU?
HEY, I DON'T MAKE STUFF UP!
DON'T TAKE IT PERSONALLY, TAMI. YOUR STORY IS TRULY INCREDIBLE.
BUT TODAY CHIEF VIVEKA SAID SHE SENSED UNREST AMONG THE SPIRITS.
AND IN THE PAST OUR PEOPLE HAVE BATTLED OTHER DEMONS LIKE RUTU.
I SUPPOSE IF RUTU HAS **TRULY** FALLEN, WE WILL RECEIVE WORD.
WHO WAS RUTU?
PERHAPS IN YOUR LANDS YOU KNEW HIM BY ANOTHER NAME.
RUTU WAS A DEMON OF DEATH WHO PUNISHED THE SOULS OF THE WICKED.
BUT HUMAN BEINGS HAVE COMPLEX SOULS, WHICH ARE DIFFICULT TO JUDGE. IN TIME HIS PURPOSE DROVE HIM MAD.

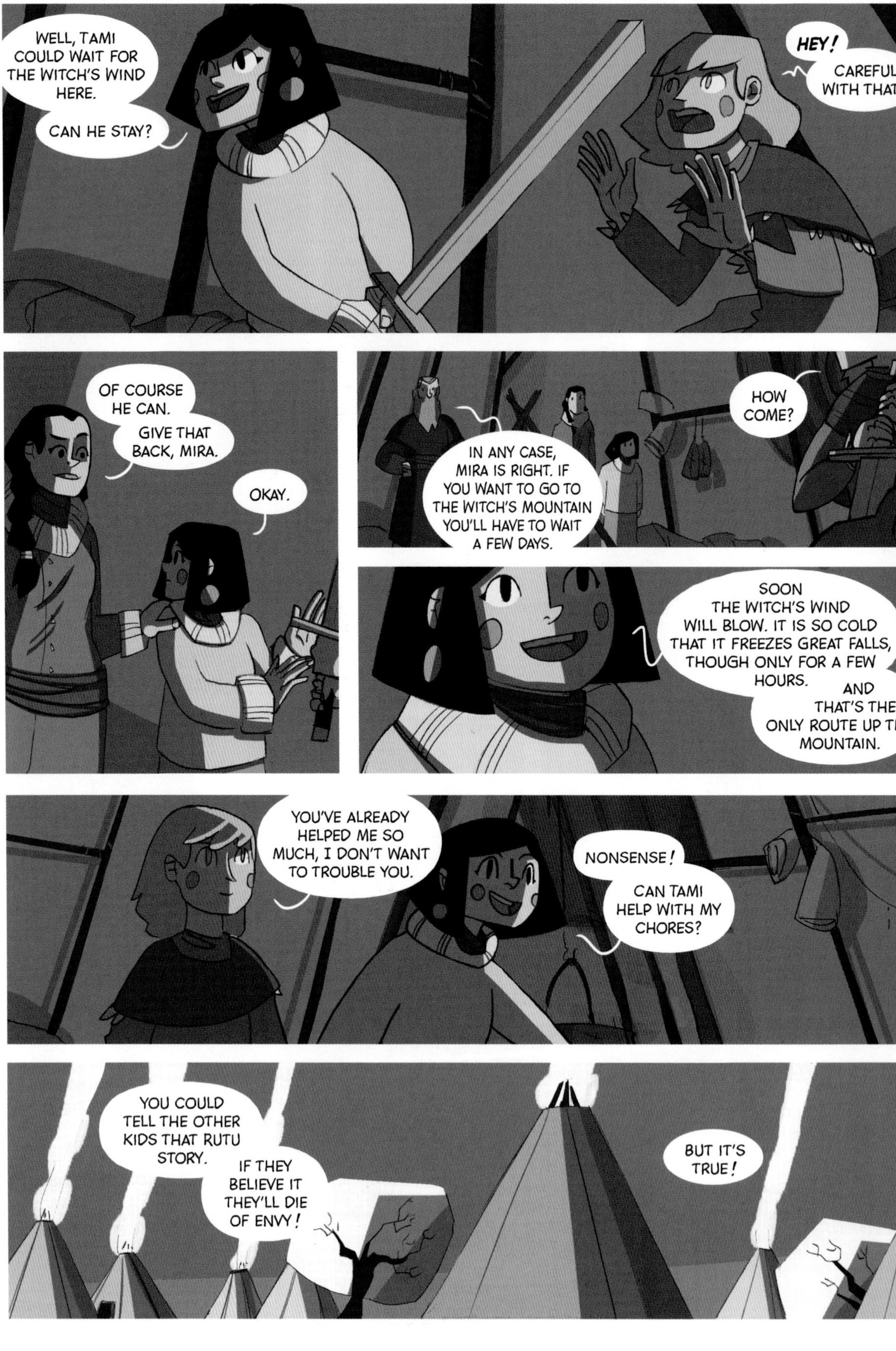

WELL, TAMI COULD WAIT FOR THE WITCH'S WIND HERE.
CAN HE STAY?
HEY!
CAREFUL WITH THAT!
OF COURSE HE CAN.
GIVE THAT BACK, MIRA.
OKAY.
IN ANY CASE, MIRA IS RIGHT. IF YOU WANT TO GO TO THE WITCH'S MOUNTAIN YOU'LL HAVE TO WAIT A FEW DAYS.
HOW COME?
SOON THE WITCH'S WIND WILL BLOW. IT IS SO COLD THAT IT FREEZES GREAT FALLS, THOUGH ONLY FOR A FEW HOURS.
AND THAT'S THE ONLY ROUTE UP THE MOUNTAIN.
YOU'VE ALREADY HELPED ME SO MUCH, I DON'T WANT TO TROUBLE YOU.
NONSENSE!
CAN TAMI HELP WITH MY CHORES?
YOU COULD TELL THE OTHER KIDS THAT RUTU STORY.
IF THEY BELIEVE IT THEY'LL DIE OF ENVY!
BUT IT'S TRUE!

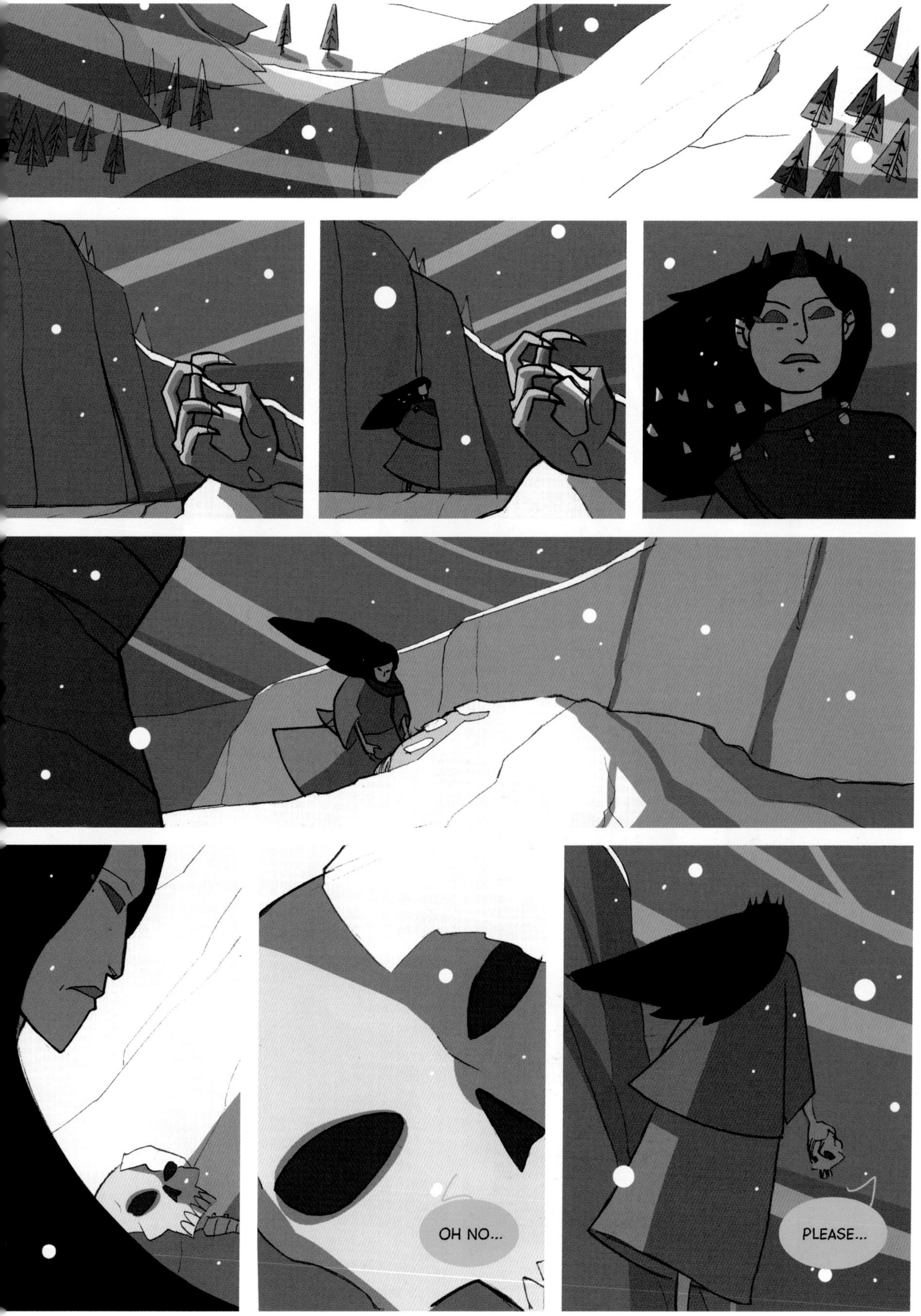
OH NO...
PLEASE...

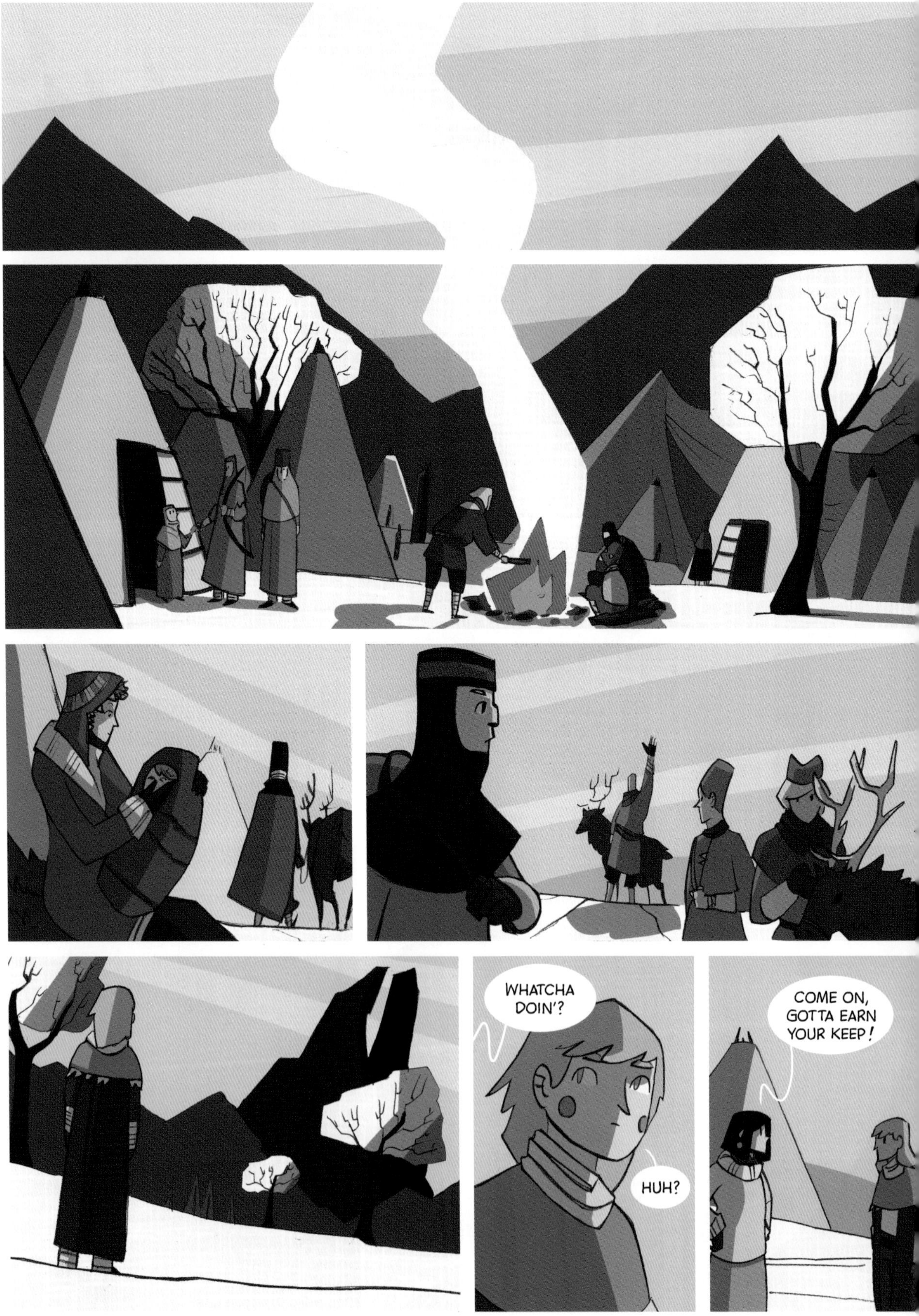
WHATCHA DOIN'?
HUH?
COME ON, GOTTA EARN YOUR KEEP!

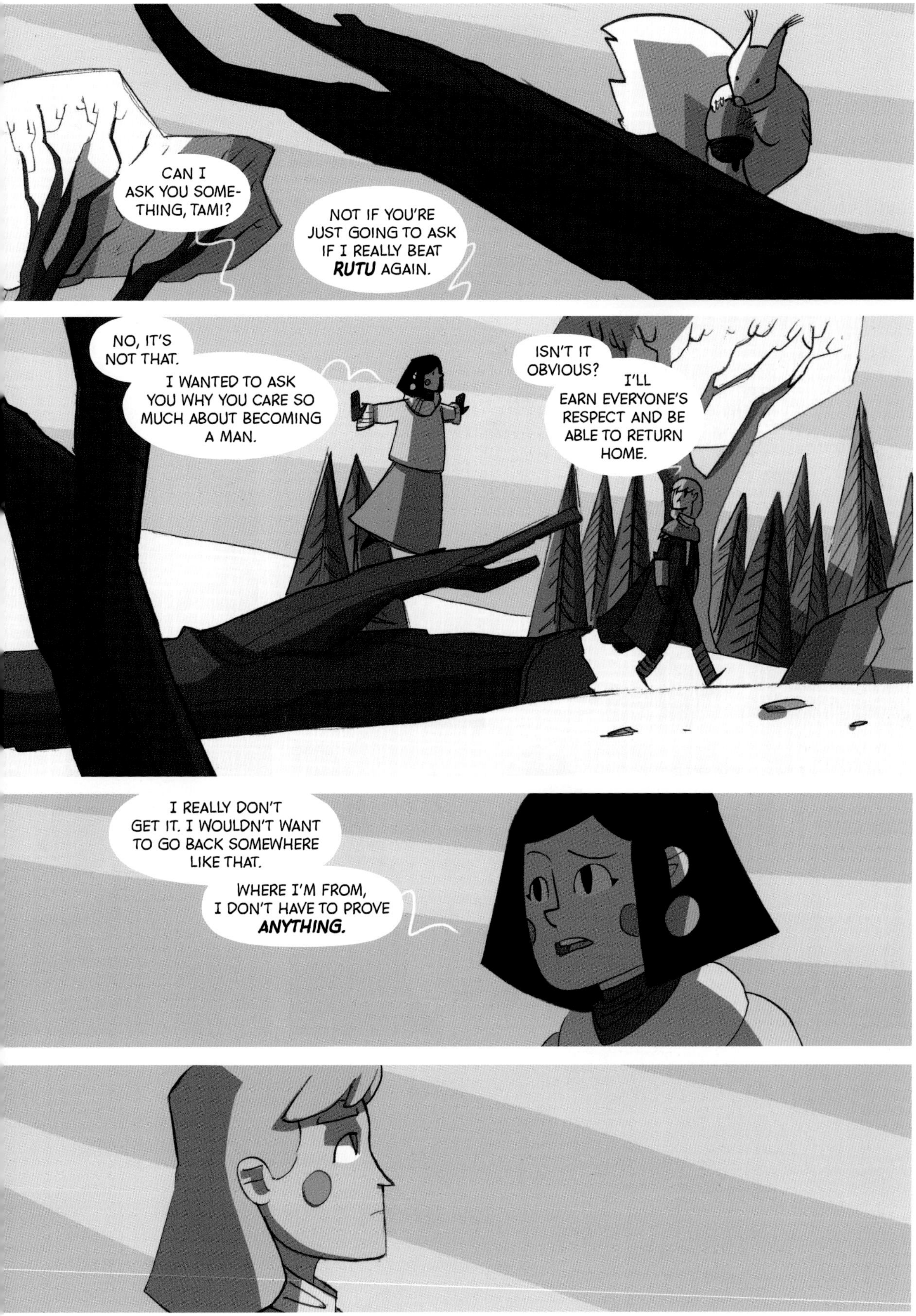
CAN I ASK YOU SOME-THING, TAMI?
NOT IF YOU'RE JUST GOING TO ASK IF I REALLY BEAT **RUTU** AGAIN.
NO, IT'S NOT THAT.
I WANTED TO ASK YOU WHY YOU CARE SO MUCH ABOUT BECOMING A MAN.
ISN'T IT OBVIOUS?
I'LL EARN EVERYONE'S RESPECT AND BE ABLE TO RETURN HOME.
I REALLY DON'T GET IT. I WOULDN'T WANT TO GO BACK SOMEWHERE LIKE THAT.
WHERE I'M FROM, I DON'T HAVE TO PROVE **ANYTHING.**

BUT I WOULD MISS MY PARENTS.

DON'T WE NEED TO GATHER WOOD FOR YOUR FATHER?

YOU MUST MISS YOUR FAMILY A LOT.

IF I WERE YOU I'D DO ANYTHING TO GET BACK, TOO.

ACTUALLY, I DON'T HAVE ANYONE.

I'M AN ORPHAN.

OH...

I... I'M SORRY, TAMI!

IT'S ALL RIGHT, IT HAPPENED WHEN I WAS VERY YOUNG.

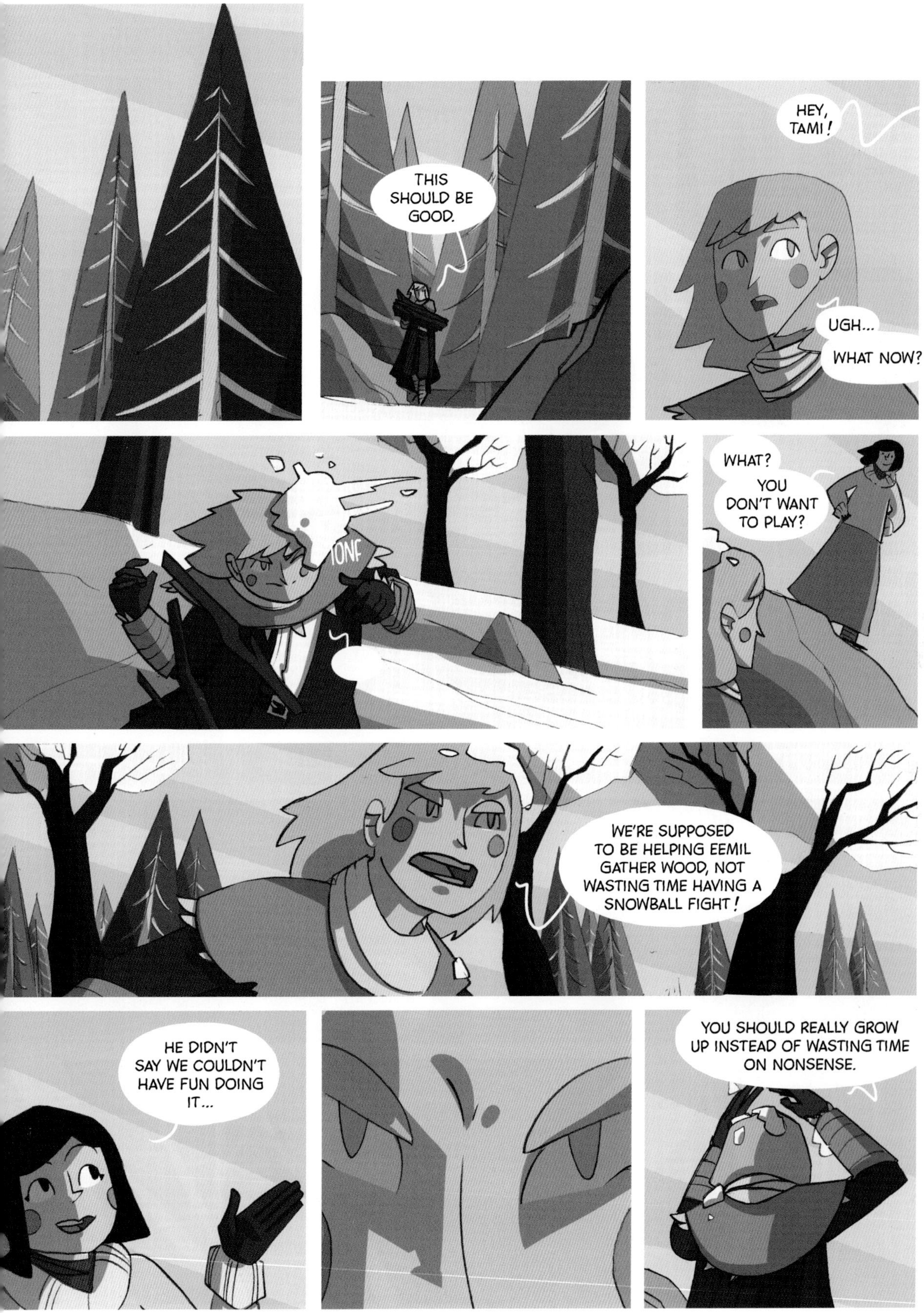
THIS SHOULD BE GOOD.
HEY, TAMI!
UGH...
WHAT NOW?
TONF
WHAT? YOU DON'T WANT TO PLAY?
WE'RE SUPPOSED TO BE HELPING EEMIL GATHER WOOD, NOT WASTING TIME HAVING A SNOWBALL FIGHT!
HE DIDN'T SAY WE COULDN'T HAVE FUN DOING IT...
YOU SHOULD REALLY GROW UP INSTEAD OF WASTING TIME ON NONSENSE.

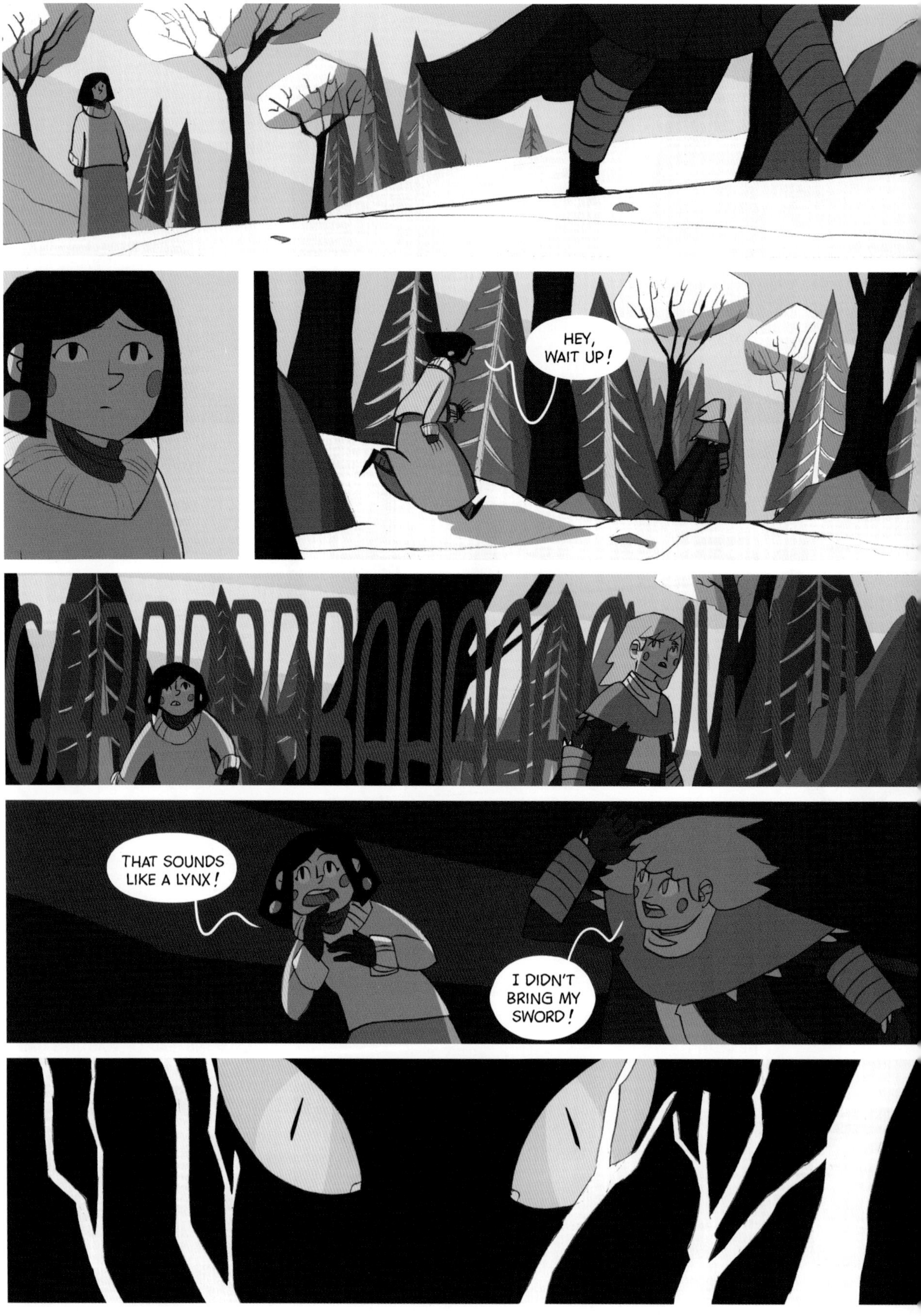
HEY, WAIT UP!
THAT SOUNDS LIKE A LYNX!
I DIDN'T BRING MY SWORD!

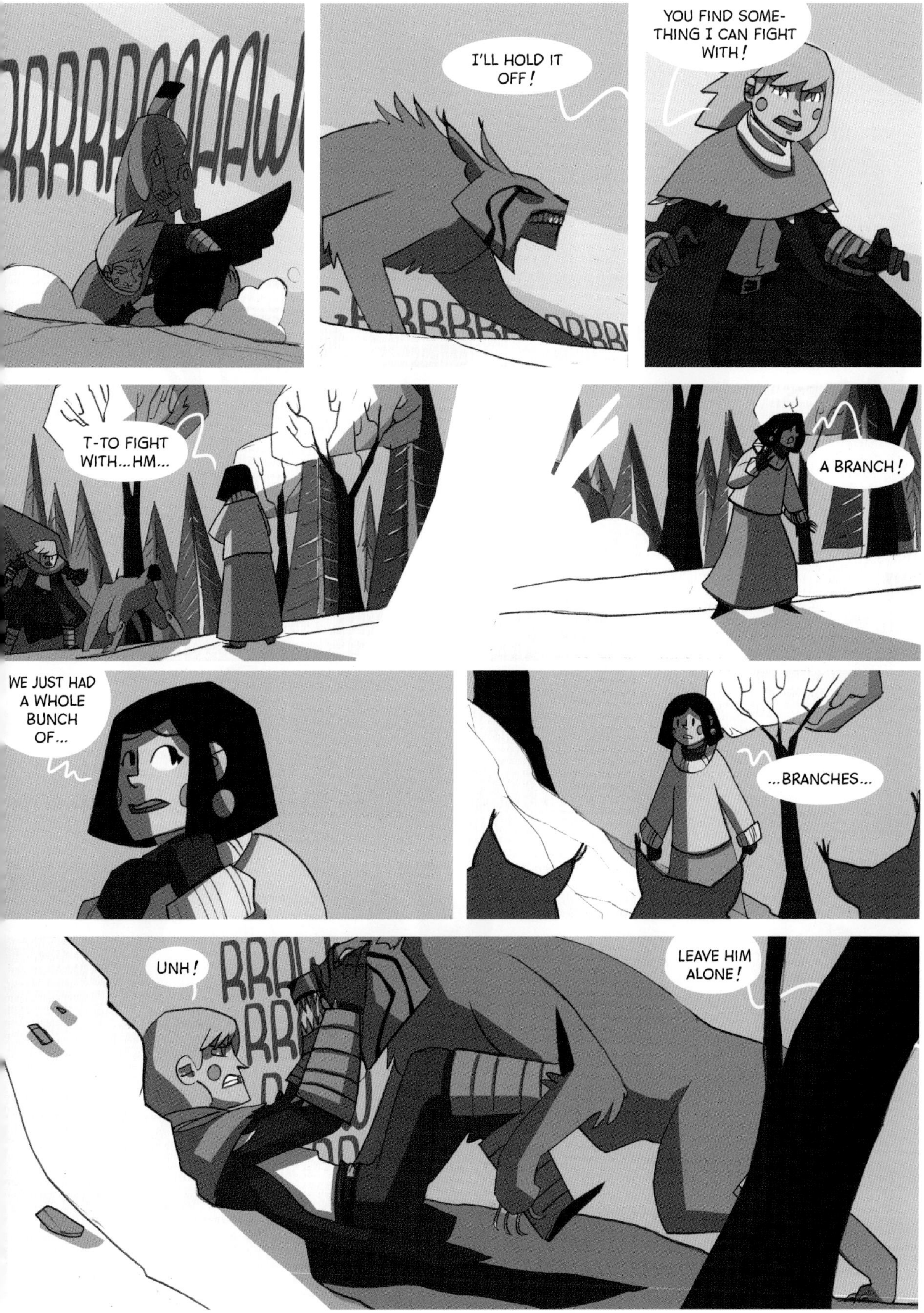
I'LL HOLD IT OFF!
YOU FIND SOMETHING I CAN FIGHT WITH!
T-TO FIGHT WITH...HM...
A BRANCH!
WE JUST HAD A WHOLE BUNCH OF...
...BRANCHES...
UNH!
LEAVE HIM ALONE!

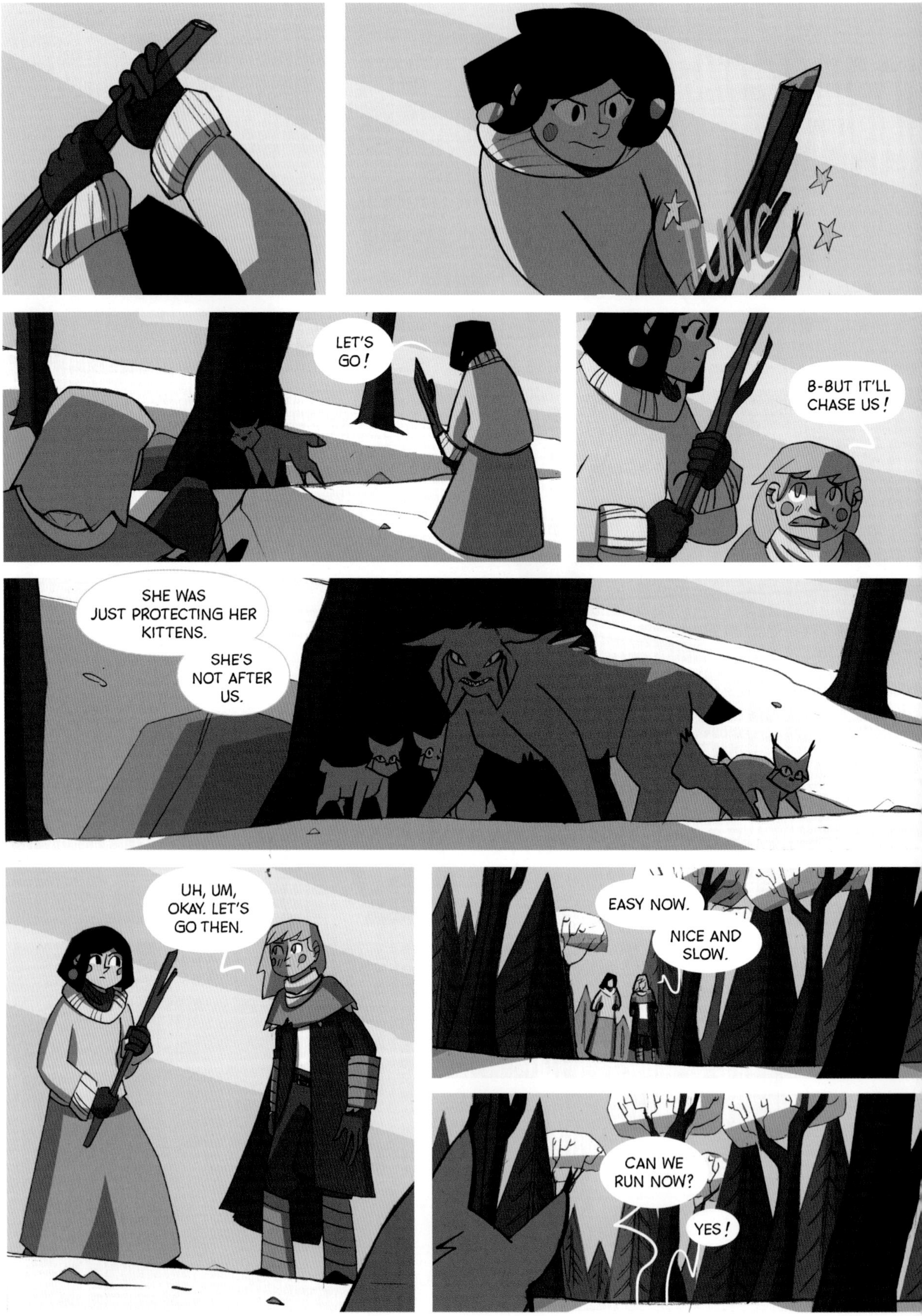
TUNC
LET'S GO!
B-BUT IT'LL CHASE US!
SHE WAS JUST PROTECTING HER KITTENS.
SHE'S NOT AFTER US.
UH, UM, OKAY. LET'S GO THEN.
EASY NOW.
NICE AND SLOW.
CAN WE RUN NOW?
YES!

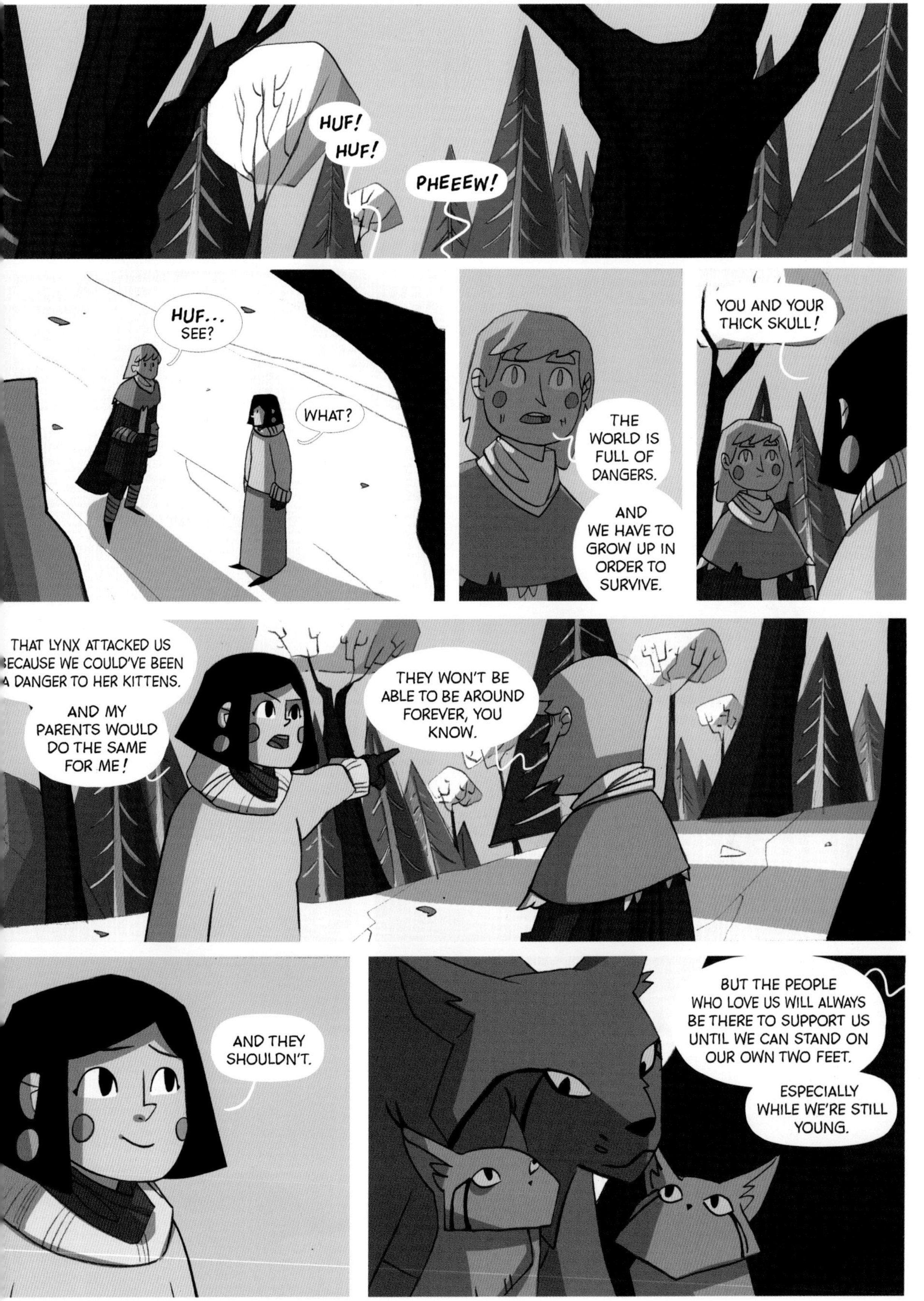

HUF!
HUF!
PHEEEW!
HUF... SEE?
WHAT?
THE WORLD IS FULL OF DANGERS.
AND WE HAVE TO GROW UP IN ORDER TO SURVIVE.
YOU AND YOUR THICK SKULL!
THAT LYNX ATTACKED US BECAUSE WE COULD'VE BEEN A DANGER TO HER KITTENS.
AND MY PARENTS WOULD DO THE SAME FOR ME!
THEY WON'T BE ABLE TO BE AROUND FOREVER, YOU KNOW.
AND THEY SHOULDN'T.
BUT THE PEOPLE WHO LOVE US WILL ALWAYS BE THERE TO SUPPORT US UNTIL WE CAN STAND ON OUR OWN TWO FEET.
ESPECIALLY WHILE WE'RE STILL YOUNG.

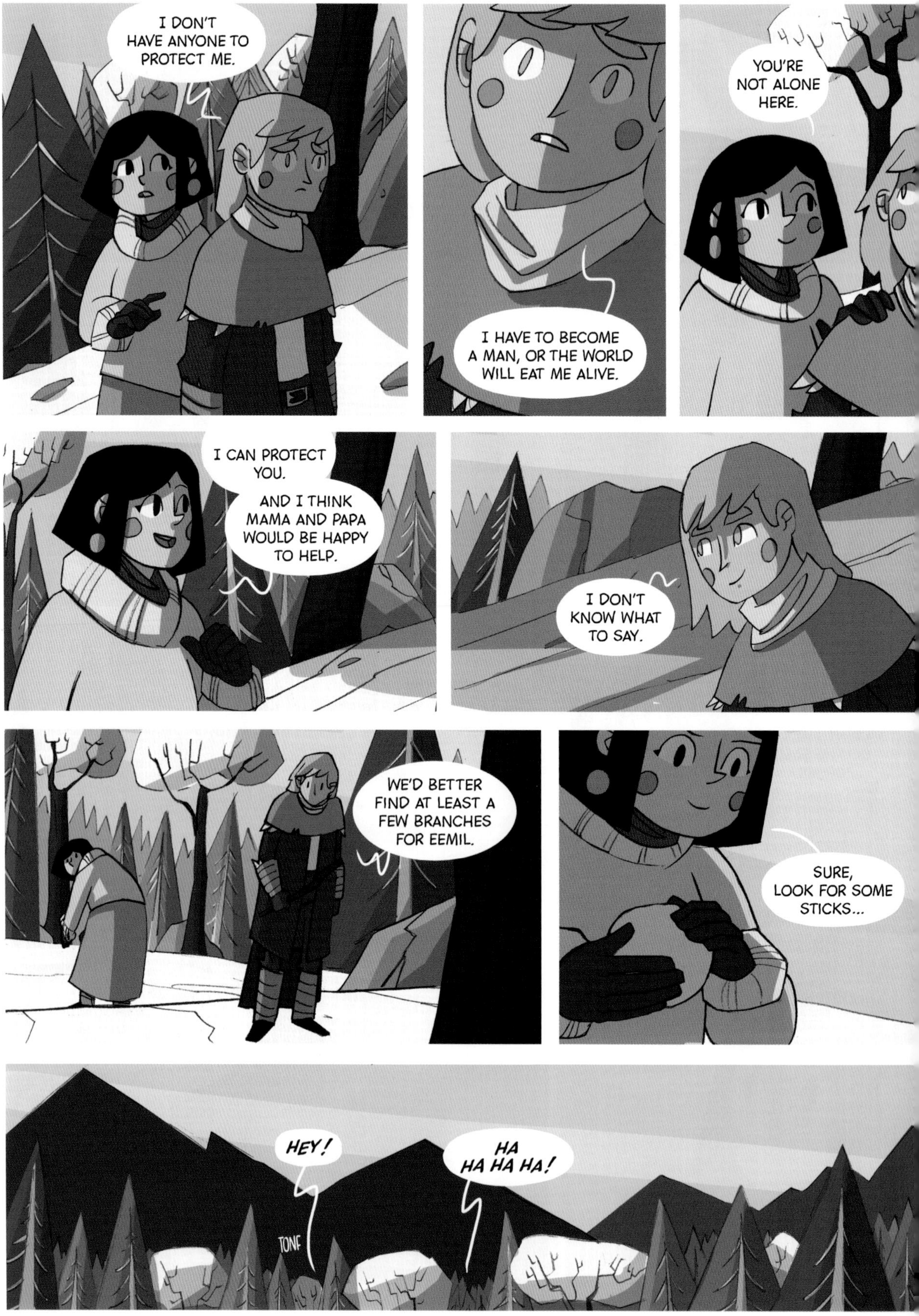
I DON'T HAVE ANYONE TO PROTECT ME.
I HAVE TO BECOME A MAN, OR THE WORLD WILL EAT ME ALIVE.
YOU'RE NOT ALONE HERE.
I CAN PROTECT YOU.
AND I THINK MAMA AND PAPA WOULD BE HAPPY TO HELP.
I DON'T KNOW WHAT TO SAY.
WE'D BETTER FIND AT LEAST A FEW BRANCHES FOR EEMIL.
SURE, LOOK FOR SOME STICKS...
HEY!
TONF
HA HA HA HA!

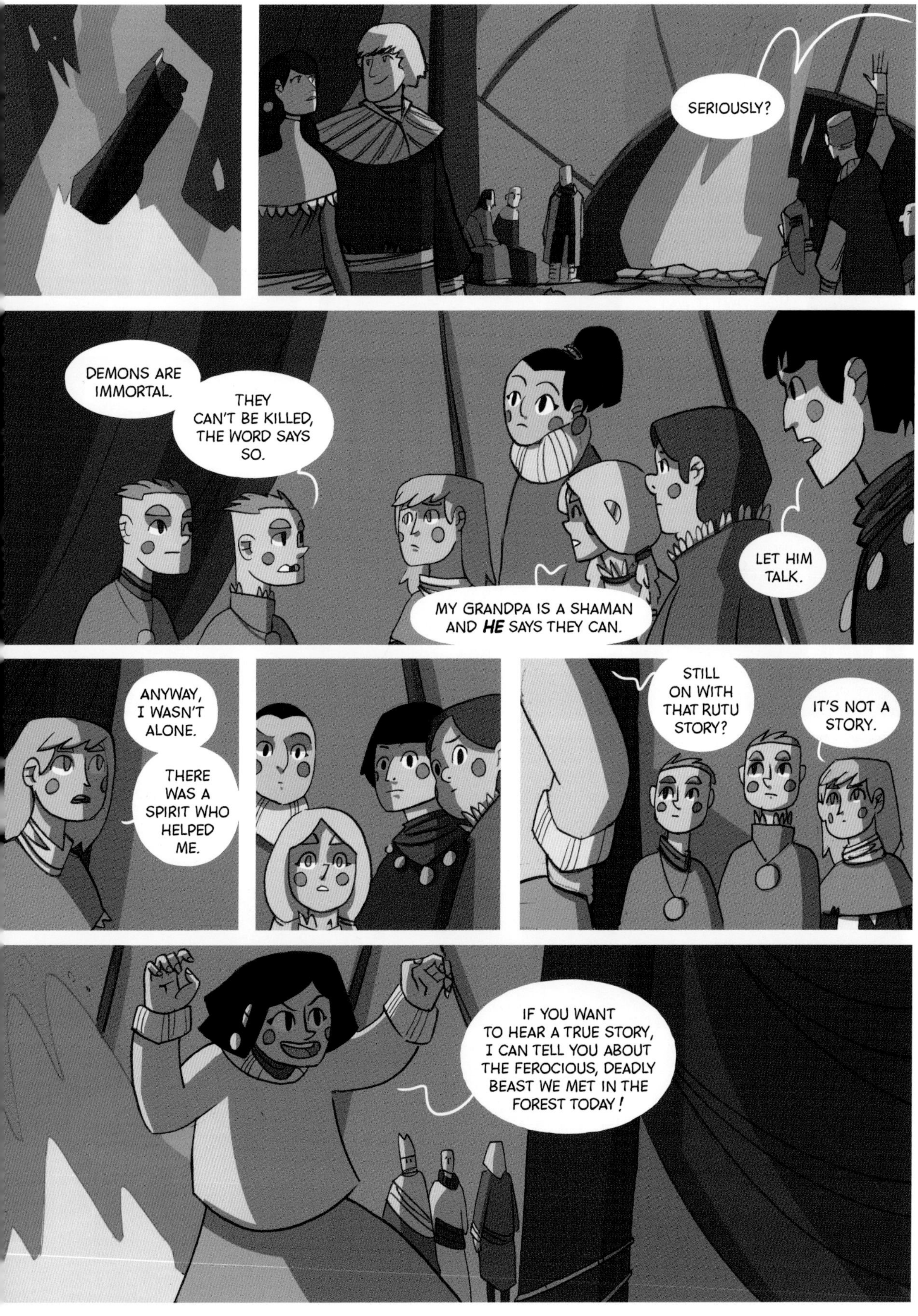
SERIOUSLY?
DEMONS ARE IMMORTAL.
THEY CAN'T BE KILLED, THE WORD SAYS SO.
MY GRANDPA IS A SHAMAN AND **HE** SAYS THEY CAN.
LET HIM TALK.
ANYWAY, I WASN'T ALONE.
THERE WAS A SPIRIT WHO HELPED ME.
STILL ON WITH THAT RUTU STORY?
IT'S NOT A STORY.
IF YOU WANT TO HEAR A TRUE STORY, I CAN TELL YOU ABOUT THE FEROCIOUS, DEADLY BEAST WE MET IN THE FOREST TODAY!

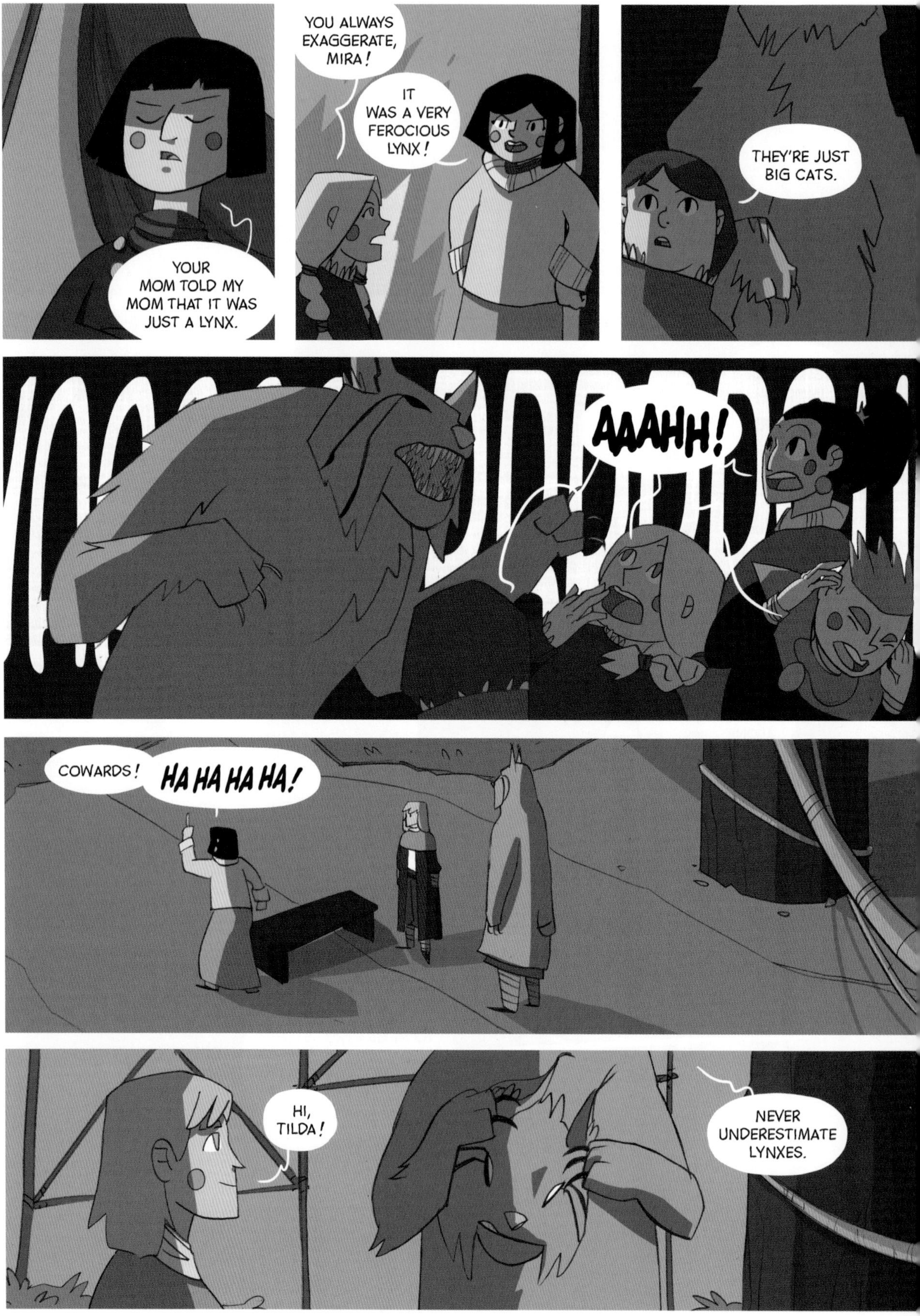
YOUR MOM TOLD MY MOM THAT IT WAS JUST A LYNX.
YOU ALWAYS EXAGGERATE, MIRA!
IT WAS A VERY FEROCIOUS LYNX!
THEY'RE JUST BIG CATS.
AAAHH!
COWARDS!
HA HA HA HA!
HI, TILDA!
NEVER UNDERESTIMATE LYNXES.

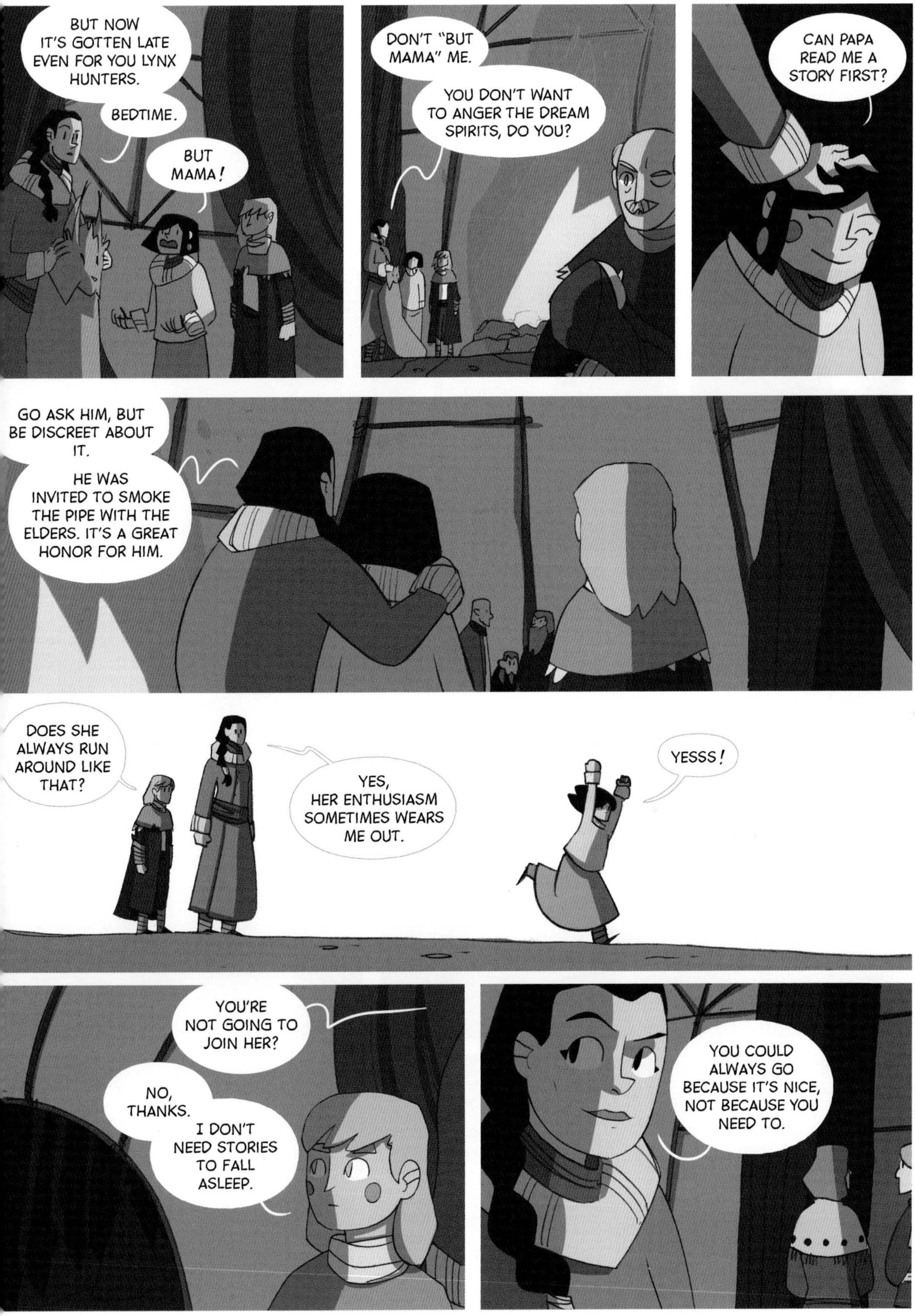
BUT NOW IT'S GOTTEN LATE EVEN FOR YOU LYNX HUNTERS.
BEDTIME.
BUT MAMA!
DON'T "BUT MAMA" ME.
YOU DON'T WANT TO ANGER THE DREAM SPIRITS, DO YOU?
CAN PAPA READ ME A STORY FIRST?
GO ASK HIM, BUT BE DISCREET ABOUT IT.
HE WAS INVITED TO SMOKE THE PIPE WITH THE ELDERS. IT'S A GREAT HONOR FOR HIM.
DOES SHE ALWAYS RUN AROUND LIKE THAT?
YES, HER ENTHUSIASM SOMETIMES WEARS ME OUT.
YESSS!
YOU'RE NOT GOING TO JOIN HER?
NO, THANKS.
I DON'T NEED STORIES TO FALL ASLEEP.
YOU COULD ALWAYS GO BECAUSE IT'S NICE, NOT BECAUSE YOU NEED TO.

LYNXES NEVER COME DOWN THIS FAR. BUT IF RUTU WERE REALLY DEAD...

NONSENSE.

AND WHY IS *HE* HERE?

YOU THINK SOMETHING IS STIRRING IN THE FOREST?

EEMIL HAS LONG BEEN AN IMPORTANT MEMBER OF OUR COMMUNITY.

IT'S TIME YOU START TO LEARN HOW THIS VILLAGE IS RUN.

I WOULD BE HONORED.

PAPA!

WILL YOU TELL ME A STORY?

A STORY? UH, I DON'T KNOW...

WHY NOT? GO AHEAD.

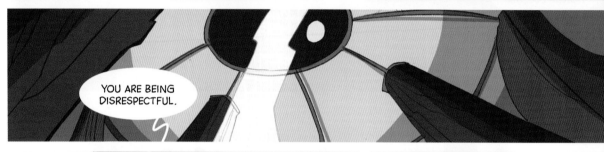

YOU ARE BEING DISRESPECTFUL.

WE'RE DISCUSSING THE FUTURE OF THE VILLAGE HERE.

NOT SHARING FAIRY TALES.

COME ON, GIVE IT A REST, KERREL.

CAN I LISTEN, TOO?

OKAY, WHICH STORY WOULD YOU LIKE?

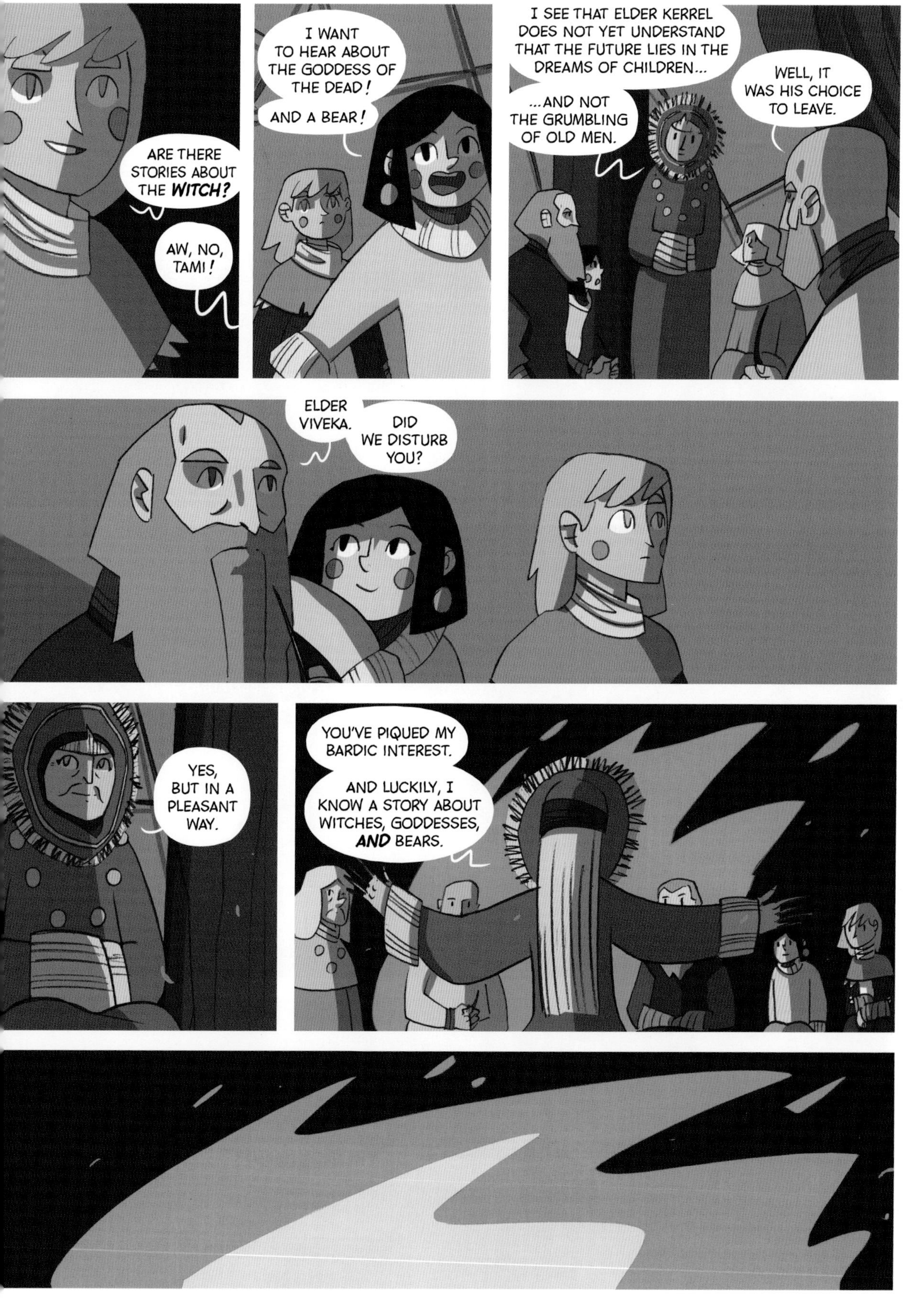
ARE THERE STORIES ABOUT THE **WITCH?**
AW, NO, TAMI!
I WANT TO HEAR ABOUT THE GODDESS OF THE DEAD!
AND A BEAR!
I SEE THAT ELDER KERREL DOES NOT YET UNDERSTAND THAT THE FUTURE LIES IN THE DREAMS OF CHILDREN...
...AND NOT THE GRUMBLING OF OLD MEN.
WELL, IT WAS HIS CHOICE TO LEAVE.
ELDER VIVEKA.
DID WE DISTURB YOU?
YES, BUT IN A PLEASANT WAY.
YOU'VE PIQUED MY BARDIC INTEREST.
AND LUCKILY, I KNOW A STORY ABOUT WITCHES, GODDESSES, **AND** BEARS.

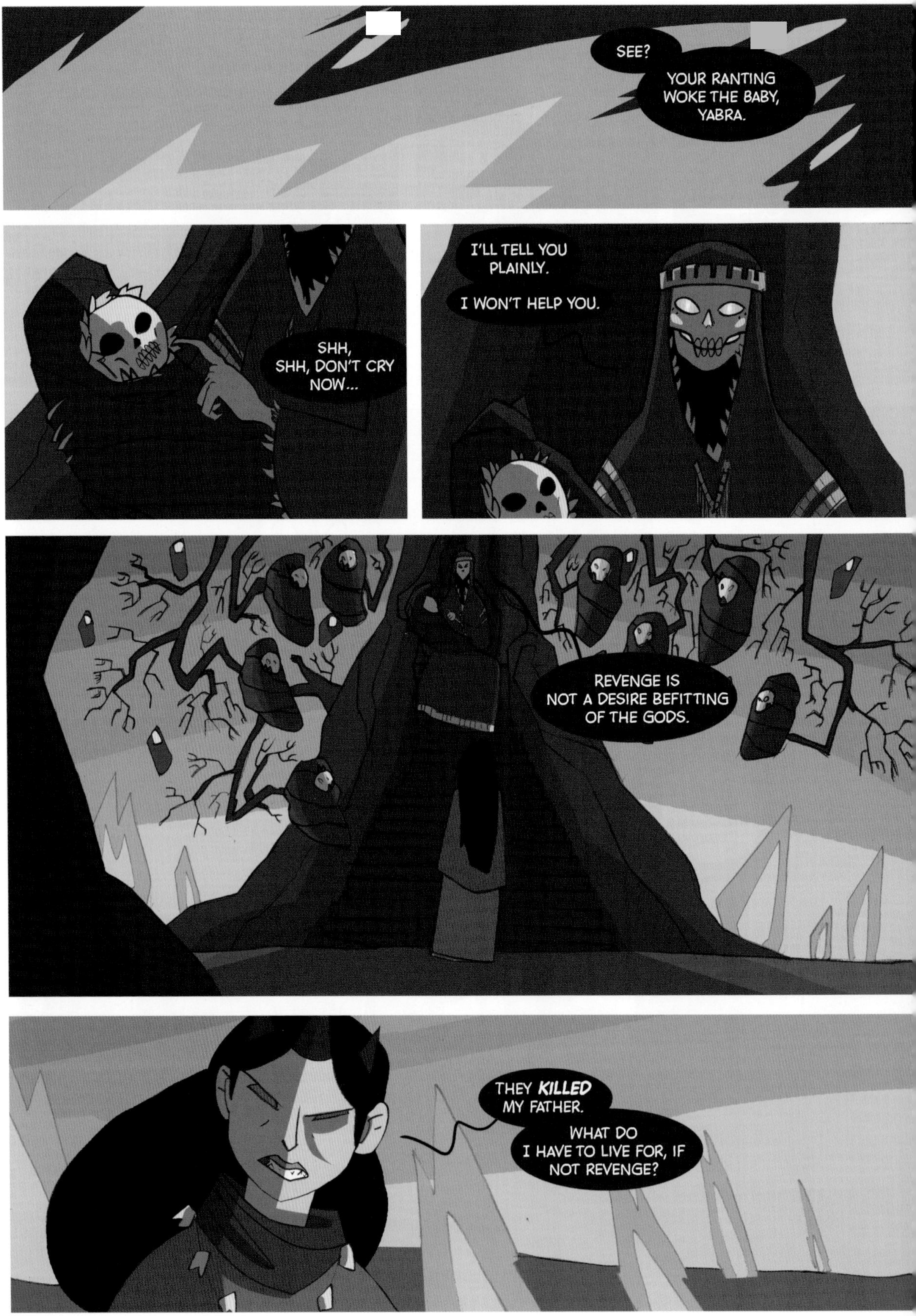
SEE?
YOUR RANTING WOKE THE BABY, YABRA.
SHH, SHH, DON'T CRY NOW...
I'LL TELL YOU PLAINLY.
I WON'T HELP YOU.
REVENGE IS NOT A DESIRE BEFITTING OF THE GODS.
THEY **KILLED** MY FATHER.
WHAT DO I HAVE TO LIVE FOR, IF NOT REVENGE?

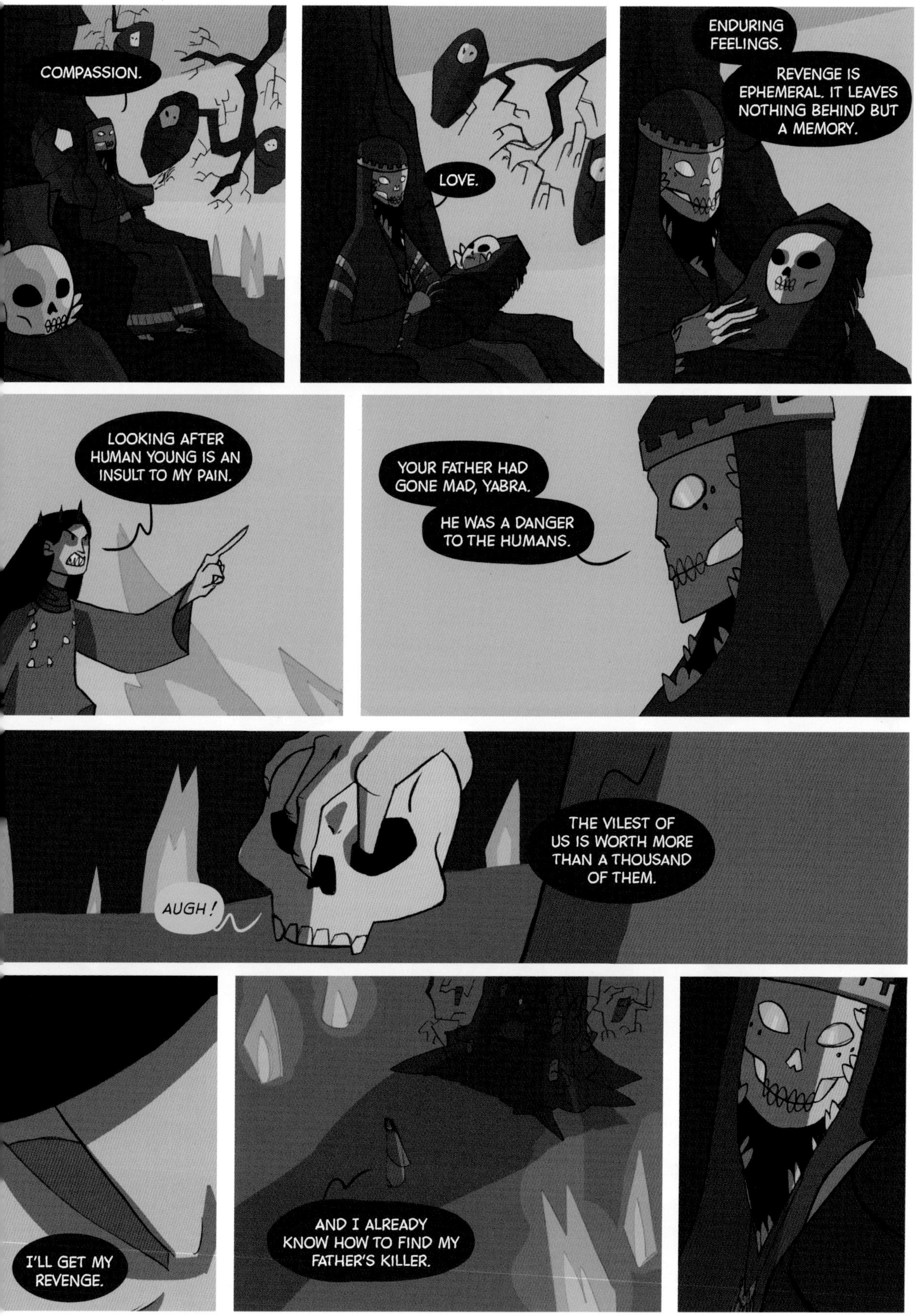
COMPASSION.
LOVE.
ENDURING FEELINGS.
REVENGE IS EPHEMERAL. IT LEAVES NOTHING BEHIND BUT A MEMORY.
LOOKING AFTER HUMAN YOUNG IS AN INSULT TO MY PAIN.
YOUR FATHER HAD GONE MAD, YABRA.
HE WAS A DANGER TO THE HUMANS.
AUGH!
THE VILEST OF US IS WORTH MORE THAN A THOUSAND OF THEM.
I'LL GET MY REVENGE.
AND I ALREADY KNOW HOW TO FIND MY FATHER'S KILLER.

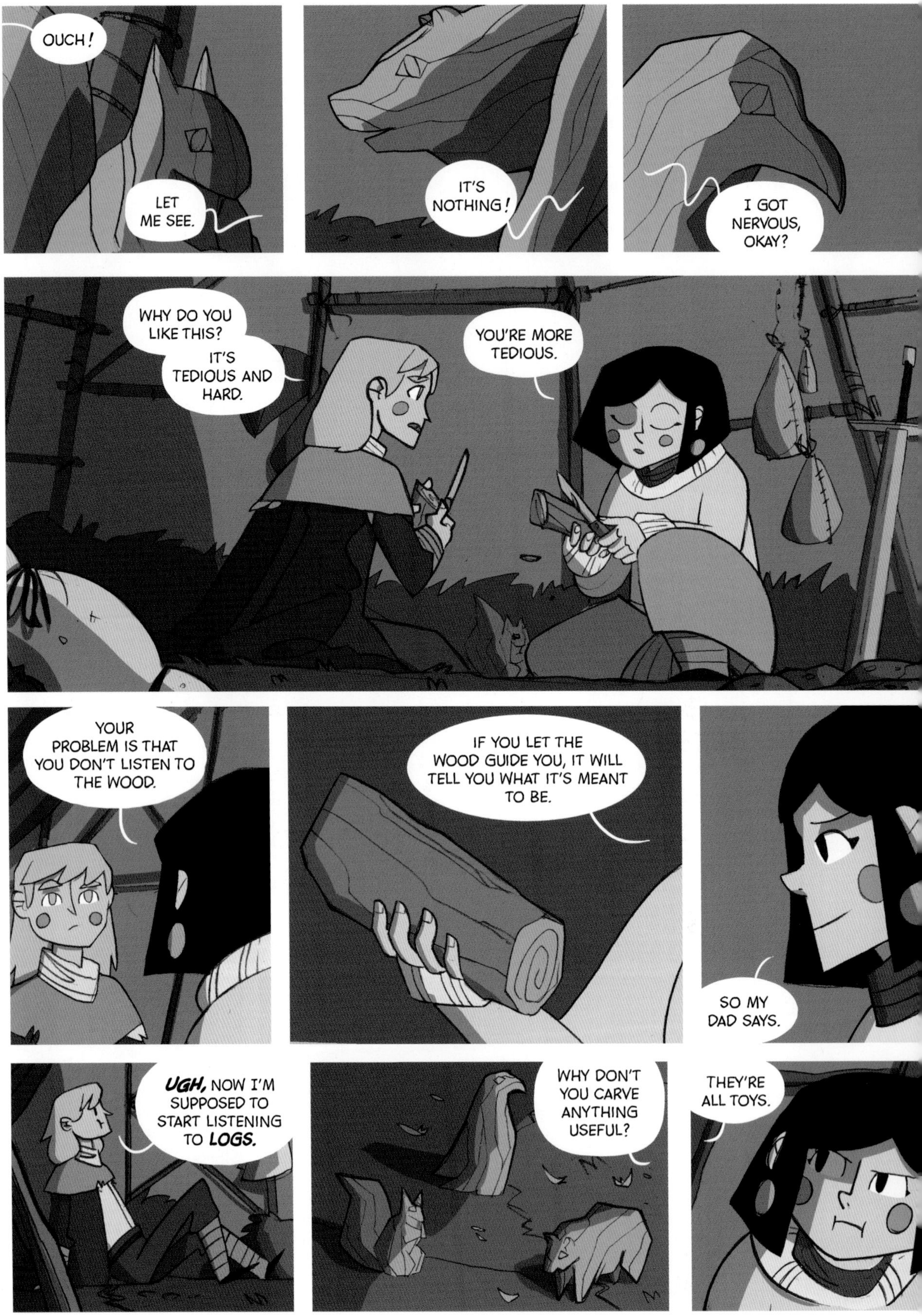
OUCH!
LET ME SEE.
IT'S NOTHING!
I GOT NERVOUS, OKAY?
WHY DO YOU LIKE THIS?
IT'S TEDIOUS AND HARD.
YOU'RE MORE TEDIOUS.
YOUR PROBLEM IS THAT YOU DON'T LISTEN TO THE WOOD.
IF YOU LET THE WOOD GUIDE YOU, IT WILL TELL YOU WHAT IT'S MEANT TO BE.
SO MY DAD SAYS.
UGH, NOW I'M SUPPOSED TO START LISTENING TO LOGS.
WHY DON'T YOU CARVE ANYTHING USEFUL?
THEY'RE ALL TOYS.

FINE, TELL ME SOMETHING "USEFUL" AND I'LL CARVE IT FOR YOU.

WELL?

GULP...

CHOOSE CAREFULLY, I'LL ONLY MAKE YOU **ONE** THING.

HMMM.

COULD YOU MAKE ME A DRAGON FIGURINE?

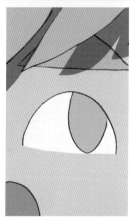

WHAT? THAT COULD BE USEFUL!

OKAY. I'LL MAKE YOU A VERY USEFUL DRAGON.

MIRA!

IS THAT THE OTHER KIDS?

YES, IT'S HIDE-AND-SEEK TODAY. WE CAN FINISH LATER.

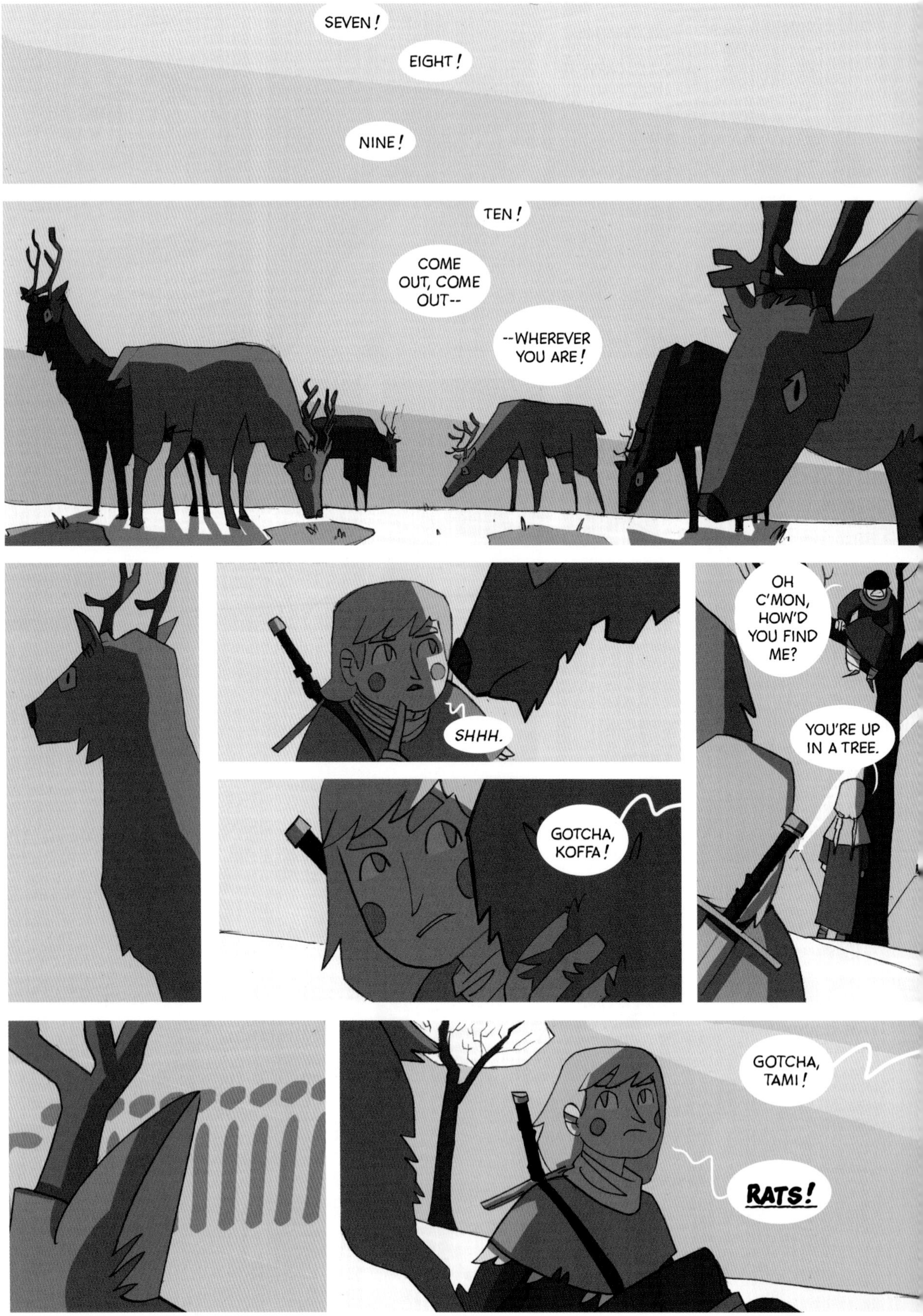

SEVEN!
EIGHT!
NINE!
TEN!
COME OUT, COME OUT--
--WHEREVER YOU ARE!
SHHH.
GOTCHA, KOFFA!
OH C'MON, HOW'D YOU FIND ME?
YOU'RE UP IN A TREE.
GOTCHA, TAMI!
RATS!

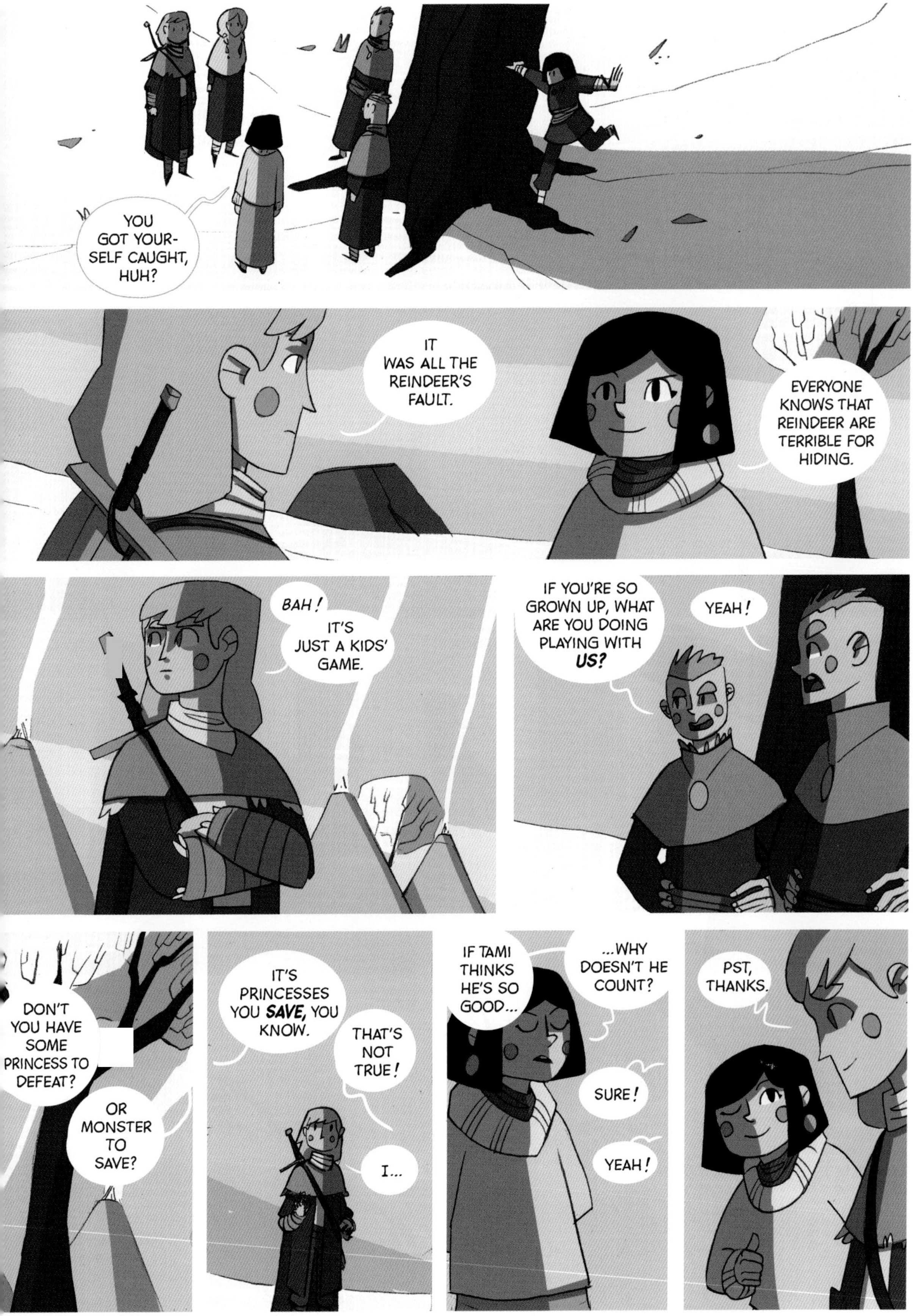
YOU GOT YOURSELF CAUGHT, HUH?
IT WAS ALL THE REINDEER'S FAULT.
EVERYONE KNOWS THAT REINDEER ARE TERRIBLE FOR HIDING.
BAH! IT'S JUST A KIDS' GAME.
IF YOU'RE SO GROWN UP, WHAT ARE YOU DOING PLAYING WITH *US?*
YEAH!
DON'T YOU HAVE SOME PRINCESS TO DEFEAT?
OR MONSTER TO SAVE?
IT'S PRINCESSES YOU *SAVE,* YOU KNOW.
THAT'S NOT TRUE!
I...
IF TAMI THINKS HE'S SO GOOD...
...WHY DOESN'T HE COUNT?
SURE!
YEAH!
PST, THANKS.

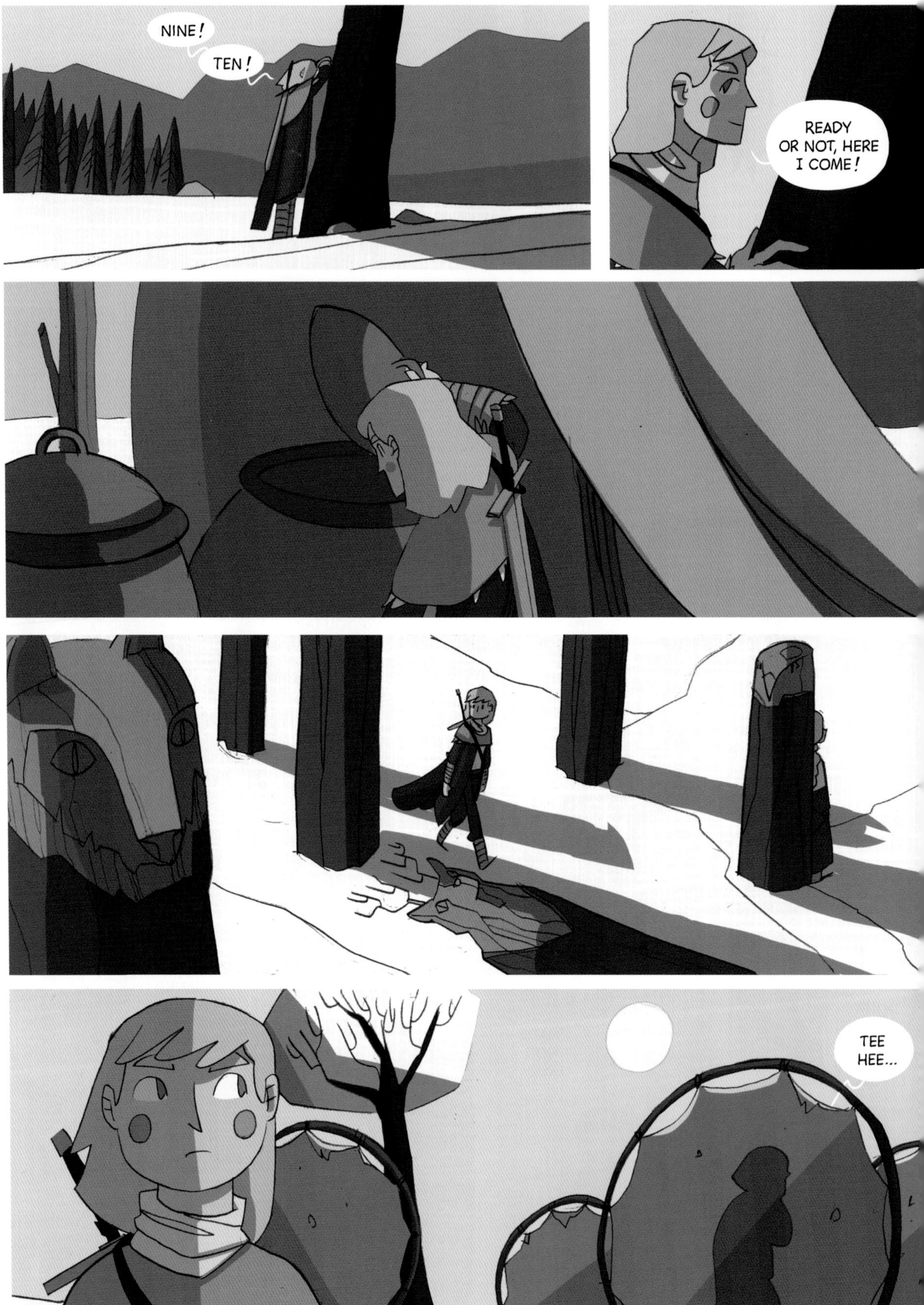
NINE!
TEN!
READY OR NOT, HERE I COME!
TEE HEE...

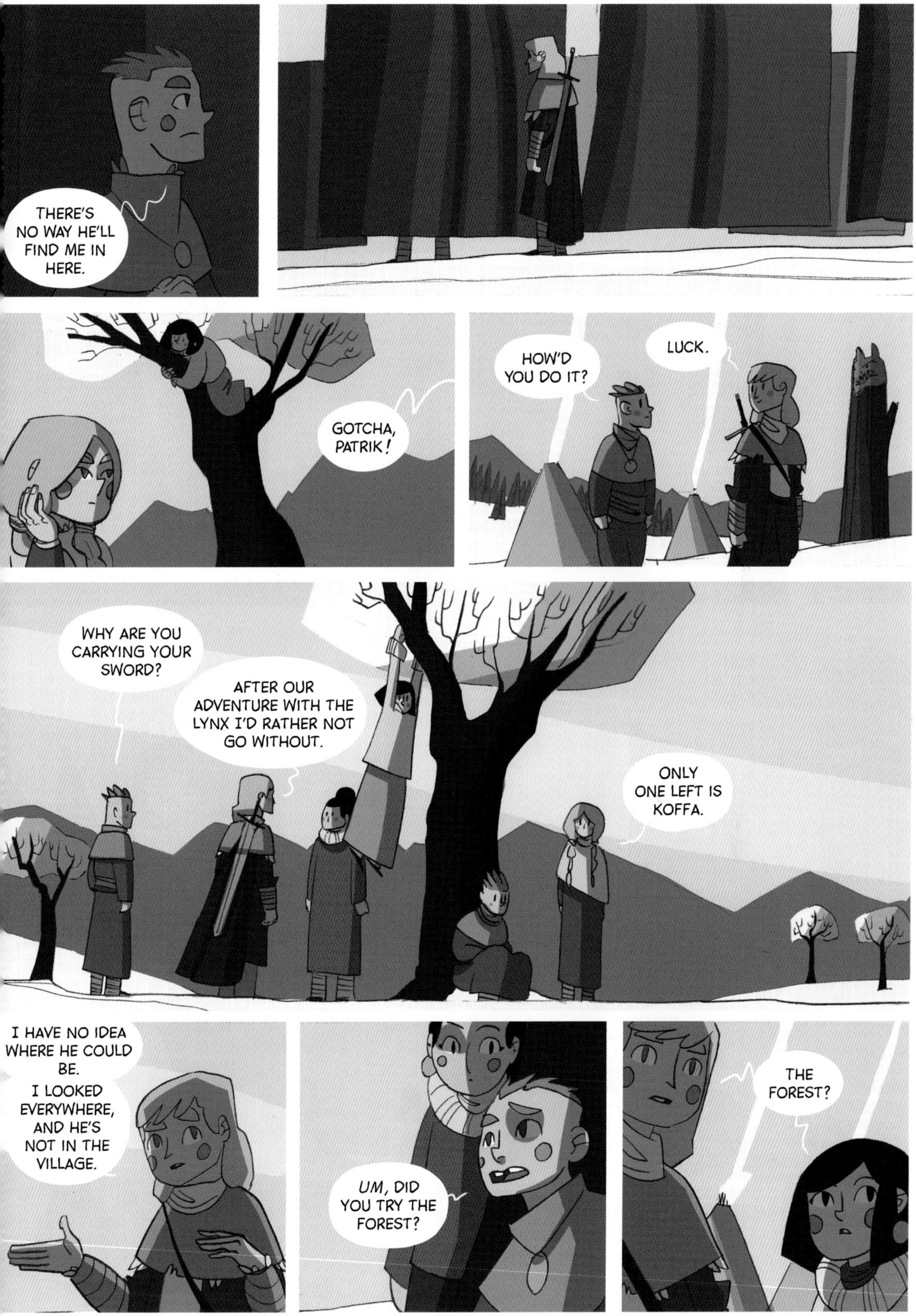
THERE'S NO WAY HE'LL FIND ME IN HERE.
GOTCHA, PATRIK!
HOW'D YOU DO IT?
LUCK.
WHY ARE YOU CARRYING YOUR SWORD?
AFTER OUR ADVENTURE WITH THE LYNX I'D RATHER NOT GO WITHOUT.
ONLY ONE LEFT IS KOFFA.
I HAVE NO IDEA WHERE HE COULD BE.
I LOOKED EVERYWHERE, AND HE'S NOT IN THE VILLAGE.
UM, DID YOU TRY THE FOREST?
THE FOREST?

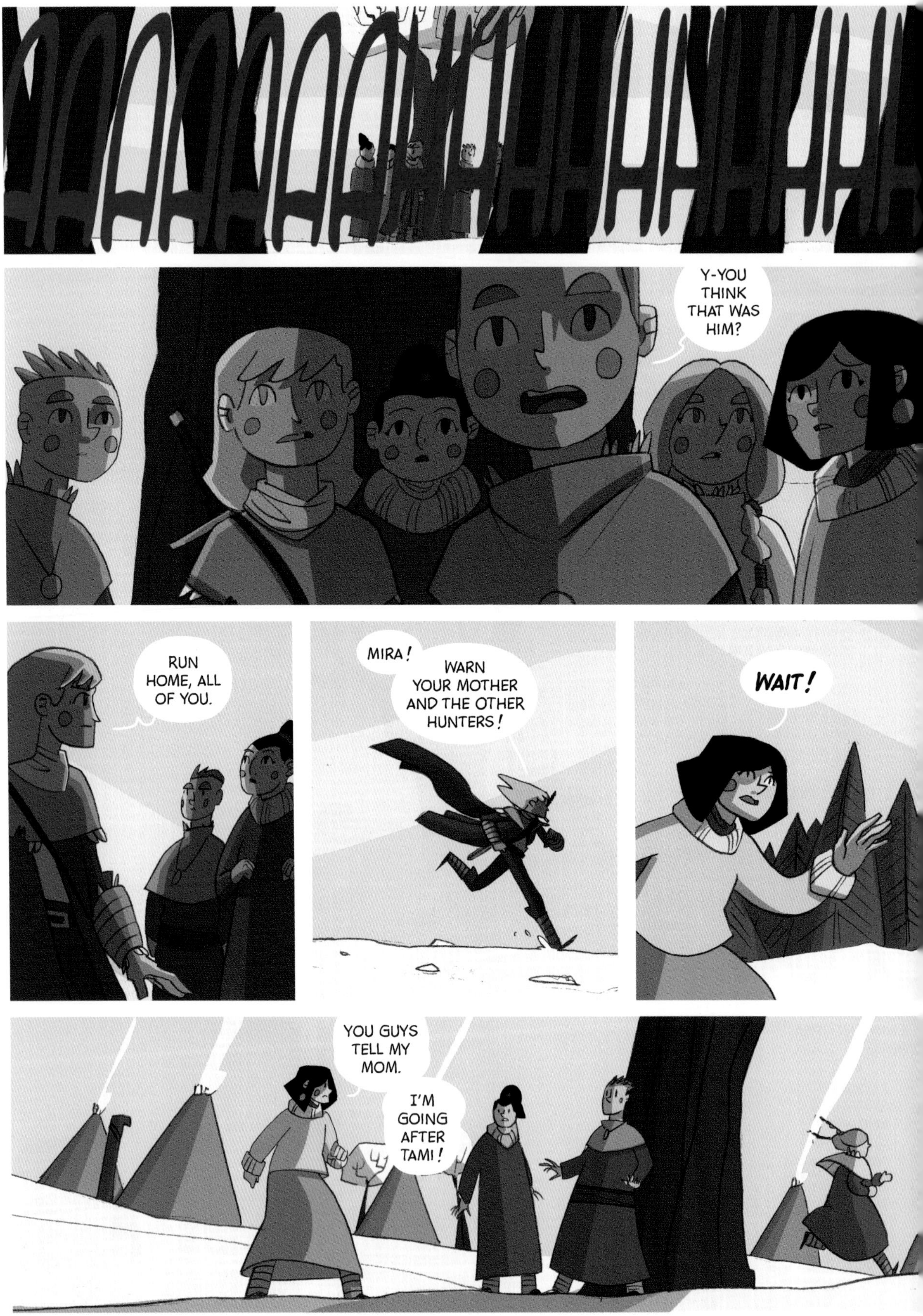

Y-YOU THINK THAT WAS HIM?
RUN HOME, ALL OF YOU.
MIRA!
WARN YOUR MOTHER AND THE OTHER HUNTERS!
WAIT!
YOU GUYS TELL MY MOM.
I'M GOING AFTER TAMI!

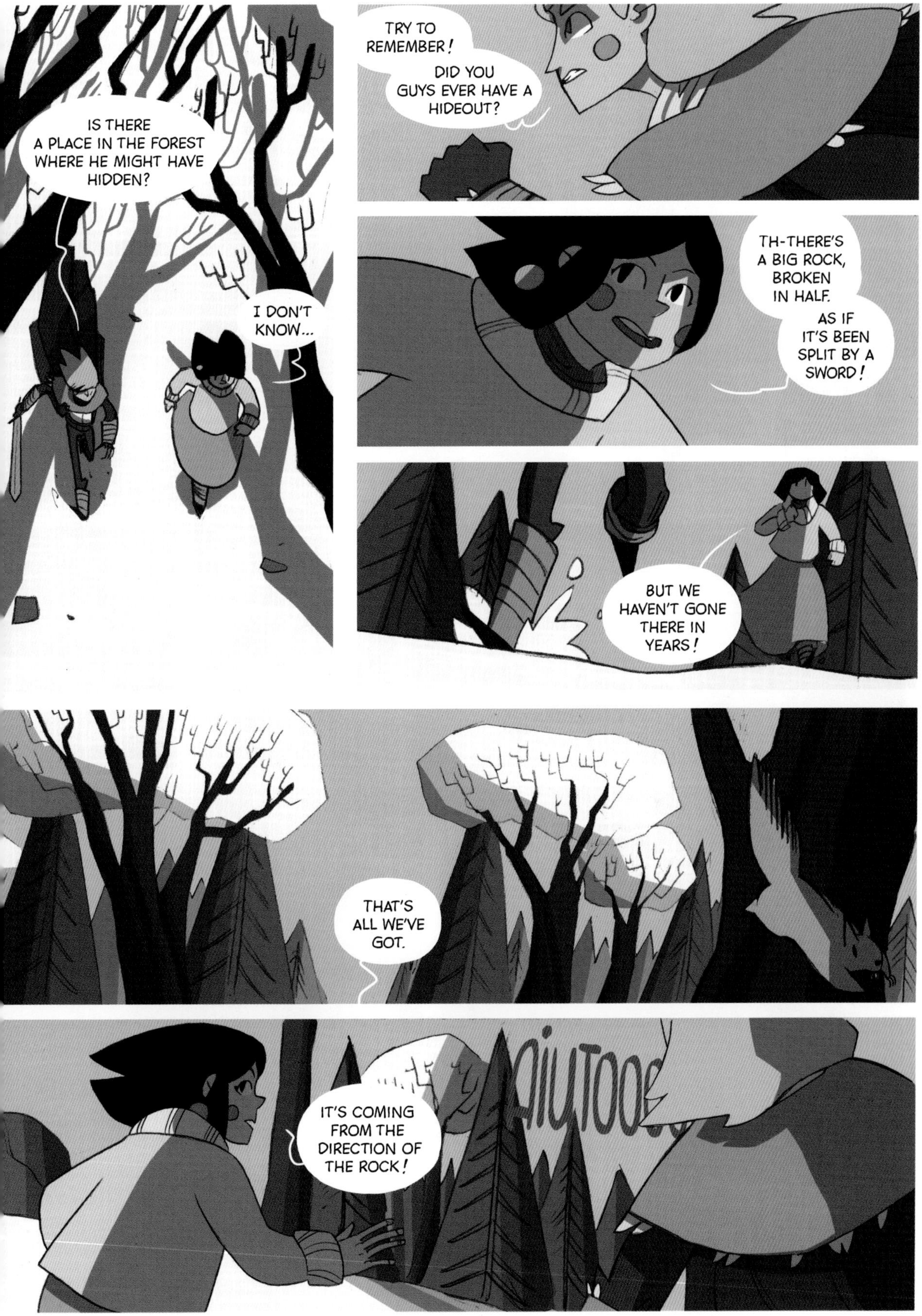
IS THERE A PLACE IN THE FOREST WHERE HE MIGHT HAVE HIDDEN?
I DON'T KNOW...
TRY TO REMEMBER!
DID YOU GUYS EVER HAVE A HIDEOUT?
TH-THERE'S A BIG ROCK, BROKEN IN HALF.
AS IF IT'S BEEN SPLIT BY A SWORD!
BUT WE HAVEN'T GONE THERE IN YEARS!
THAT'S ALL WE'VE GOT.
IT'S COMING FROM THE DIRECTION OF THE ROCK!

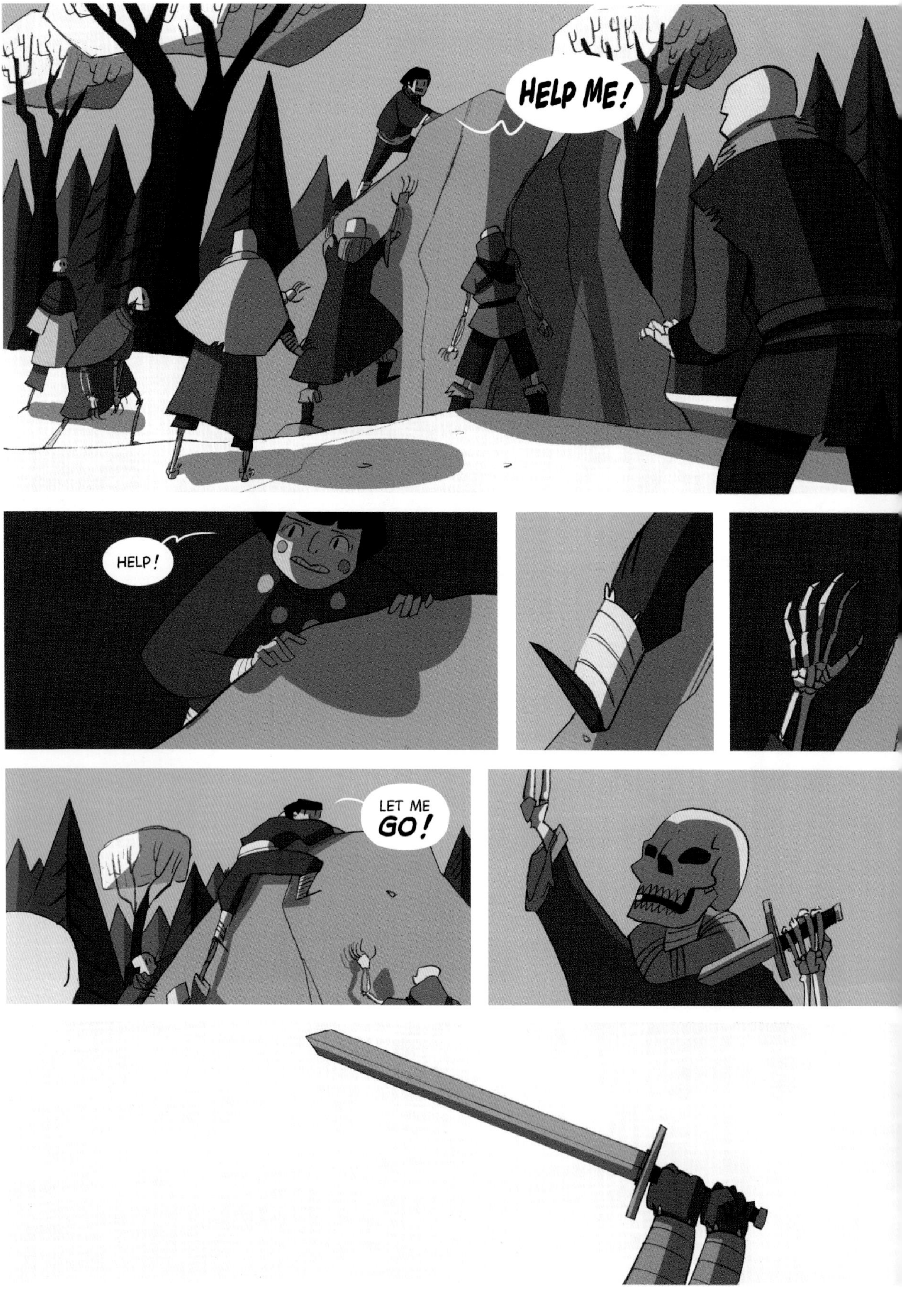
HELP ME!
HELP!
LET ME GO!

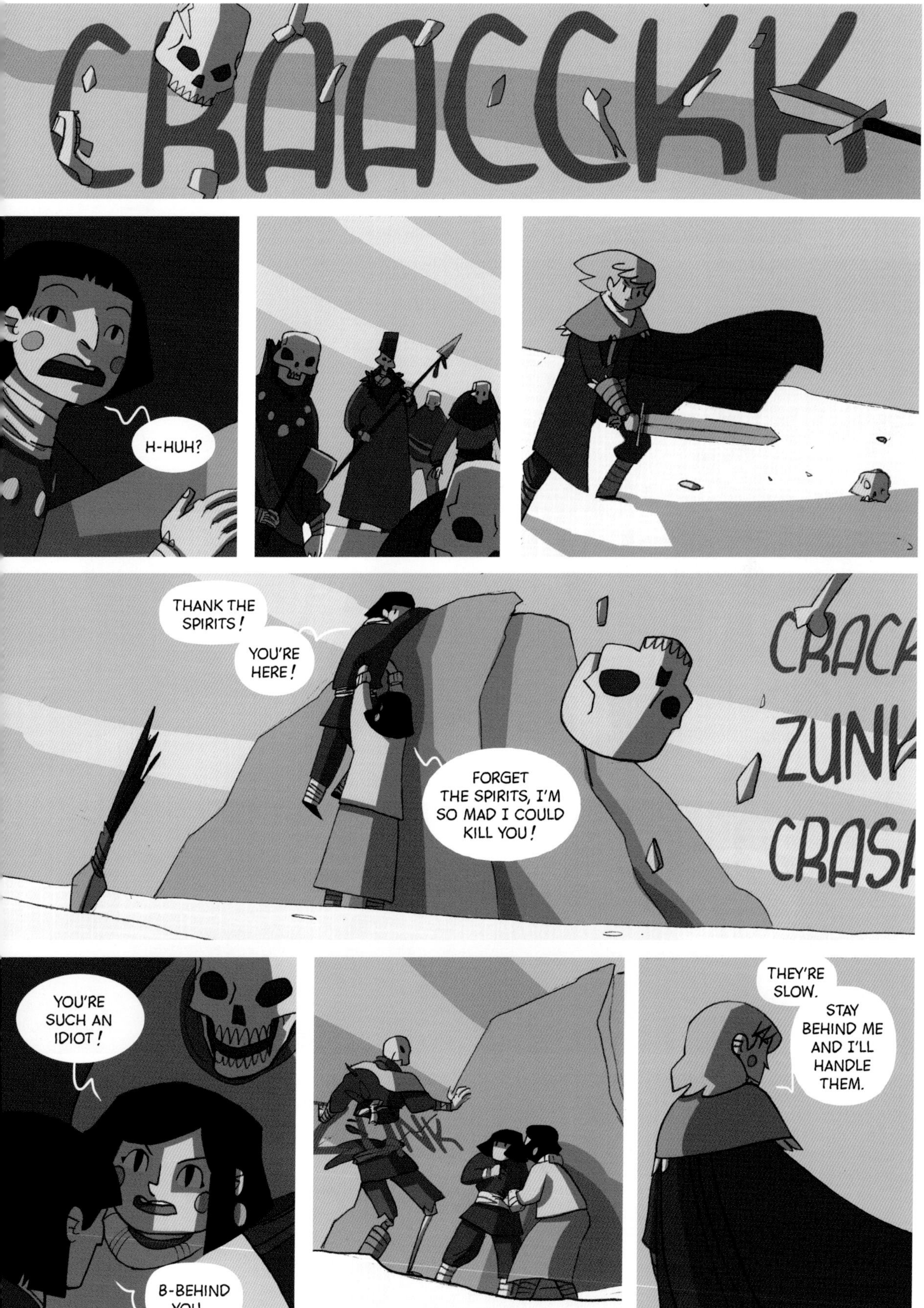
CRAACCKK
H-HUH?
THANK THE SPIRITS!
YOU'RE HERE!
FORGET THE SPIRITS, I'M SO MAD I COULD KILL YOU!
CRACK
ZUNK
CRASH
YOU'RE SUCH AN IDIOT!
B-BEHIND YOU...
THEY'RE SLOW.
STAY BEHIND ME AND I'LL HANDLE THEM.

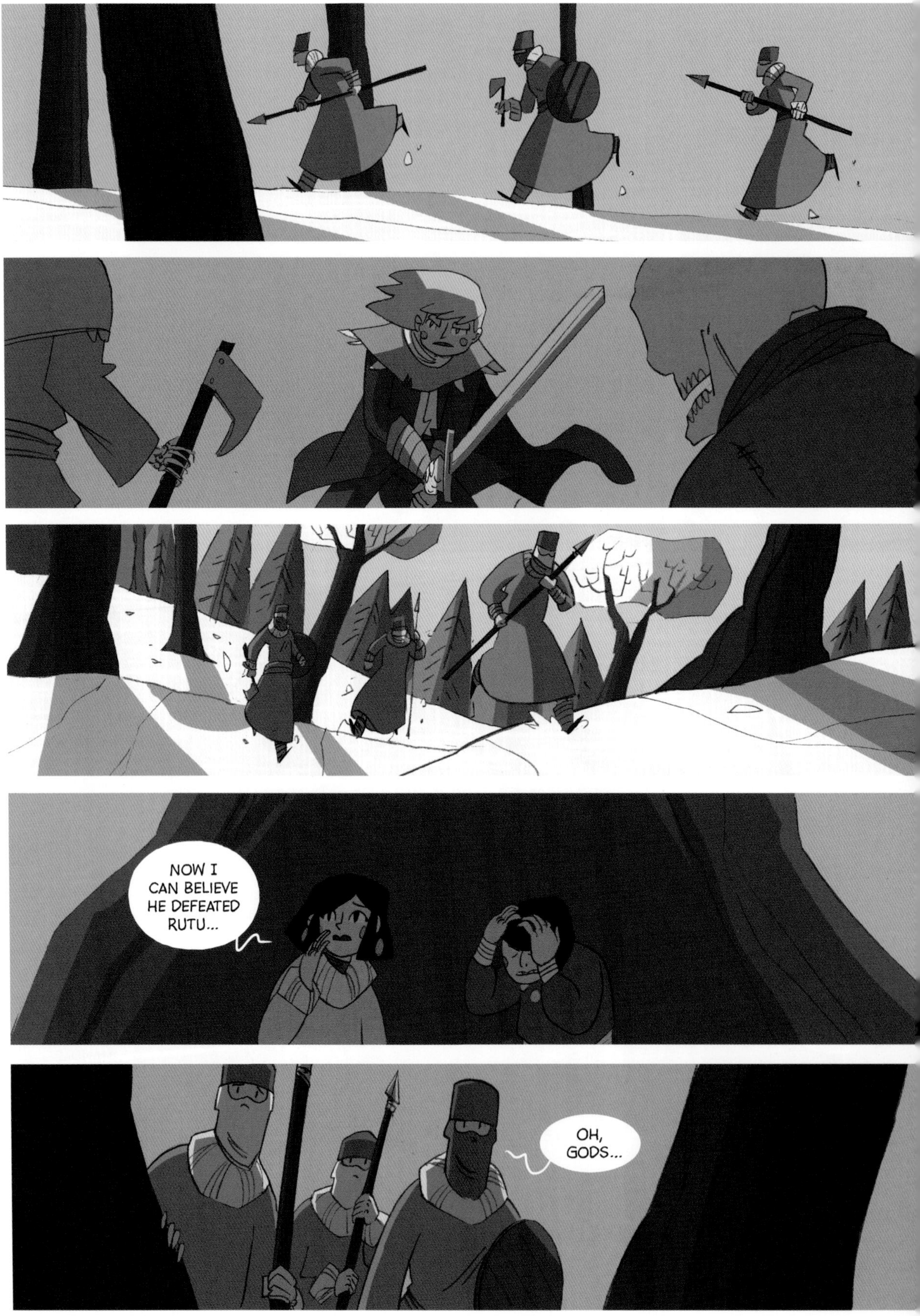
NOW I CAN BELIEVE HE DEFEATED RUTU...
OH, GODS...

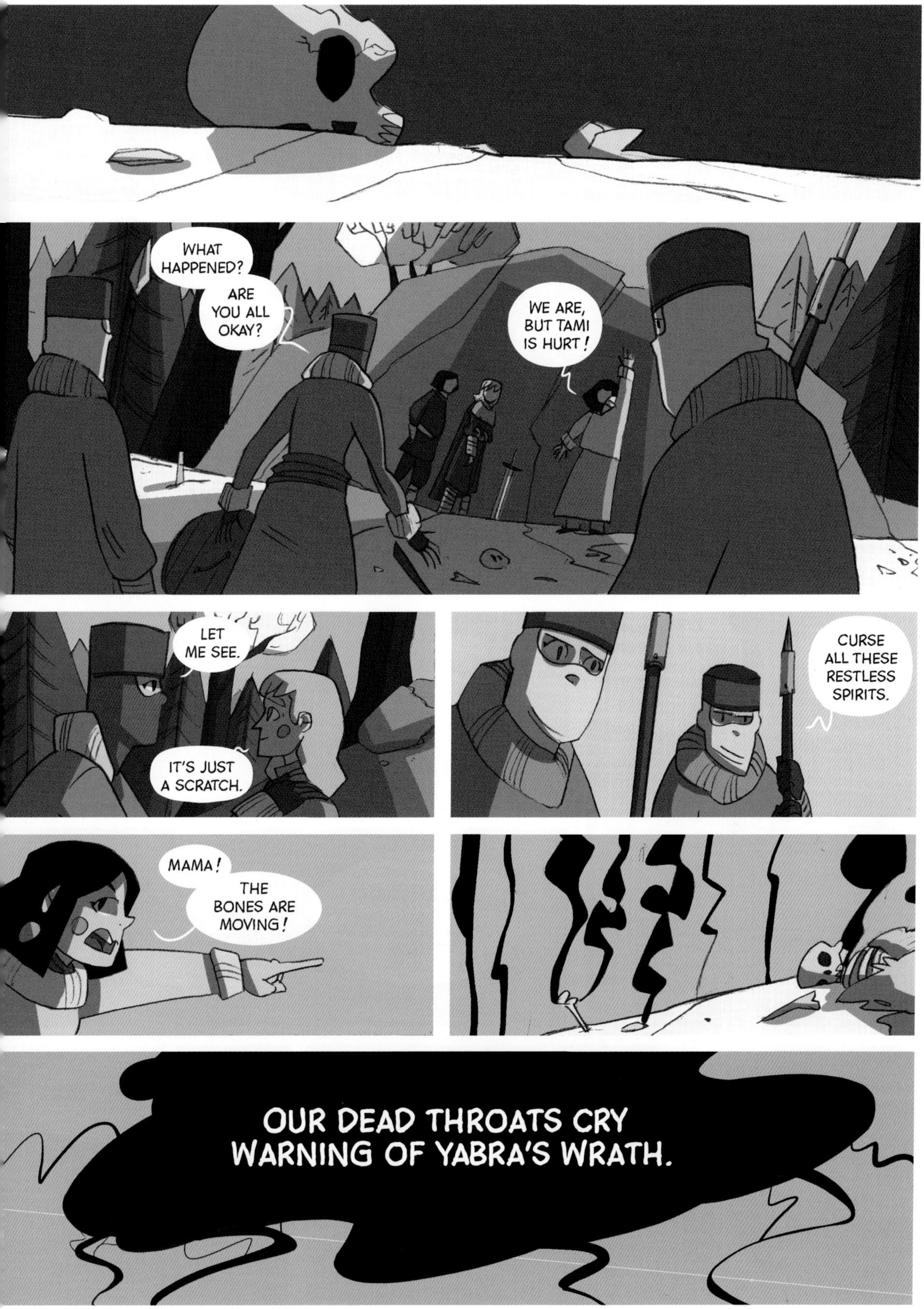
WHAT HAPPENED?
ARE YOU ALL OKAY?
WE ARE, BUT TAMI IS HURT!
LET ME SEE.
IT'S JUST A SCRATCH.
CURSE ALL THESE RESTLESS SPIRITS.
MAMA!
THE BONES ARE MOVING!
OUR DEAD THROATS CRY WARNING OF YABRA'S WRATH.

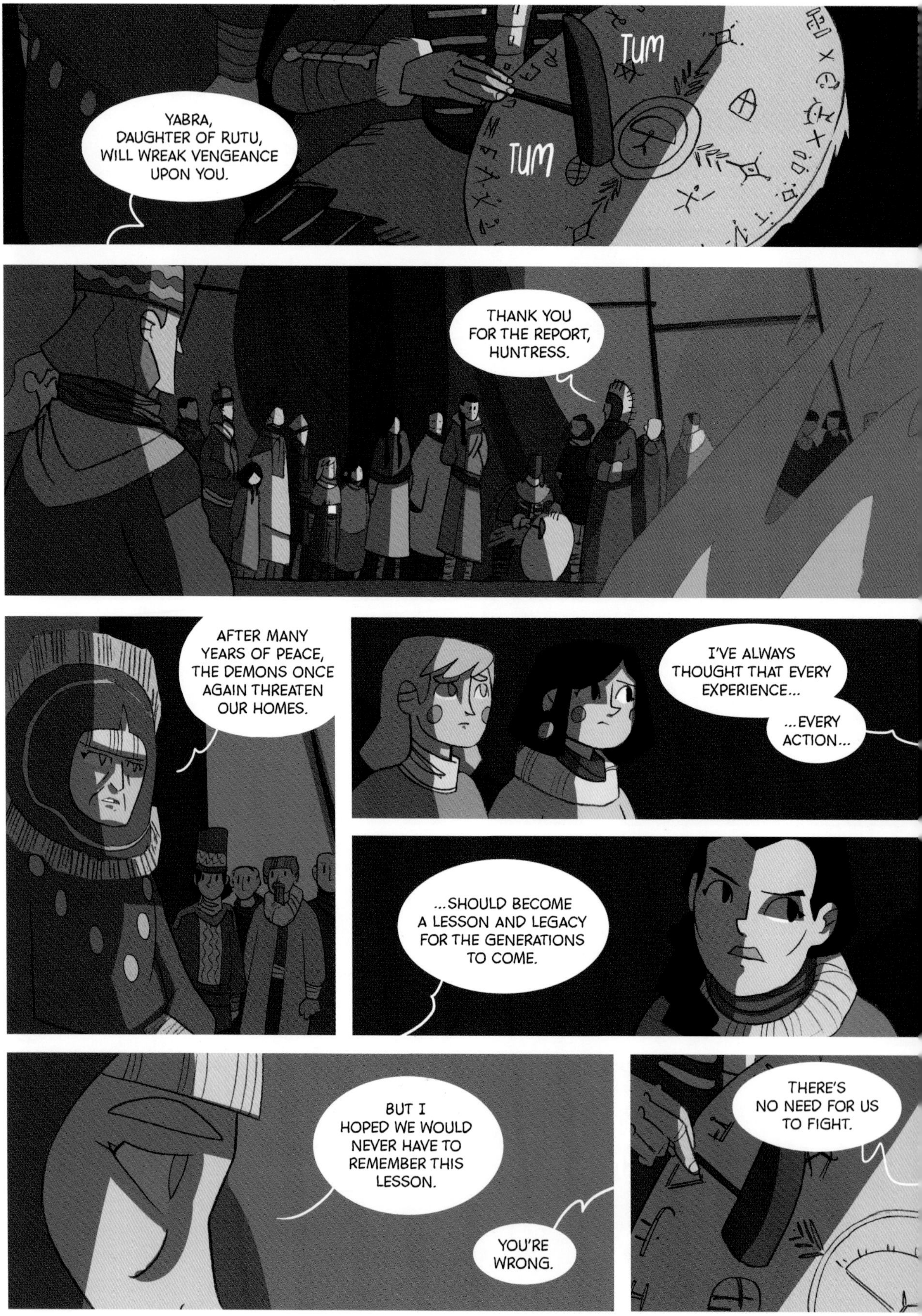
TUM
TUM
YABRA, DAUGHTER OF RUTU, WILL WREAK VENGEANCE UPON YOU.
THANK YOU FOR THE REPORT, HUNTRESS.
AFTER MANY YEARS OF PEACE, THE DEMONS ONCE AGAIN THREATEN OUR HOMES.
I'VE ALWAYS THOUGHT THAT EVERY EXPERIENCE...
...EVERY ACTION...
...SHOULD BECOME A LESSON AND LEGACY FOR THE GENERATIONS TO COME.
BUT I HOPED WE WOULD NEVER HAVE TO REMEMBER THIS LESSON.
YOU'RE WRONG.
THERE'S NO NEED FOR US TO FIGHT.

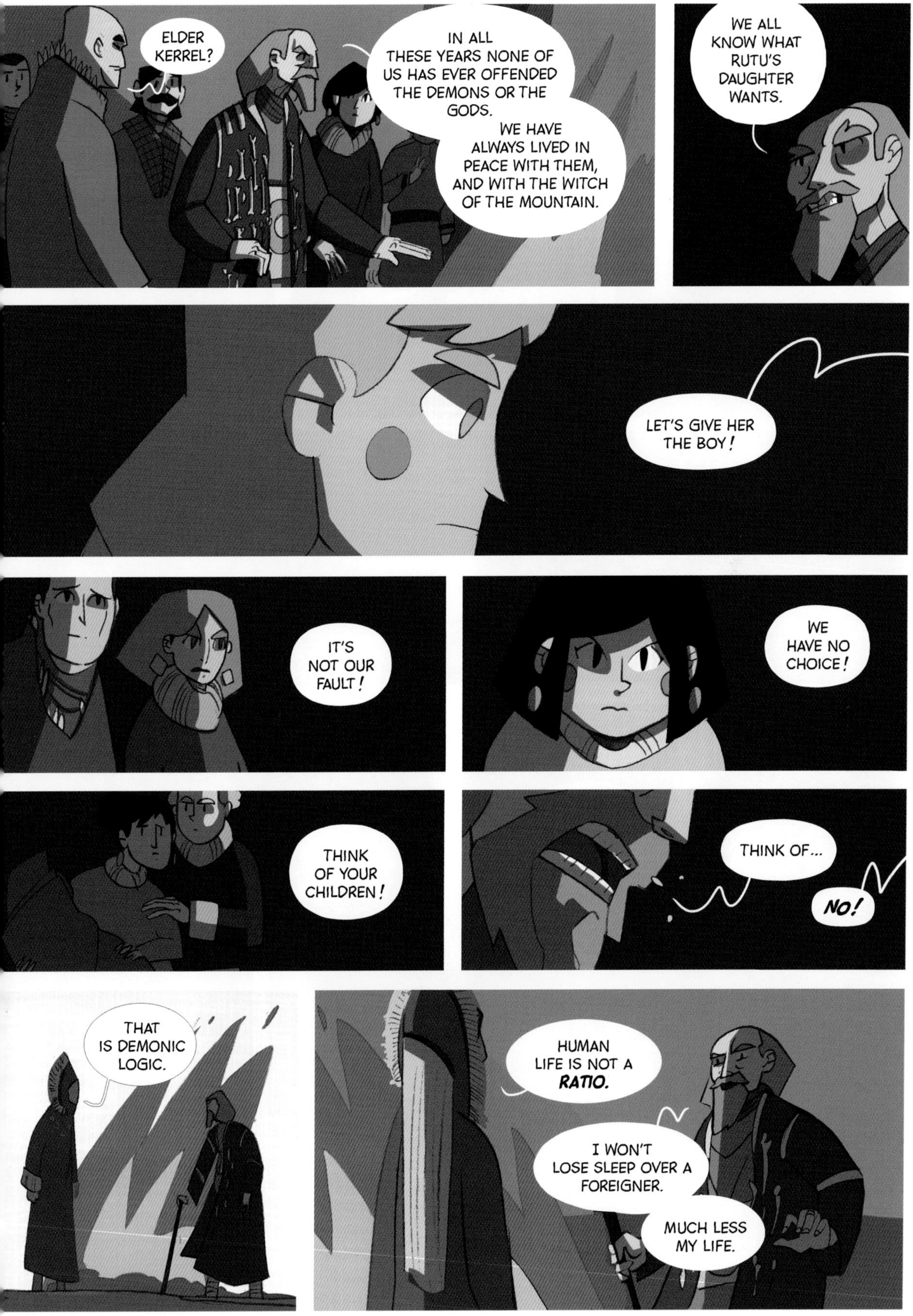
ELDER KERREL?
IN ALL THESE YEARS NONE OF US HAS EVER OFFENDED THE DEMONS OR THE GODS.
WE HAVE ALWAYS LIVED IN PEACE WITH THEM, AND WITH THE WITCH OF THE MOUNTAIN.
WE ALL KNOW WHAT RUTU'S DAUGHTER WANTS.
LET'S GIVE HER THE BOY!
IT'S NOT OUR FAULT!
WE HAVE NO CHOICE!
THINK OF YOUR CHILDREN!
THINK OF...
NO!
THAT IS DEMONIC LOGIC.
HUMAN LIFE IS NOT A RATIO.
I WON'T LOSE SLEEP OVER A FOREIGNER.
MUCH LESS MY LIFE.

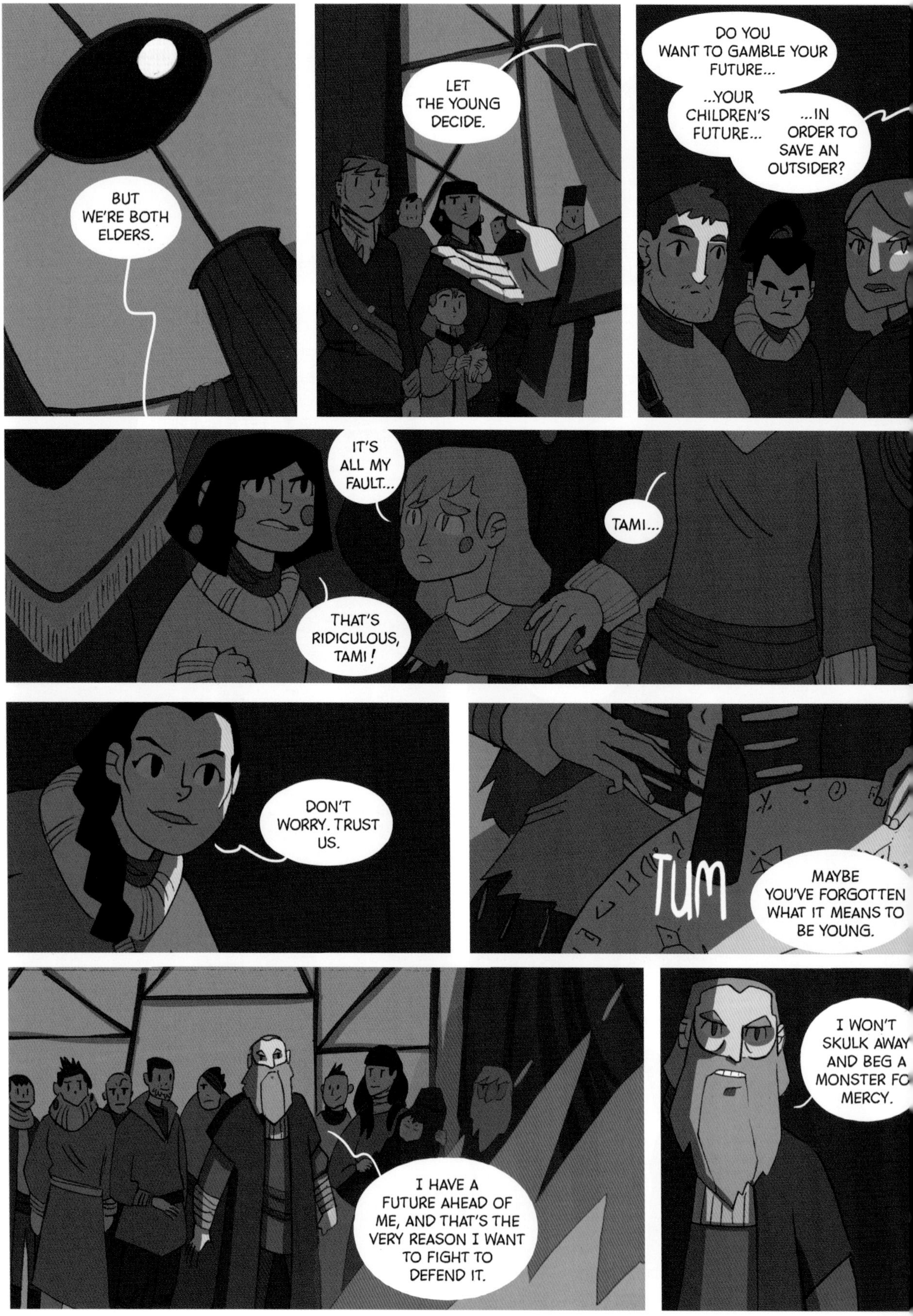
BUT WE'RE BOTH ELDERS.
LET THE YOUNG DECIDE.
DO YOU WANT TO GAMBLE YOUR FUTURE...
...YOUR CHILDREN'S FUTURE...
...IN ORDER TO SAVE AN OUTSIDER?
IT'S ALL MY FAULT...
THAT'S RIDICULOUS, TAMI!
TAMI...
DON'T WORRY. TRUST US.
TUM
MAYBE YOU'VE FORGOTTEN WHAT IT MEANS TO BE YOUNG.
I HAVE A FUTURE AHEAD OF ME, AND THAT'S THE VERY REASON I WANT TO FIGHT TO DEFEND IT.
I WON'T SKULK AWAY AND BEG A MONSTER FO MERCY.

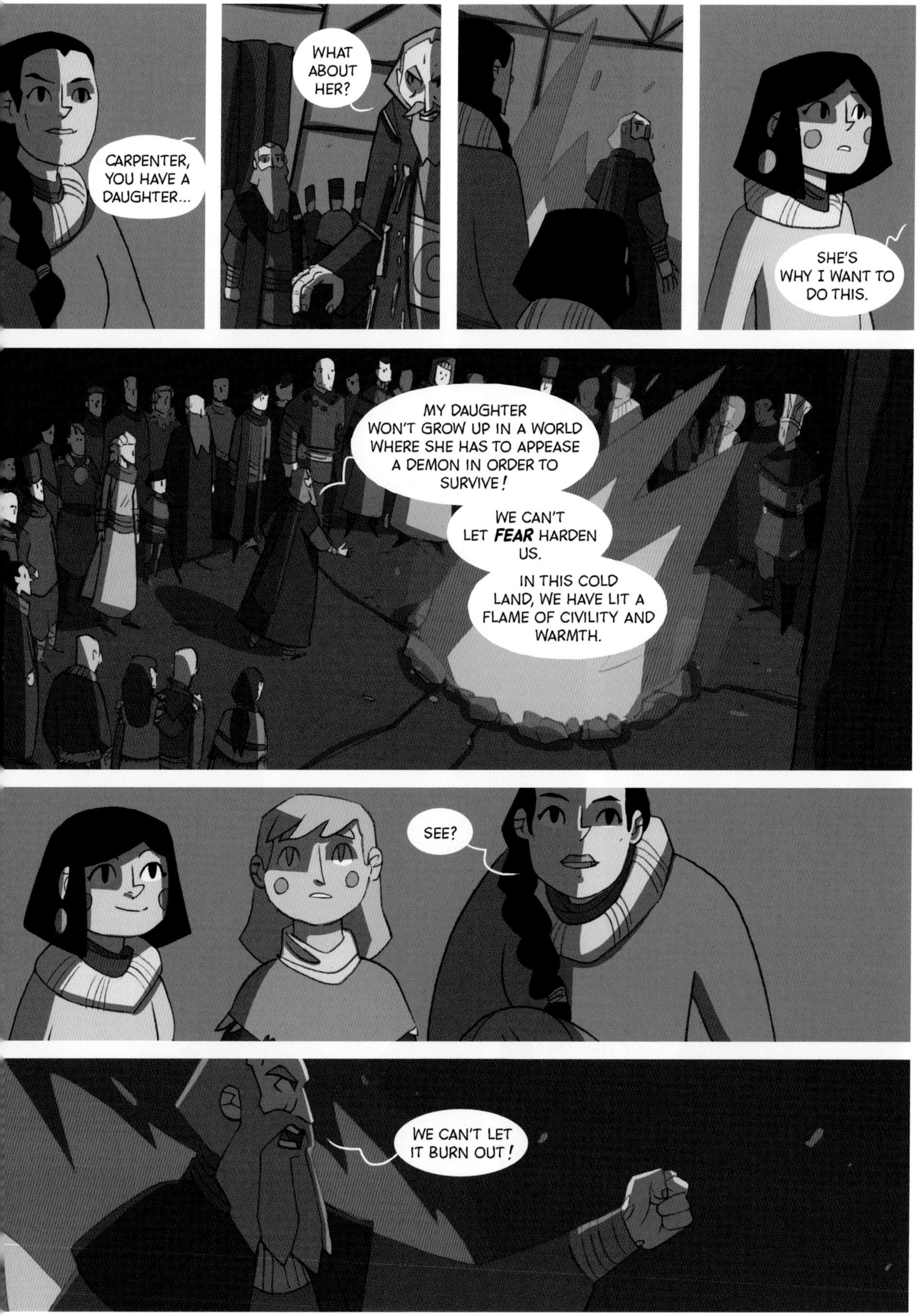
CARPENTER, YOU HAVE A DAUGHTER...
WHAT ABOUT HER?
SHE'S WHY I WANT TO DO THIS.
MY DAUGHTER WON'T GROW UP IN A WORLD WHERE SHE HAS TO APPEASE A DEMON IN ORDER TO SURVIVE!
WE CAN'T LET FEAR HARDEN US.
IN THIS COLD LAND, WE HAVE LIT A FLAME OF CIVILITY AND WARMTH.
SEE?
WE CAN'T LET IT BURN OUT!

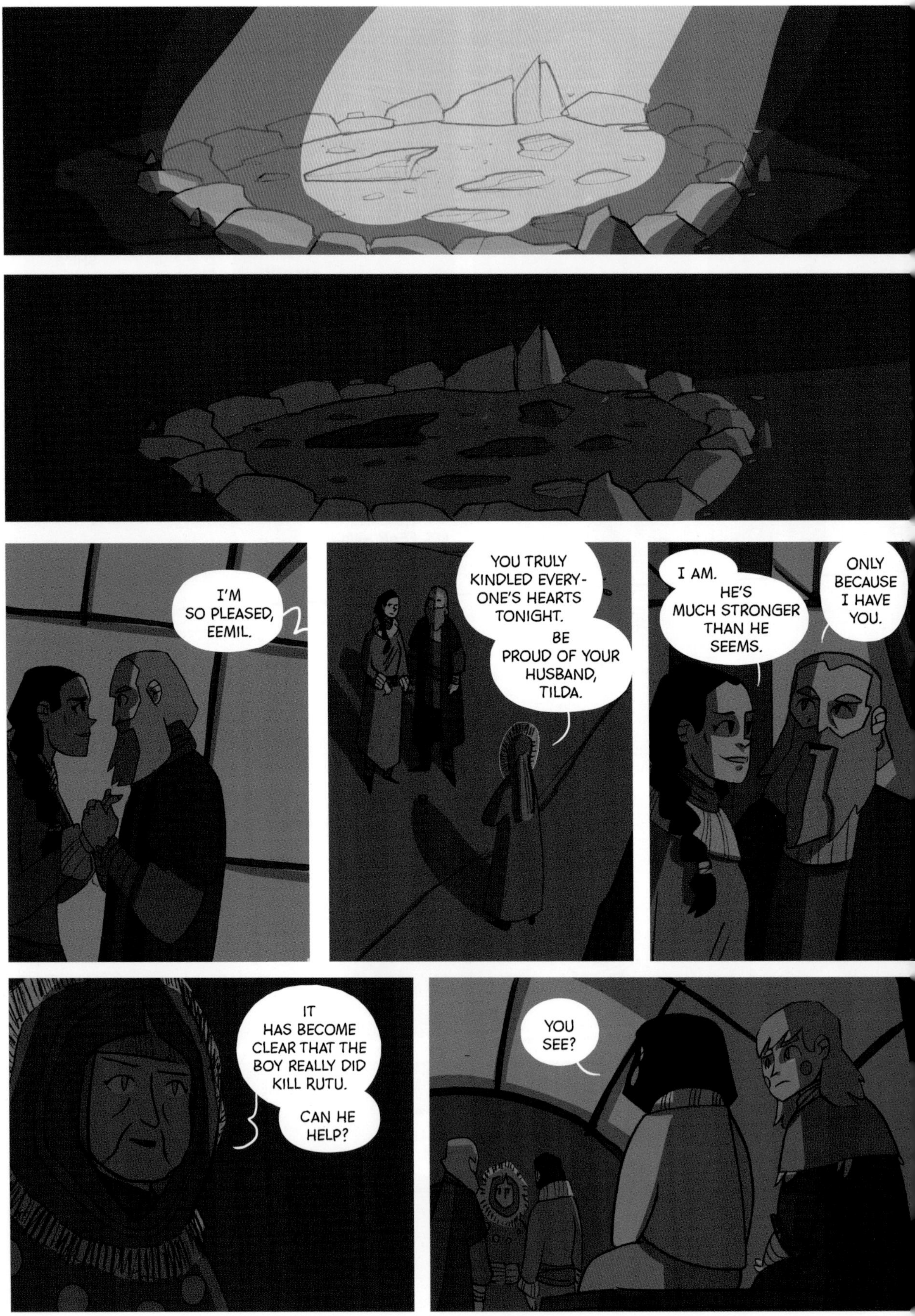
I'M SO PLEASED, EEMIL.
YOU TRULY KINDLED EVERY-ONE'S HEARTS TONIGHT.
BE PROUD OF YOUR HUSBAND, TILDA.
I AM.
HE'S MUCH STRONGER THAN HE SEEMS.
ONLY BECAUSE I HAVE YOU.
IT HAS BECOME CLEAR THAT THE BOY REALLY DID KILL RUTU.
CAN HE HELP?
YOU SEE?

I KNEW THEY WOULDN'T ABANDON YOU.

I DON'T KNOW. MAYBE THE ELDER IS RIGHT.

RUTU ATTACKED YOU AND YOU DEFENDED YOURSELF.

IT WASN'T YOUR FAULT!

MIRA! TAMI!

STOP LOOKING FOR REASONS TO FEEL GUILTY.

COME ON, LET'S GO!

PLUS, IF YOU FIGHT WITH US, THERE'S NO WAY WE'LL LOSE.

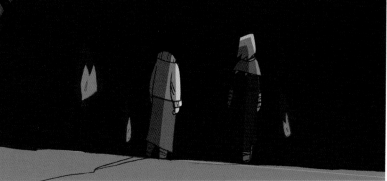

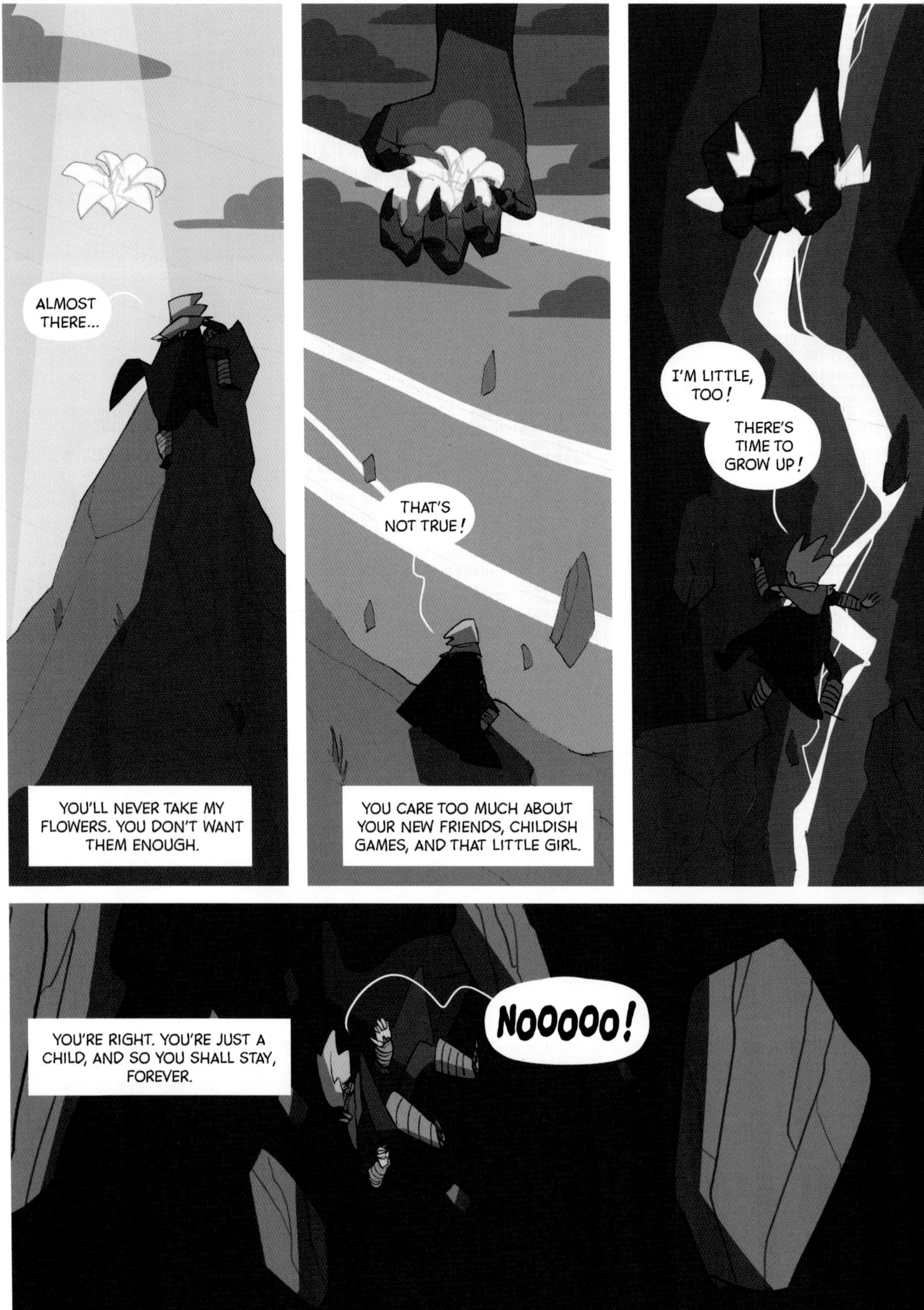
ALMOST THERE...
YOU'LL NEVER TAKE MY FLOWERS. YOU DON'T WANT THEM ENOUGH.
THAT'S NOT TRUE!
YOU CARE TOO MUCH ABOUT YOUR NEW FRIENDS, CHILDISH GAMES, AND THAT LITTLE GIRL.
I'M LITTLE, TOO!
THERE'S TIME TO GROW UP!
YOU'RE RIGHT. YOU'RE JUST A CHILD, AND SO YOU SHALL STAY, FOREVER.
NOOOOO!

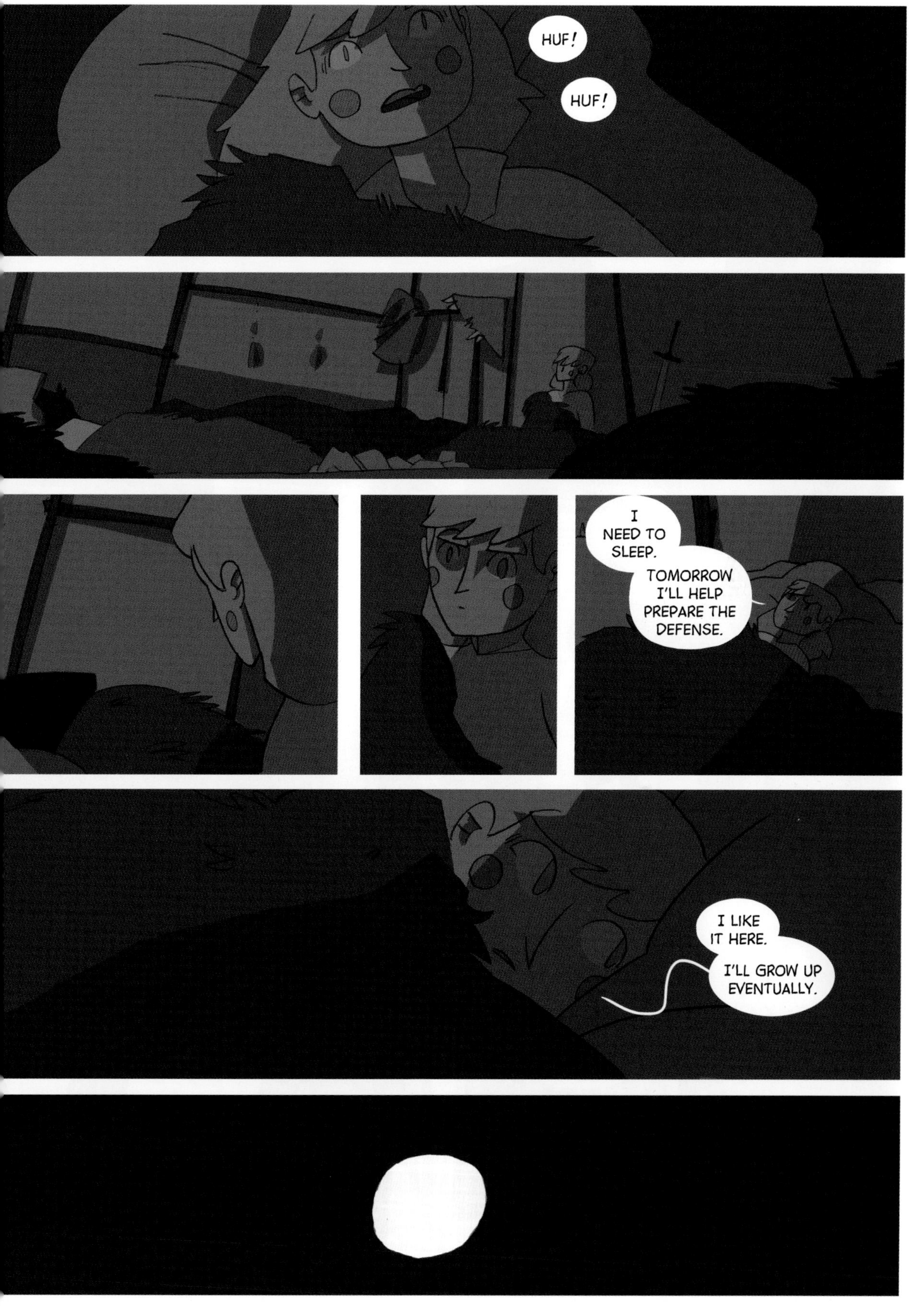
HUF!
HUF!
I NEED TO SLEEP.
TOMORROW I'LL HELP PREPARE THE DEFENSE.
I LIKE IT HERE.
I'LL GROW UP EVENTUALLY.

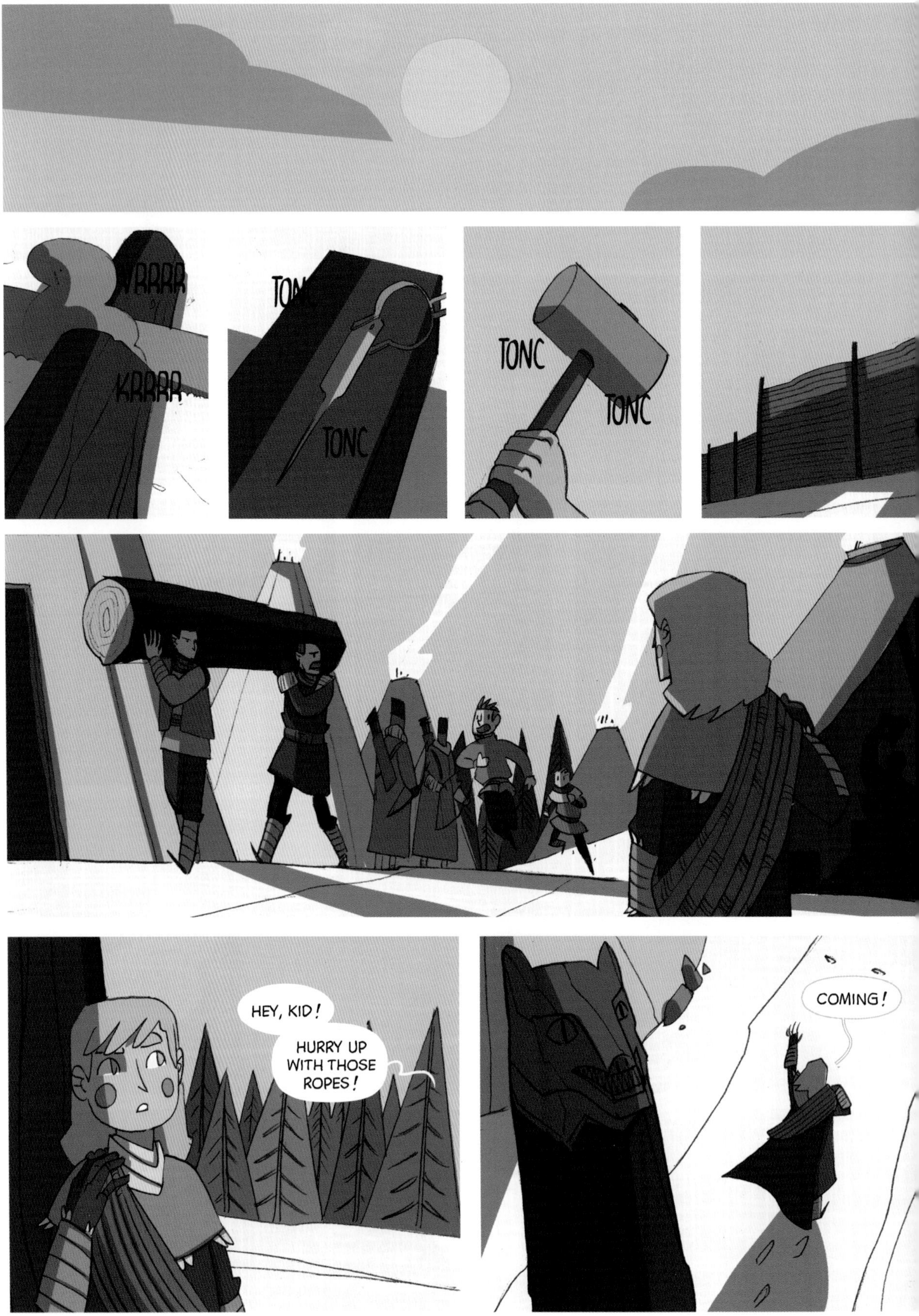

KRRRR
KRRRR
TONC
TONC
TONC
TONC
HEY, KID!
HURRY UP WITH THOSE ROPES!
COMING!

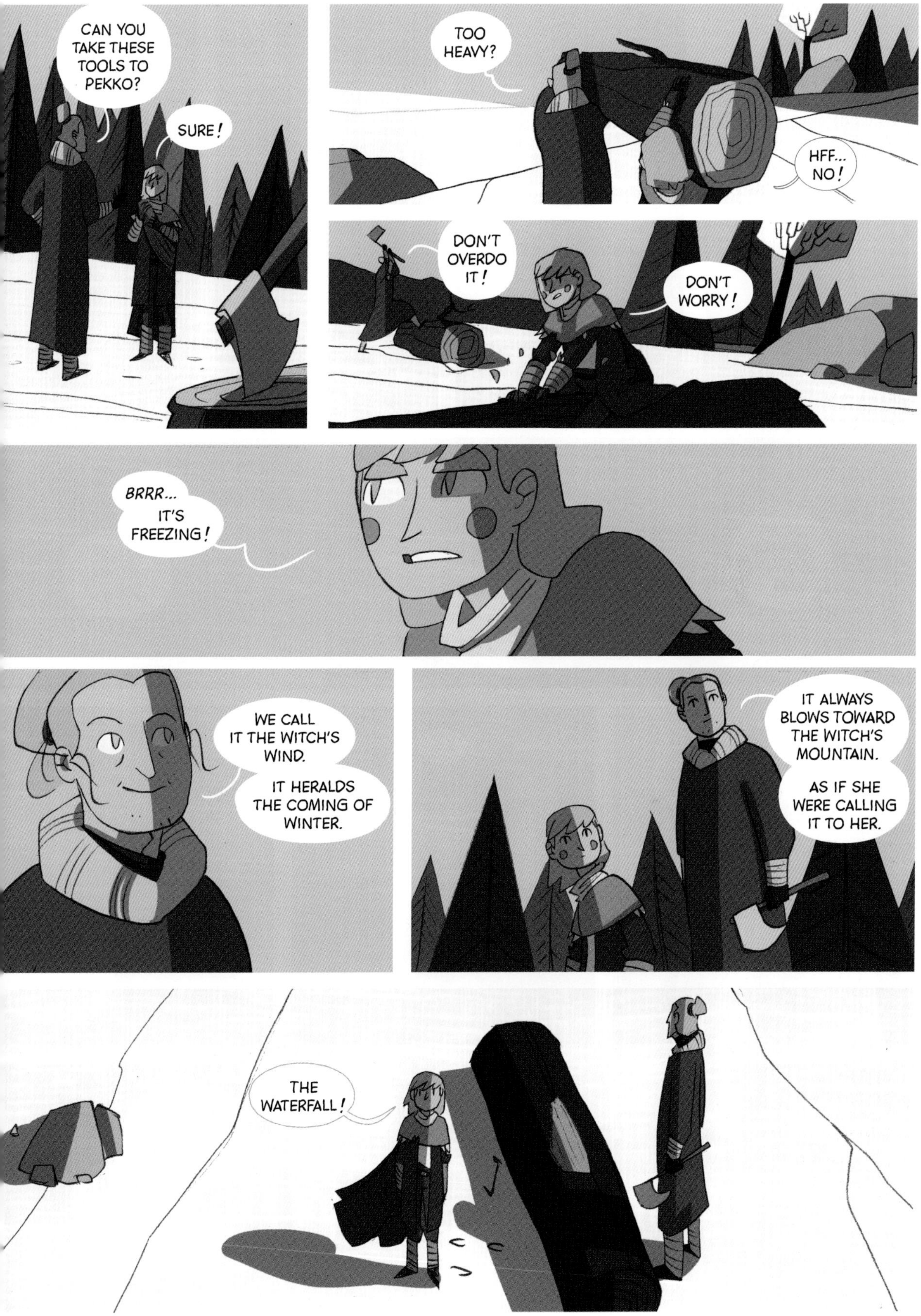
CAN YOU TAKE THESE TOOLS TO PEKKO?
SURE!
TOO HEAVY?
HFF... NO!
DON'T OVERDO IT!
DON'T WORRY!
BRRR... IT'S FREEZING!
WE CALL IT THE WITCH'S WIND.
IT HERALDS THE COMING OF WINTER.
IT ALWAYS BLOWS TOWARD THE WITCH'S MOUNTAIN.
AS IF SHE WERE CALLING IT TO HER.
THE WATERFALL!

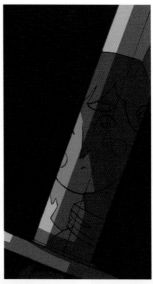

I CAN GET THE FLOWERS AND...

WHERE ARE YOU GOING?

TAMI?

I...

YOU'RE LEAVING, AREN'T YOU?

THE WATERFALL IS FROZEN OVER.

I'M GOING TO GET THE FLOWERS.

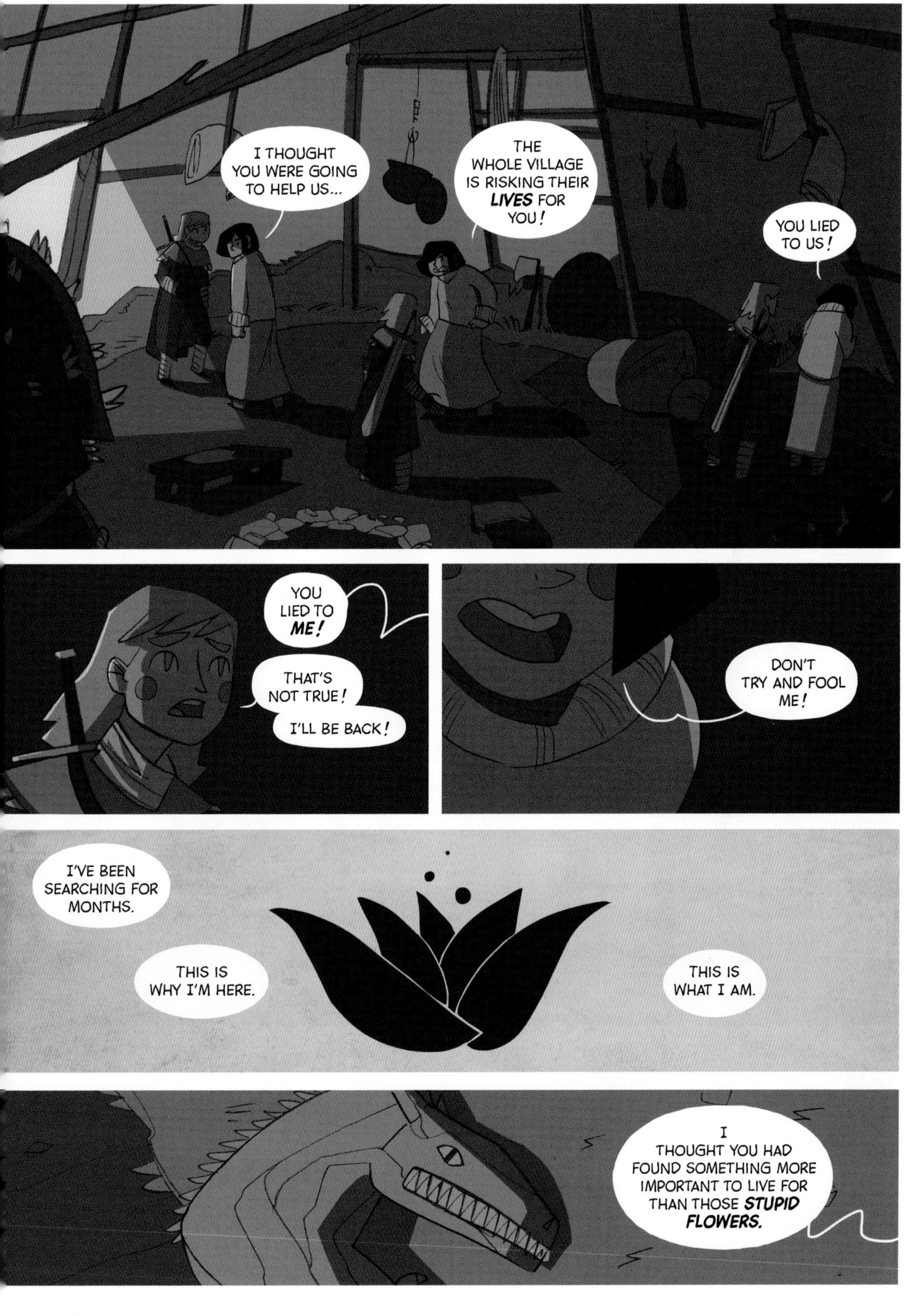
I THOUGHT YOU WERE GOING TO HELP US...
THE WHOLE VILLAGE IS RISKING THEIR **LIVES** FOR YOU!
YOU LIED TO US!
YOU LIED TO **ME!**
THAT'S NOT TRUE!
I'LL BE BACK!
DON'T TRY AND FOOL ME!
I'VE BEEN SEARCHING FOR MONTHS.
THIS IS WHY I'M HERE.
THIS IS WHAT I AM.
I THOUGHT YOU HAD FOUND SOMETHING MORE IMPORTANT TO LIVE FOR THAN THOSE **STUPID FLOWERS.**

I THOUGHT YOU CARED ABOUT US.

GET OUT OF MY HOUSE.

MIRA...

BECOME A MAN AND GO BACK TO YOUR STUPID VILLAGE! THAT'S WHAT YOU'VE ALWAYS WANTED, ISN'T IT?

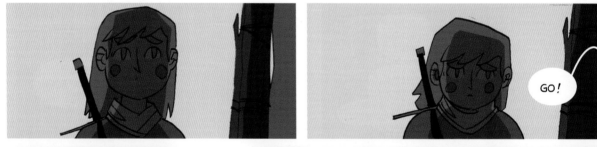

GO!

I CAN DO THIS.

I'LL BE BACK.

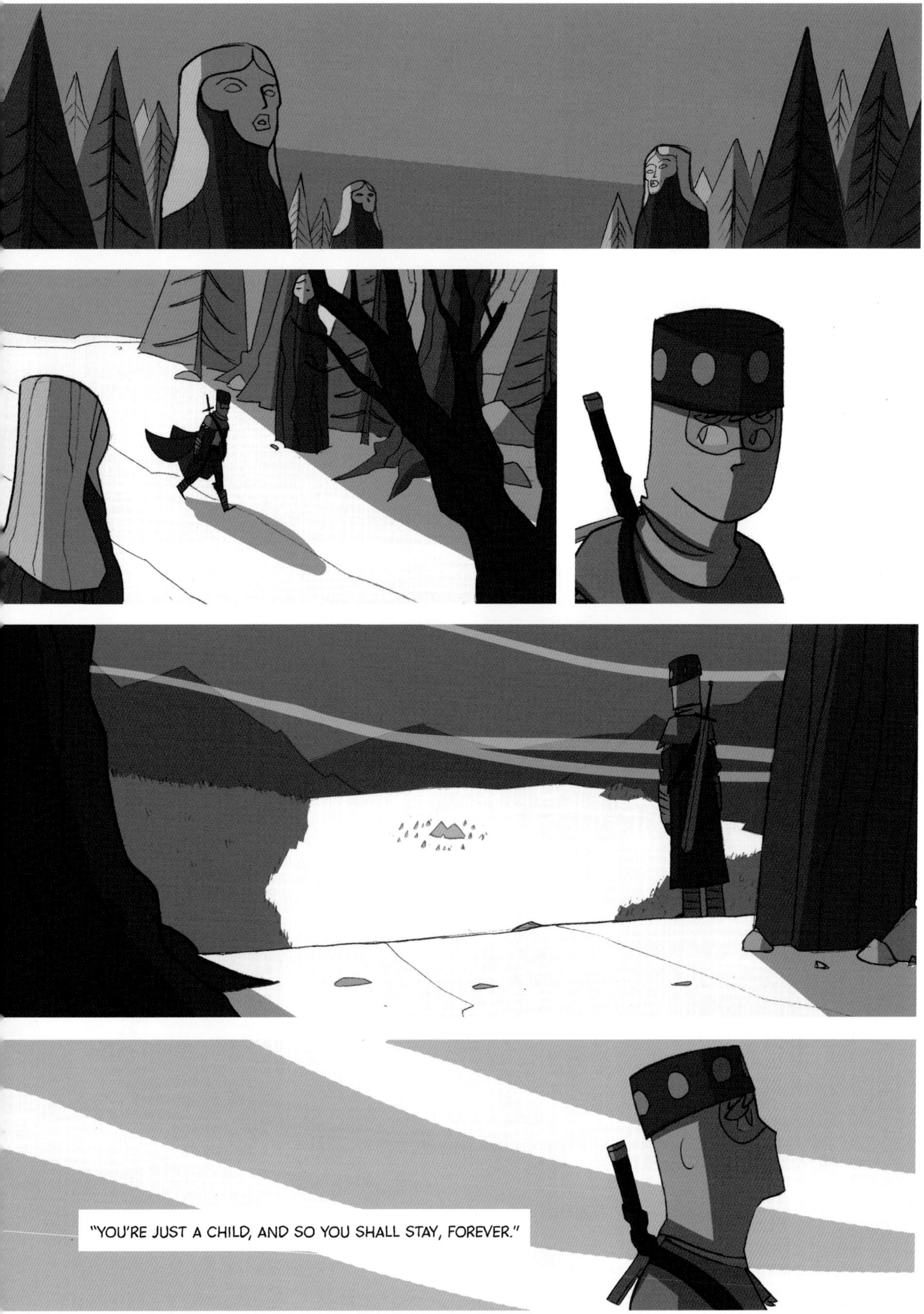
"YOU'RE JUST A CHILD, AND SO YOU SHALL STAY, FOREVER."

LOOKS LIKE THIS REALLY IS THE ONLY PATH.

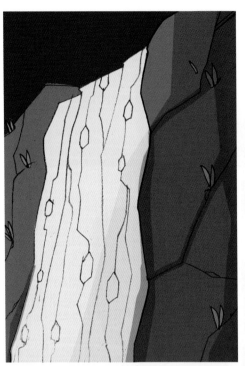

ZUNK

ZUNK

ZUNK

ZCRRACK

UH OH...

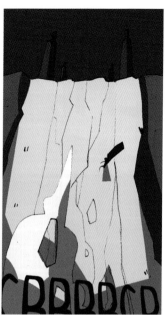

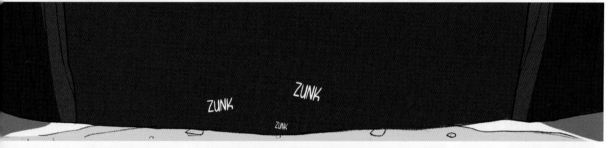

ZUNK

ZUNK

ZUNK

WELL, BESIDES NEARLY **DYING...** ...IT WASN'T SO HARD AFTER ALL.

IT'LL BE EASY ENOUGH TO GO BA--

OH NO...

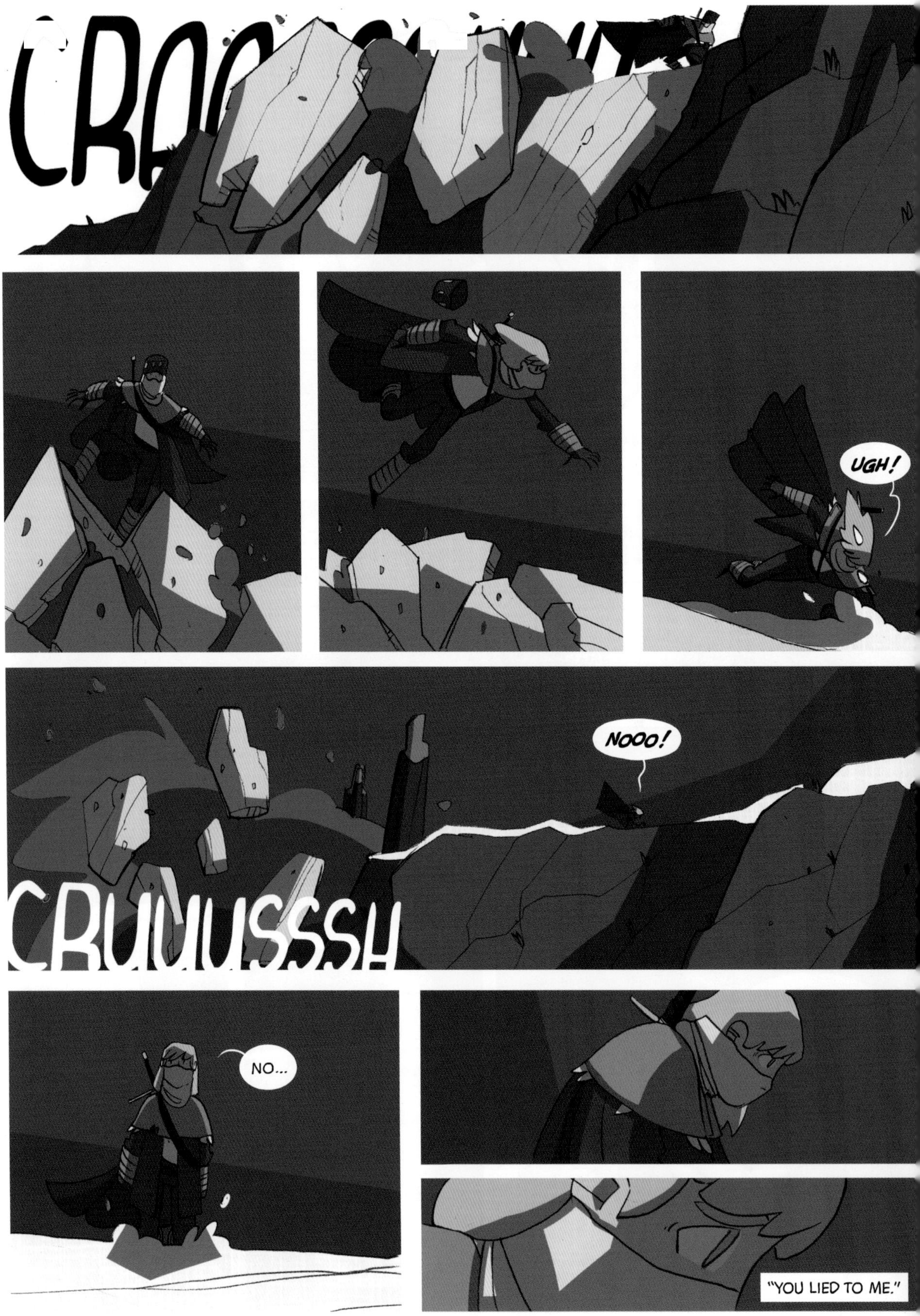
UGH!
NOOO!
CRUUUSSSH
NO...
"YOU LIED TO ME."

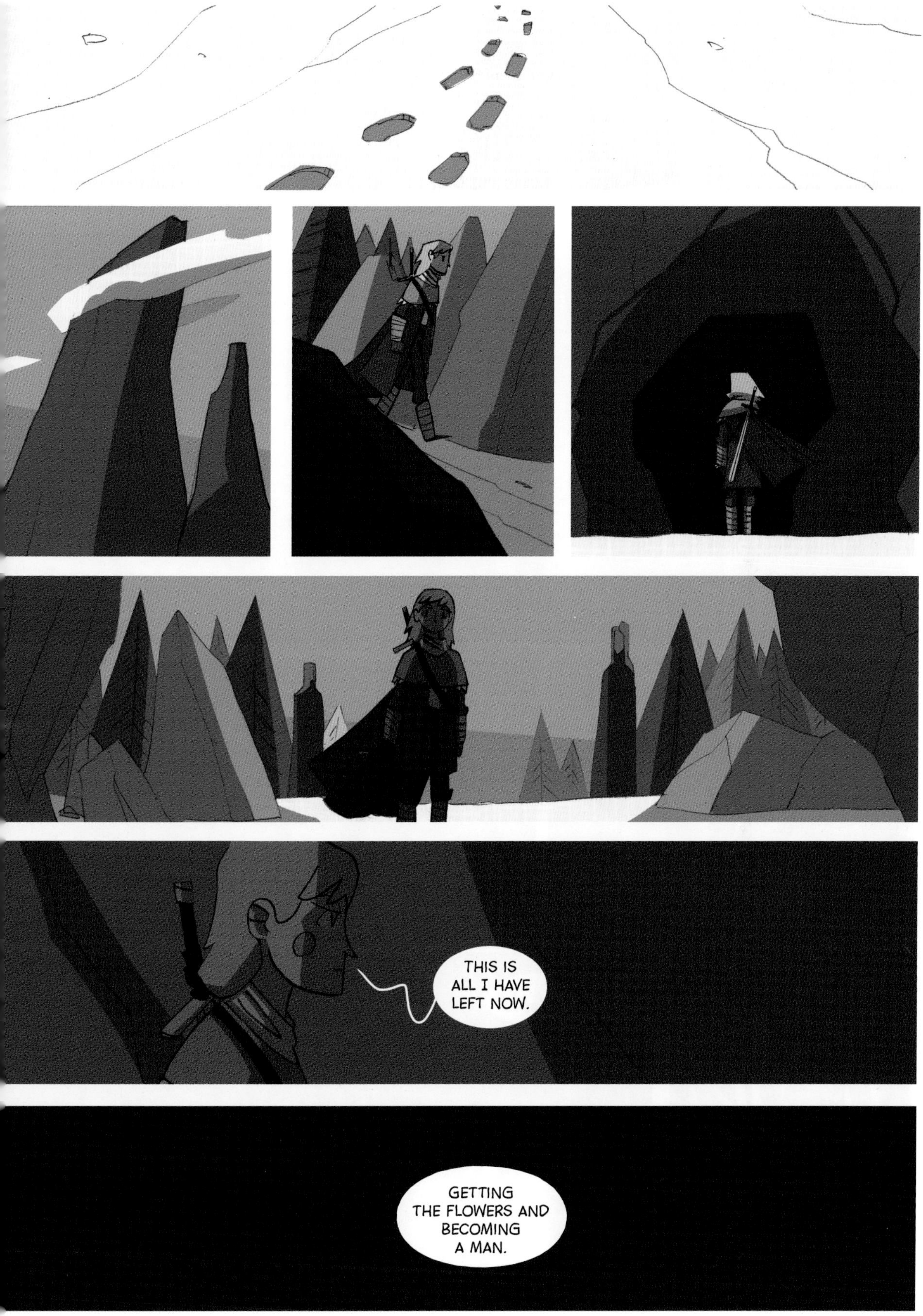
THIS IS ALL I HAVE LEFT NOW.
GETTING THE FLOWERS AND BECOMING A MAN.

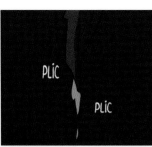

PLIC

PLIC

NOW WHAT?

HUH?

CRAKK

AAAAAH!

CROOCK

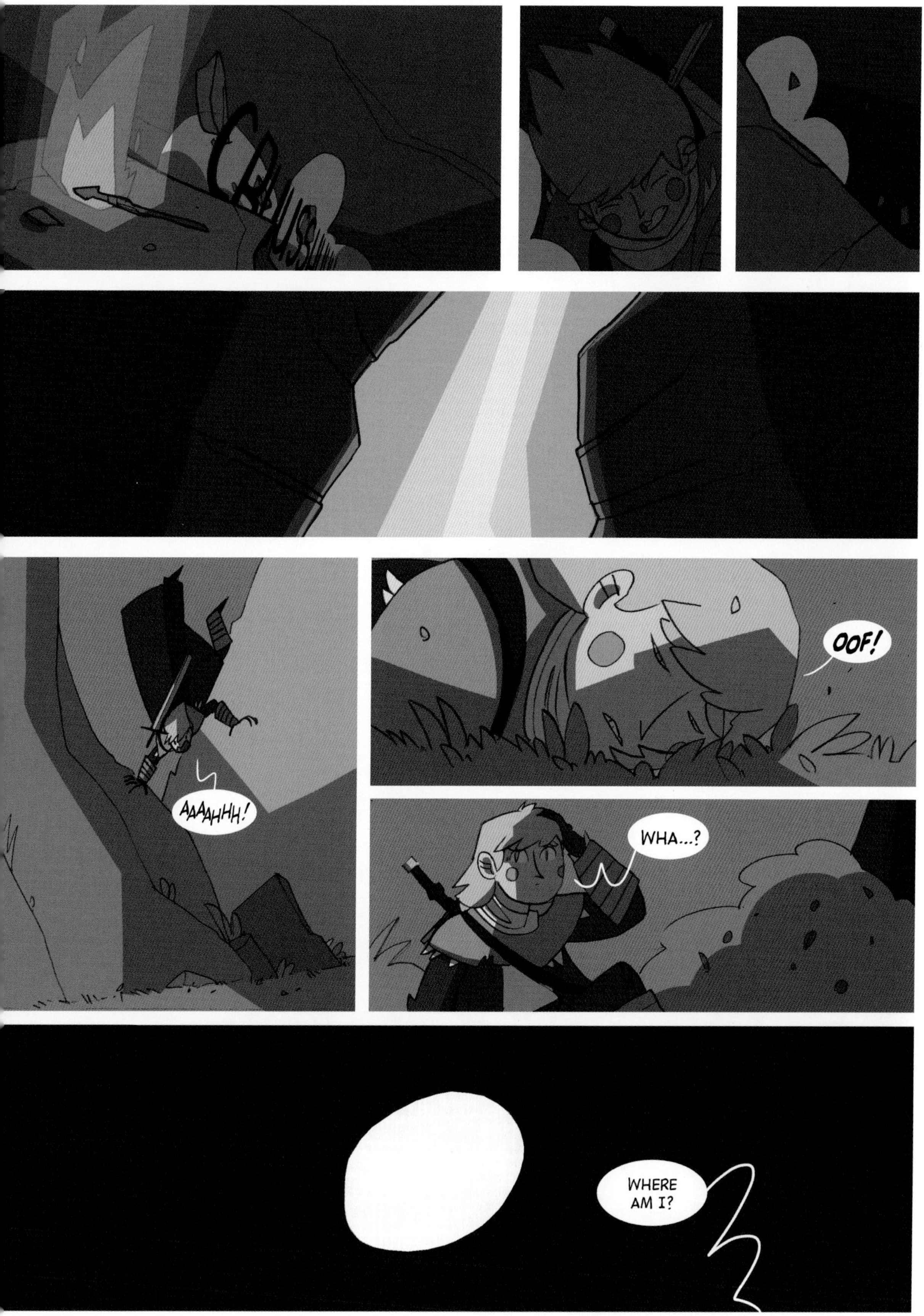
CRUSSHHH
AAAAHHH!
OOF!
WHA...?
WHERE AM I?

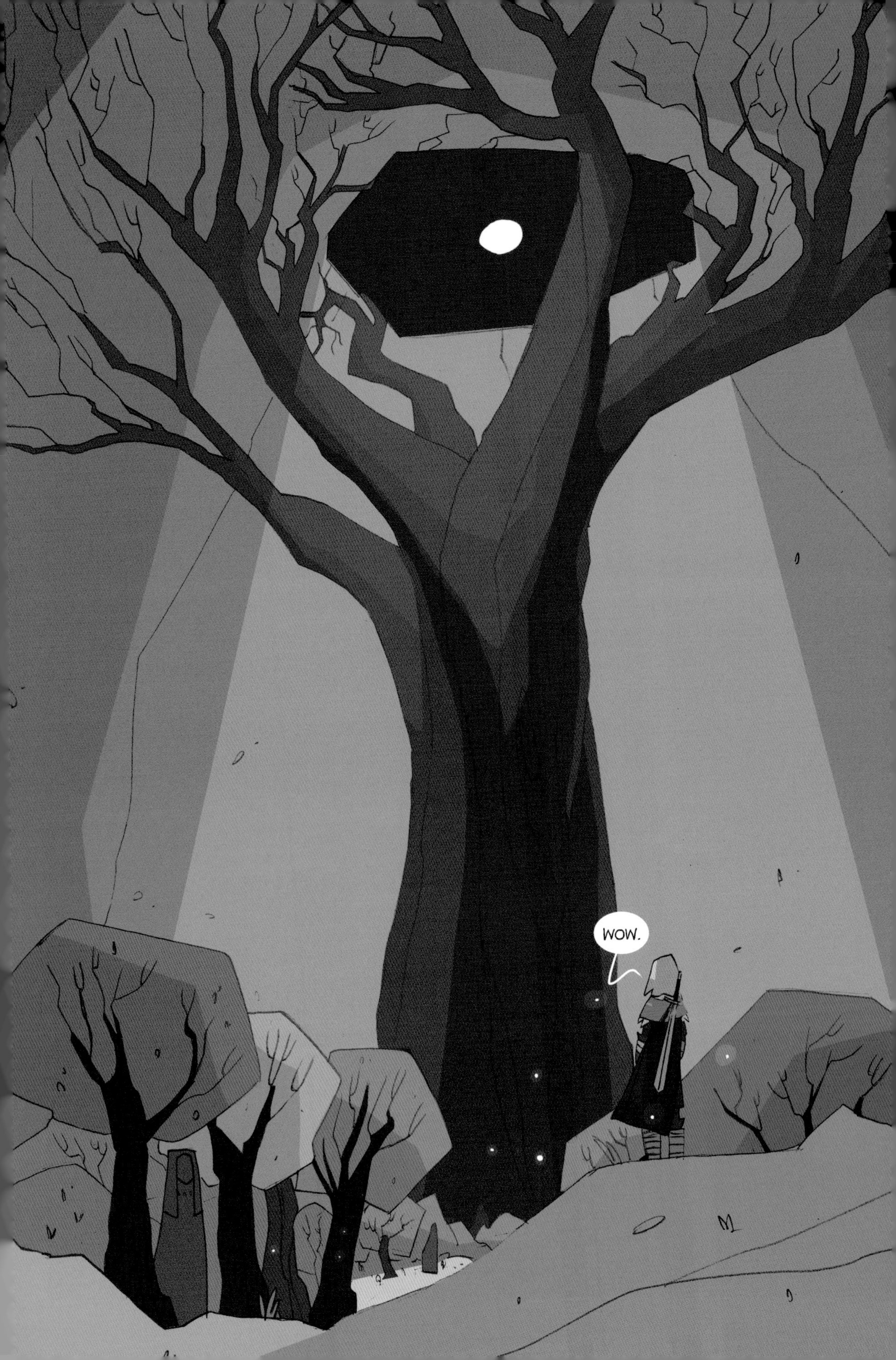
WOW.

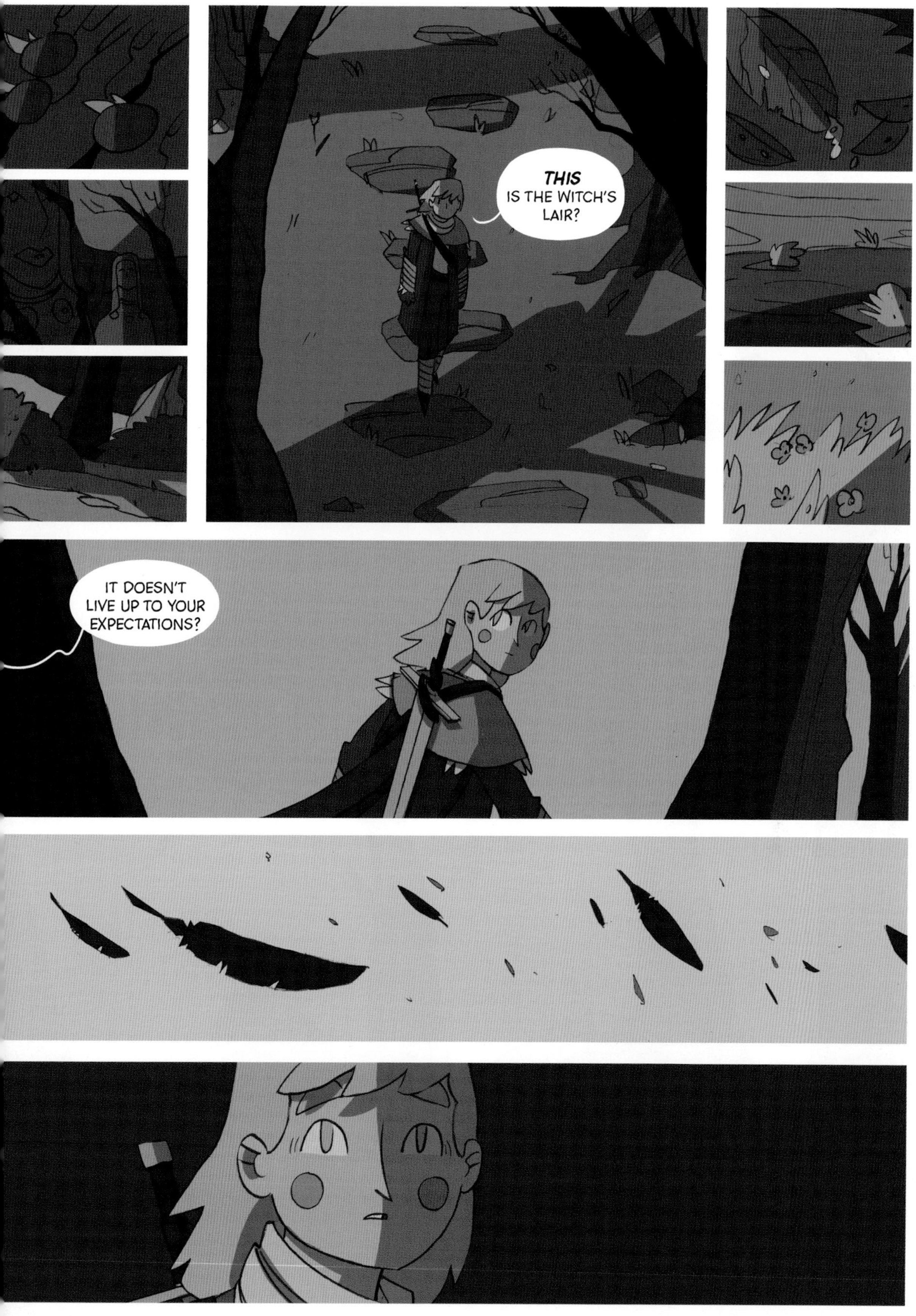
THIS
IS THE WITCH'S
LAIR?
IT DOESN'T
LIVE UP TO YOUR
EXPECTATIONS?

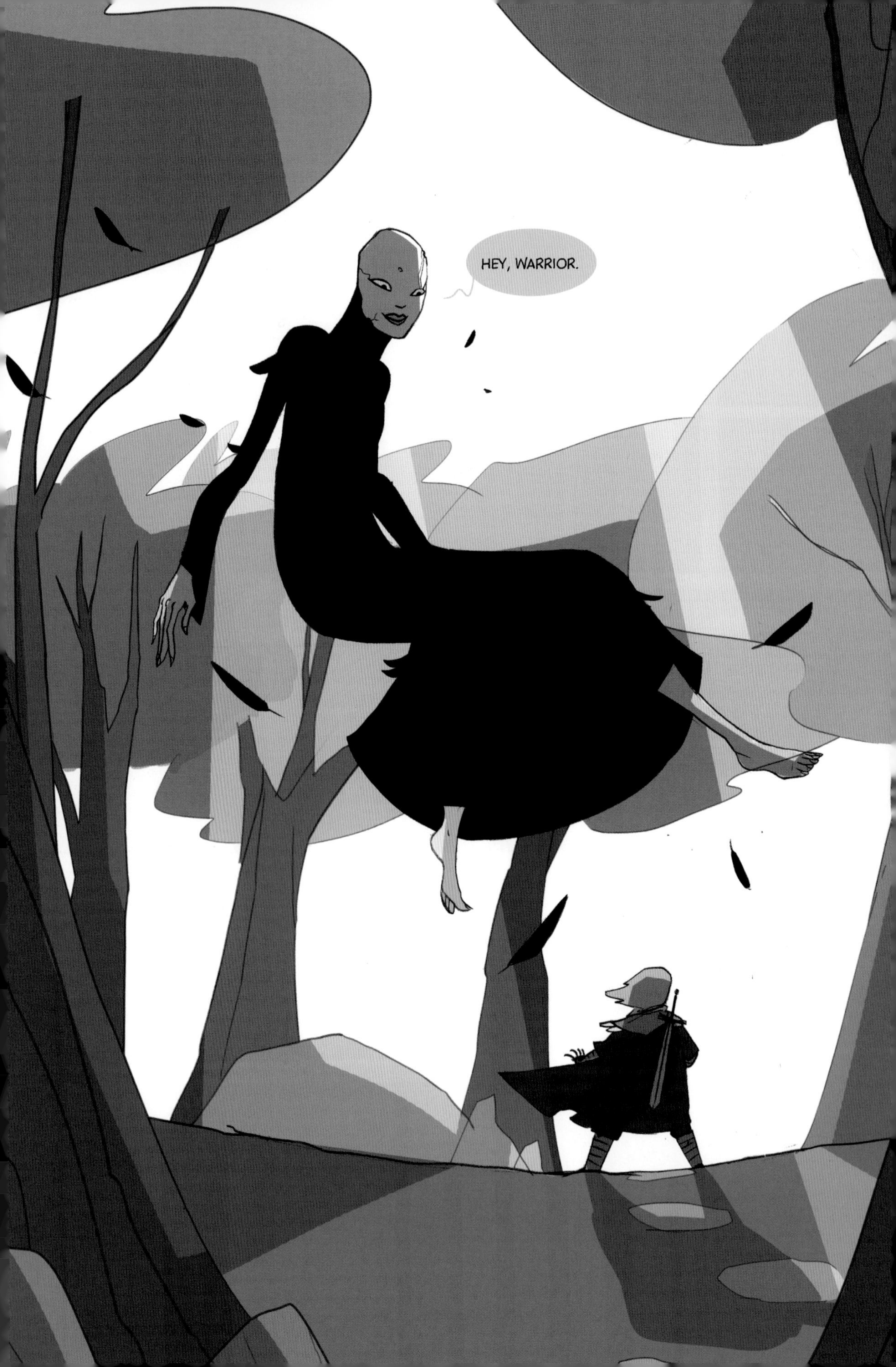
HEY, WARRIOR.

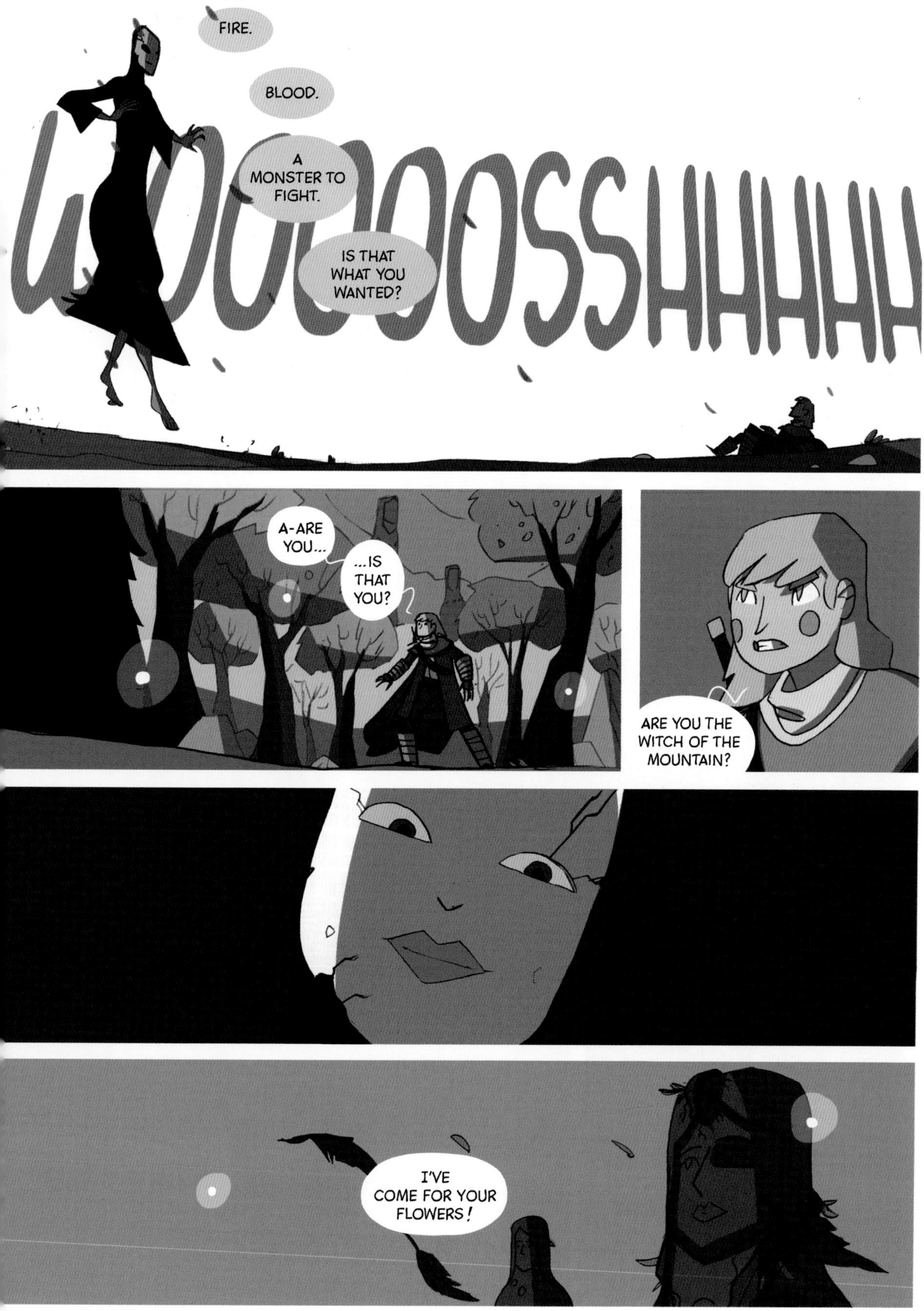
FIRE.
BLOOD.
WOOOOOOSSHHHHHH
A MONSTER TO FIGHT.
IS THAT WHAT YOU WANTED?
A-ARE YOU...
...IS THAT YOU?
ARE YOU THE WITCH OF THE MOUNTAIN?
I'VE COME FOR YOUR FLOWERS!

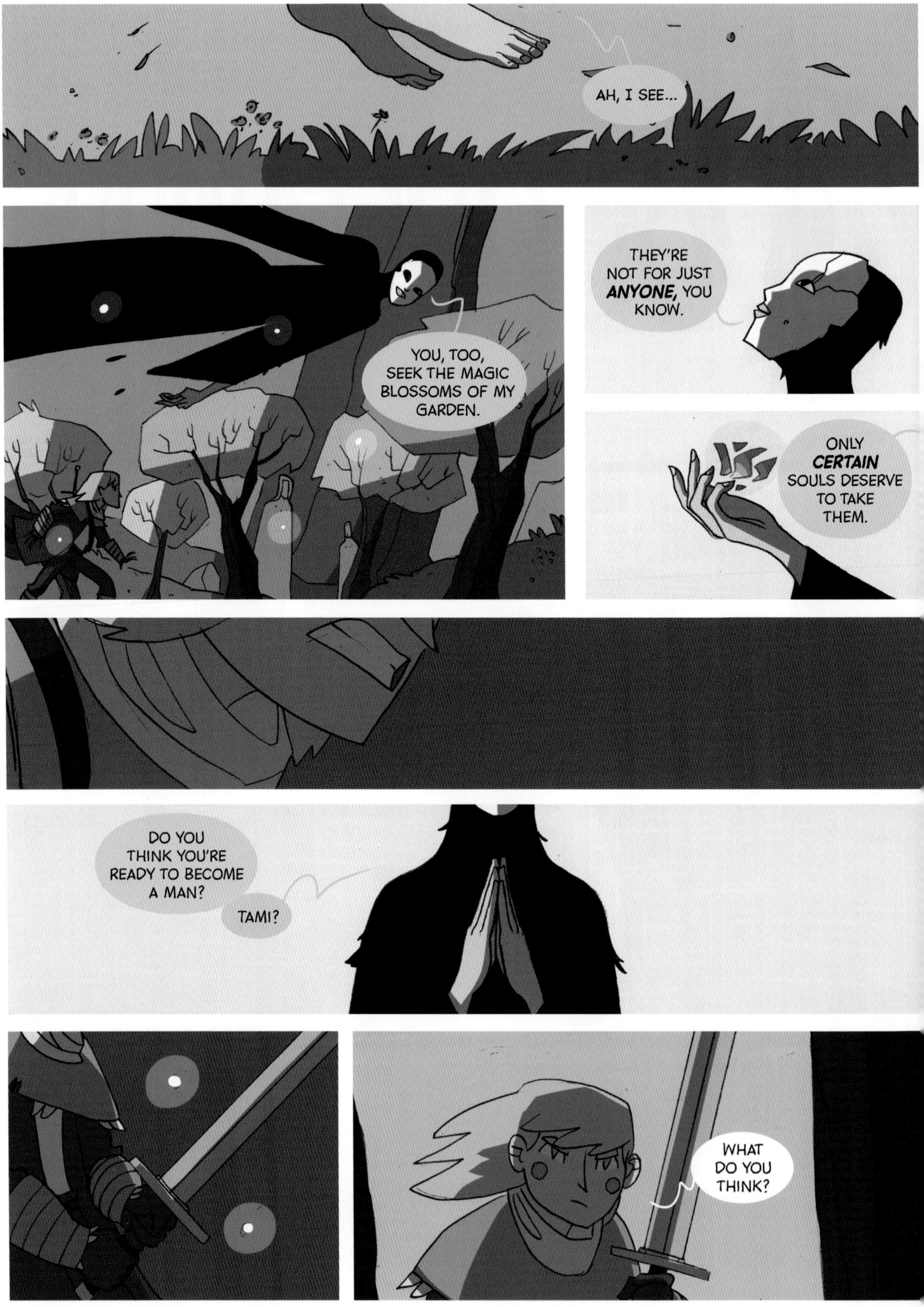
AH, I SEE...
YOU, TOO, SEEK THE MAGIC BLOSSOMS OF MY GARDEN.
THEY'RE NOT FOR JUST **ANYONE,** YOU KNOW.
ONLY **CERTAIN** SOULS DESERVE TO TAKE THEM.
DO YOU THINK YOU'RE READY TO BECOME A MAN?
TAMI?
WHAT DO YOU THINK?

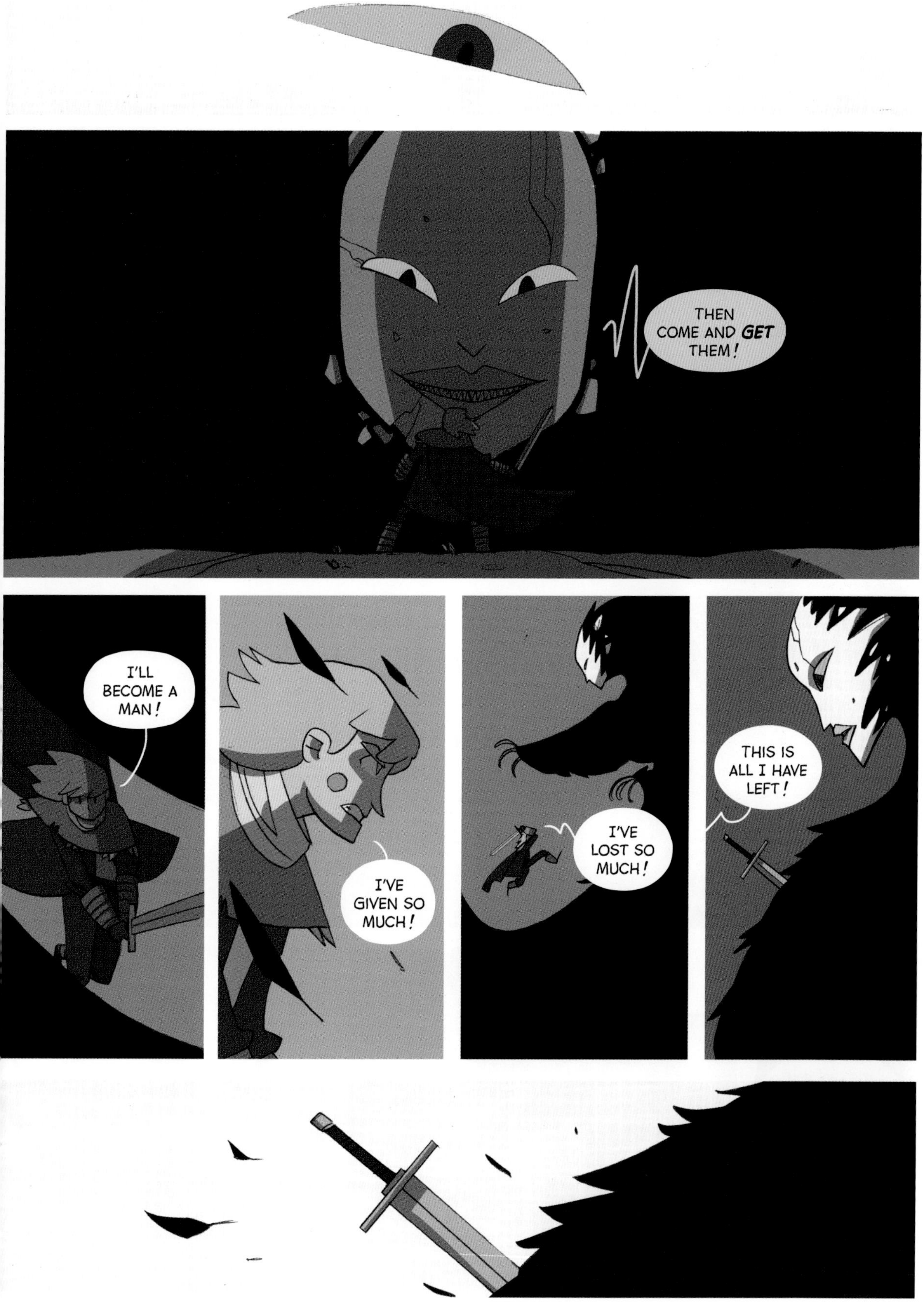
THEN COME AND GET THEM!
I'LL BECOME A MAN!
I'VE GIVEN SO MUCH!
I'VE LOST SO MUCH!
THIS IS ALL I HAVE LEFT!

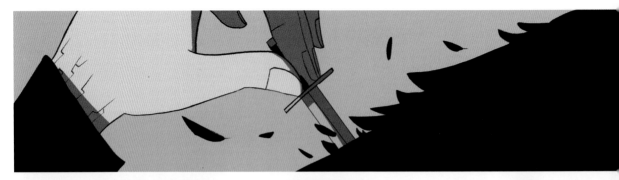

I BELIEVE THIS BELONGS TO YOU.

RELAX, I WAS JUST PLAYING.

YOU DON'T HAVE TO FIGHT, YOU'VE ALREADY PROVEN THAT YOU DESERVE MY FLOWERS.

I HAVE? HOW?

IT'S LIKE YOU SAID. YOU GAVE UP EVERYTHING AND EVERYONE...

...JUST TO PICK MY FLOWERS AND BECOME A MAN.

NO...

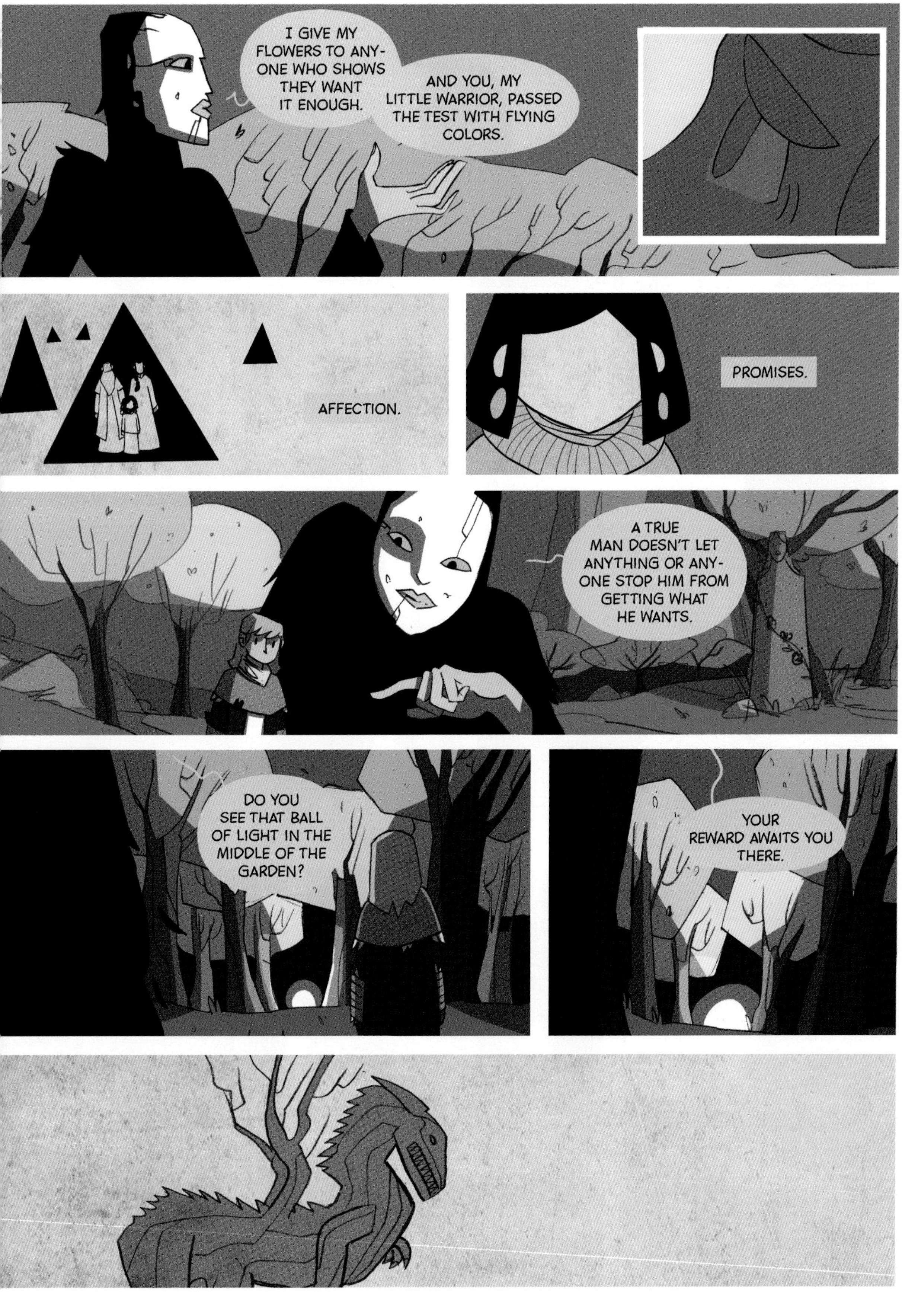
I GIVE MY FLOWERS TO ANY-ONE WHO SHOWS THEY WANT IT ENOUGH.
AND YOU, MY LITTLE WARRIOR, PASSED THE TEST WITH FLYING COLORS.
AFFECTION.
PROMISES.
A TRUE MAN DOESN'T LET ANYTHING OR ANY-ONE STOP HIM FROM GETTING WHAT HE WANTS.
DO YOU SEE THAT BALL OF LIGHT IN THE MIDDLE OF THE GARDEN?
YOUR REWARD AWAITS YOU THERE.

I DON'T WANT THEM ANY- MORE.

WHAT?

I DON'T WANT YOUR STUPID **FLOWERS!**

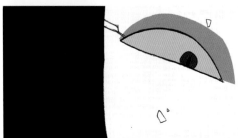

HONESTLY...

I THOUGHT THAT ONCE I BECAME A MAN--

I JUST WANTED TO BE ACCEPTED.

LOVED.

I DIDN'T REALIZE THAT MIRA, EEMIL, TILDA, AND THE OTHERS HAD ALREADY DONE THAT.

SPLAH

WITH THEM, IT WAS ENOUGH TO JUST BE MYSELF.

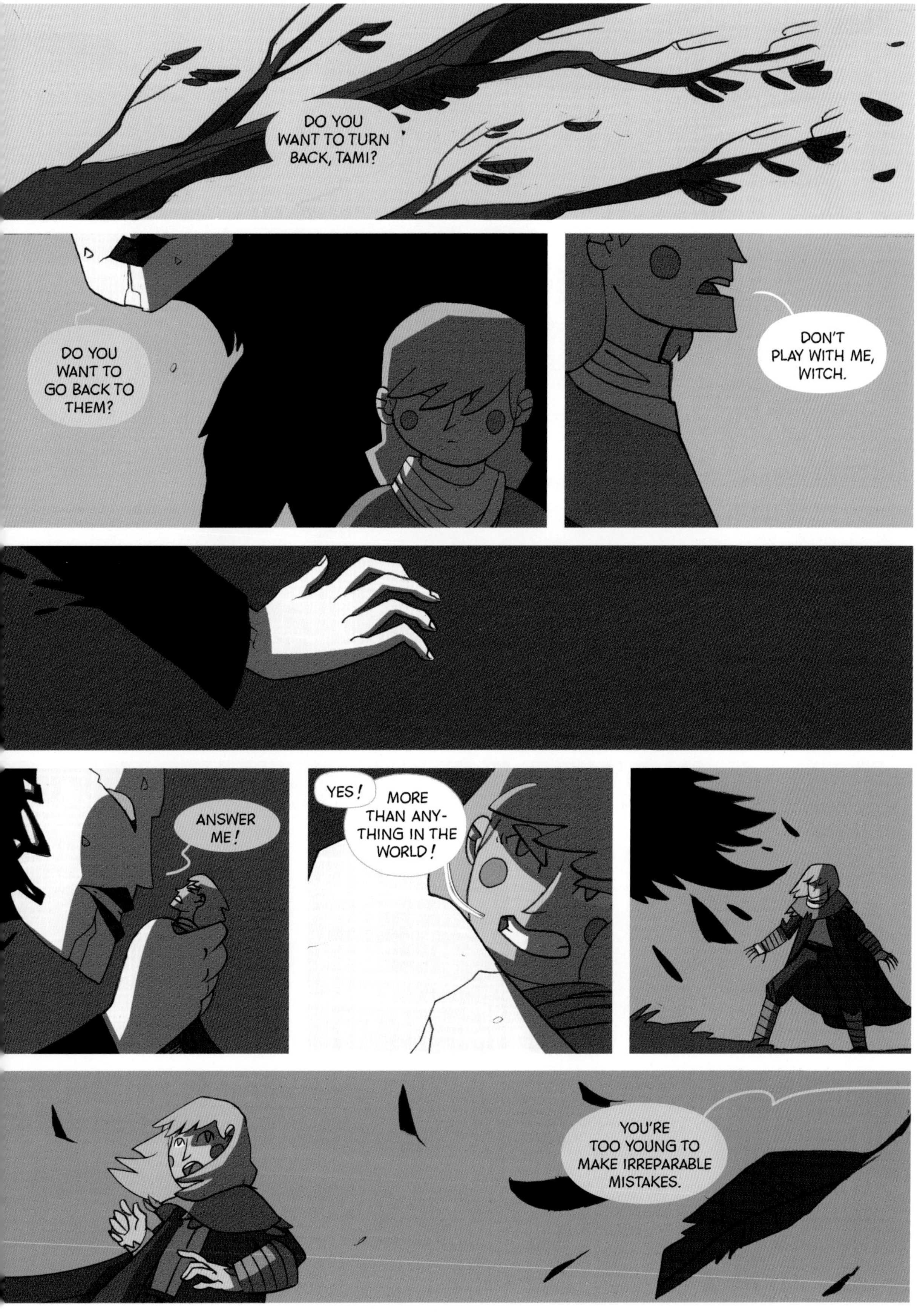
DO YOU WANT TO TURN BACK, TAMI?
DO YOU WANT TO GO BACK TO THEM?
DON'T PLAY WITH ME, WITCH.
ANSWER ME!
YES!
MORE THAN ANY-THING IN THE WORLD!
YOU'RE TOO YOUNG TO MAKE IRREPARABLE MISTAKES.

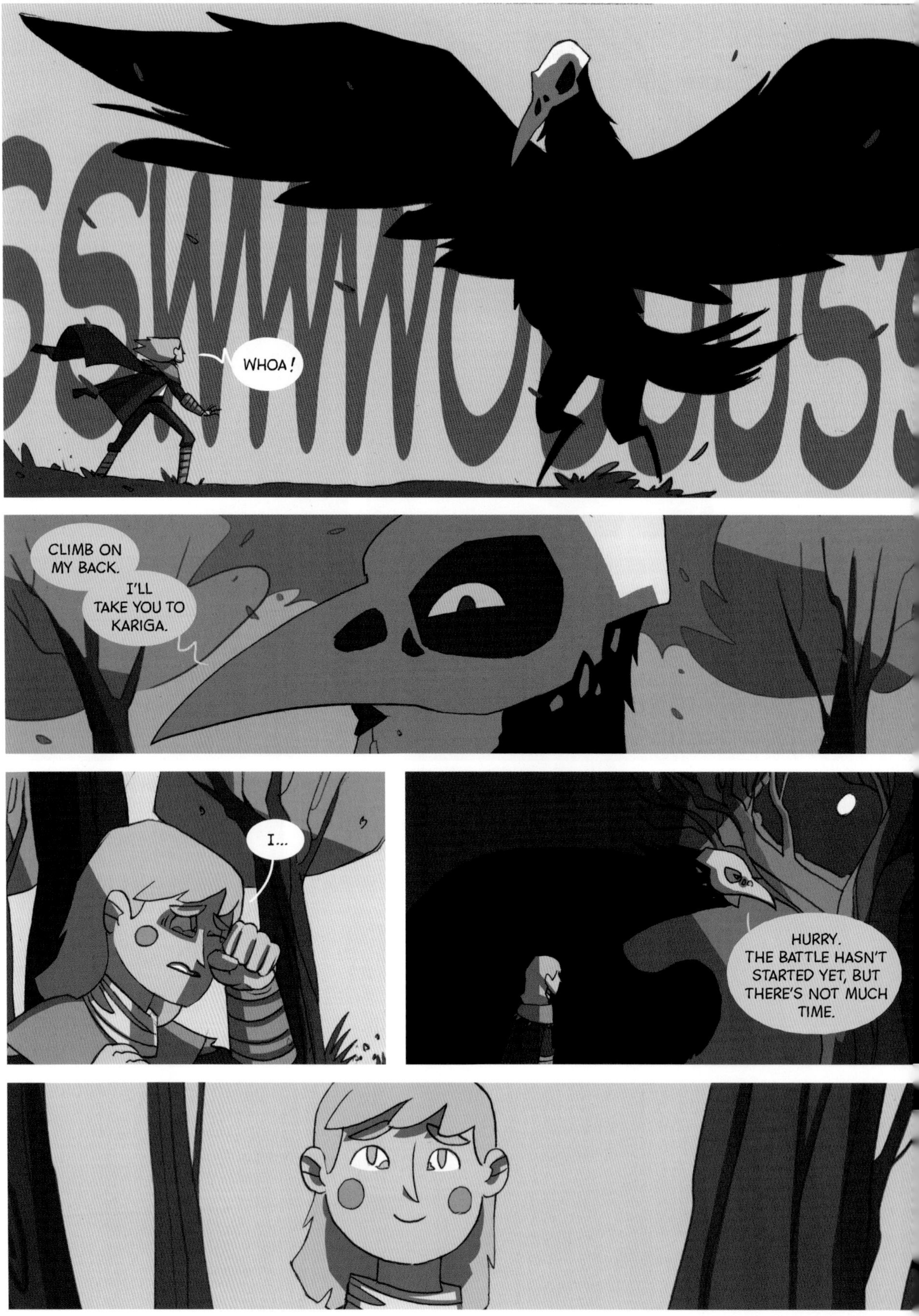
SSWWWOOOSS
WHOA!
CLIMB ON MY BACK.
I'LL TAKE YOU TO KARIGA.
I...
HURRY. THE BATTLE HASN'T STARTED YET, BUT THERE'S NOT MUCH TIME.

I'M NOT JUST HANDING YOU YOUR HAPPY ENDING.

YOU WILL SUFFER, AND YOU MAY FAIL.

AND EVEN IF YOU ARE VICTORIOUS IN BATTLE, YOUR CHOICES HAVE CONSEQUENCES.

FINE BY ME.

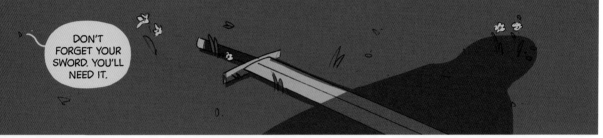

DON'T FORGET YOUR SWORD. YOU'LL NEED IT.

WITCHES AREN'T SO DIFFERENT FROM HUMANS, YOU KNOW.

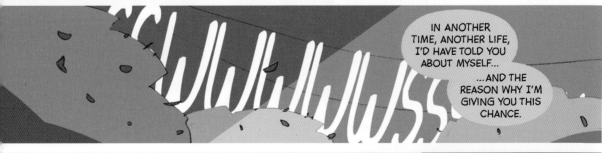

IN ANOTHER TIME, ANOTHER LIFE, I'D HAVE TOLD YOU ABOUT MYSELF...

...AND THE REASON WHY I'M GIVING YOU THIS CHANCE.

BUT THIS IS **YOUR** STORY.

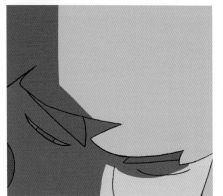

YOU REALIZE WHAT YOU HAVE TO DO, RIGHT?

YES, BUT I DON'T KNOW IF I CAN.

YOU'LL HAVE TO TRY.

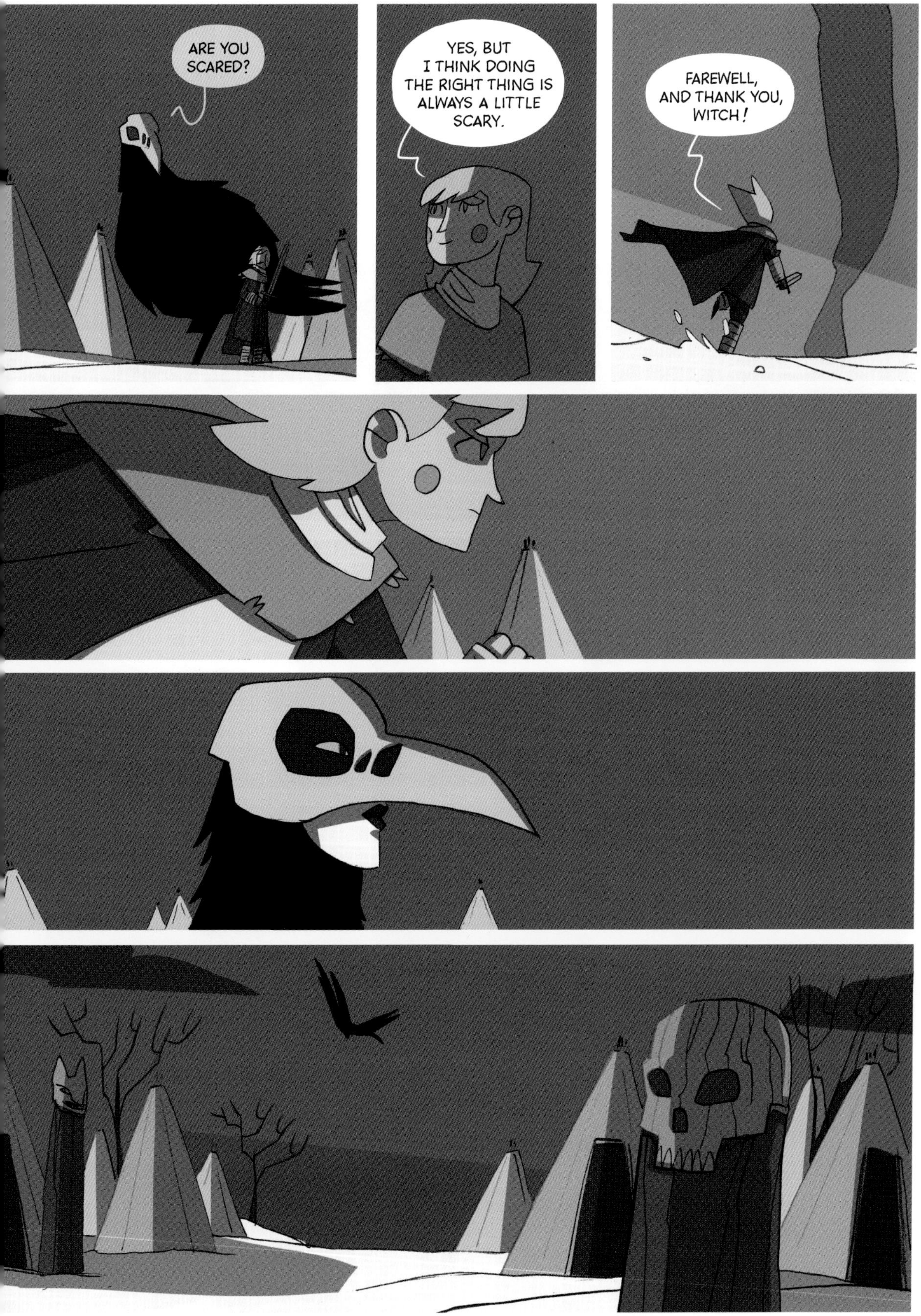
ARE YOU SCARED?
YES, BUT I THINK DOING THE RIGHT THING IS ALWAYS A LITTLE SCARY.
FAREWELL, AND THANK YOU, WITCH!

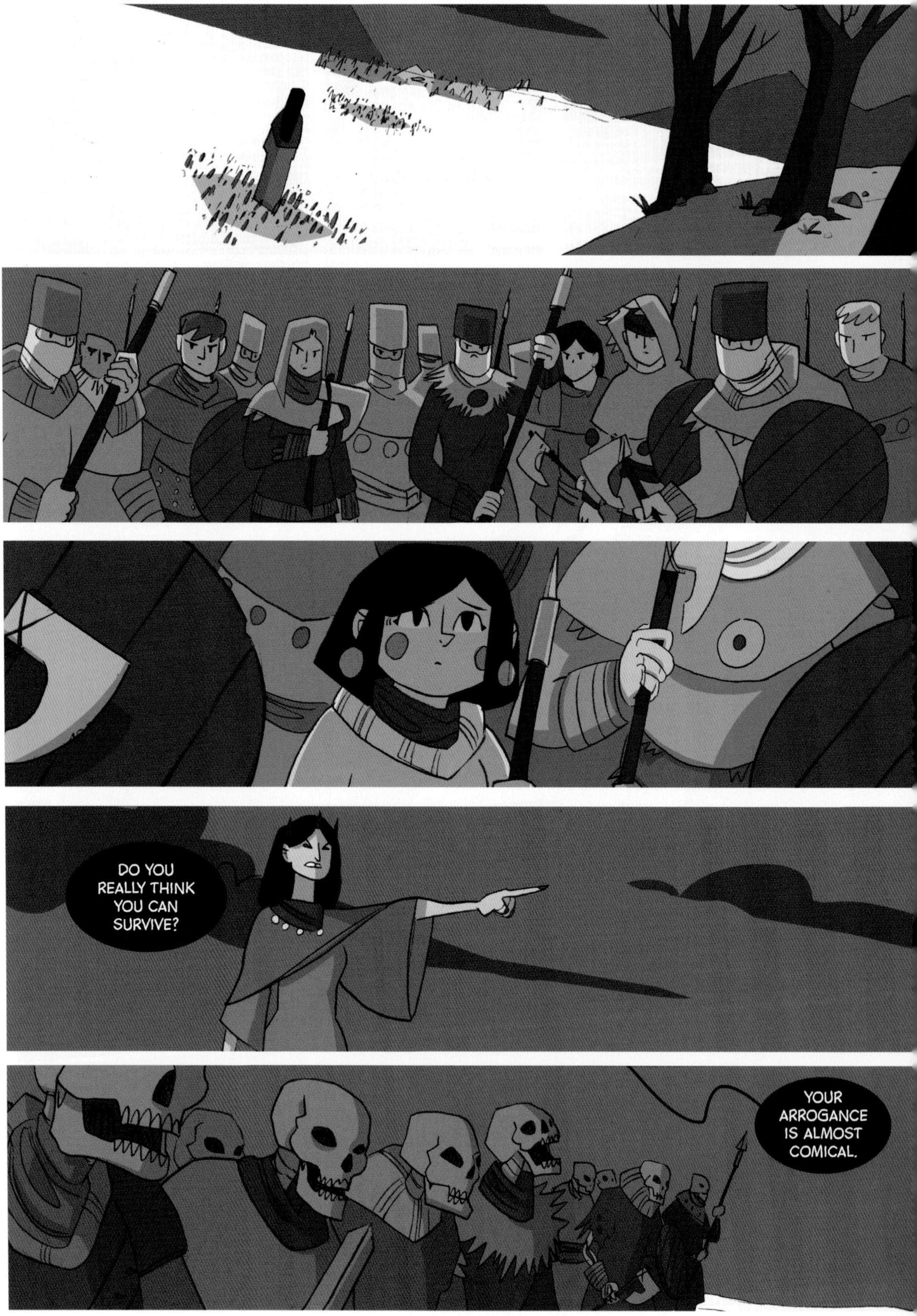
DO YOU REALLY THINK YOU CAN SURVIVE?
YOUR ARROGANCE IS ALMOST COMICAL.

YABRA!

I'M THE ONE WHO KILLED YOUR FATHER!

IF YOU WANT REVENGE...

...HERE I AM!

THE FOREIGNER.

HE'S BACK!

YOU FOOL!

≷SHUDDER≷

DO YOU REALLY THINK YOUR LIFE IS ENOUGH TO PAY FOR MY **FATHER'S?**

IT'S A START.

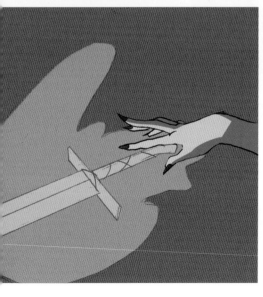

SO BE IT!

≷GULP≷

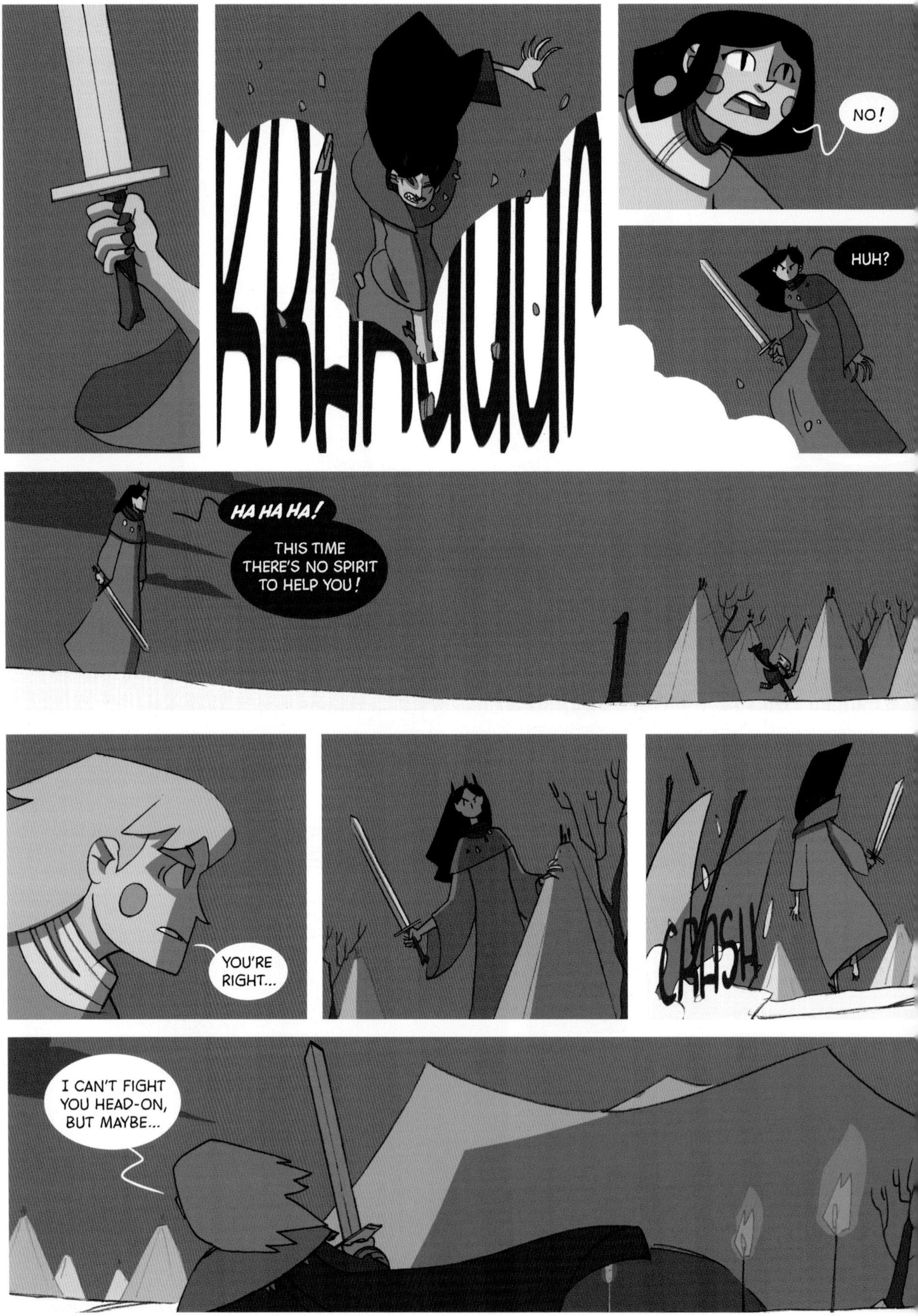
NO!
HUH?
HA HA HA!
THIS TIME THERE'S NO SPIRIT TO HELP YOU!
YOU'RE RIGHT...
CRASH
I CAN'T FIGHT YOU HEAD-ON, BUT MAYBE...

COME ON!

WE MUST TAKE THEM DOWN WHILE YABRA IS DISTRACTED BY THE BOY!

PAPA!

MIRA! WHY ARE YOU HERE?

W-WE HAVE TO HELP TAMI!

LET'S GO.

HE'S STRONG, BUT HE WON'T LAST LONG AGAINST YABRA.

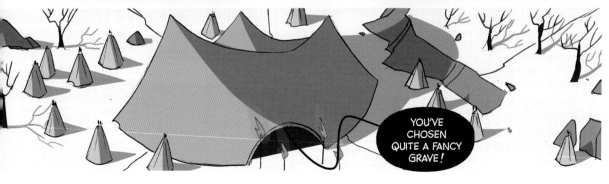
YOU'VE CHOSEN QUITE A FANCY GRAVE!

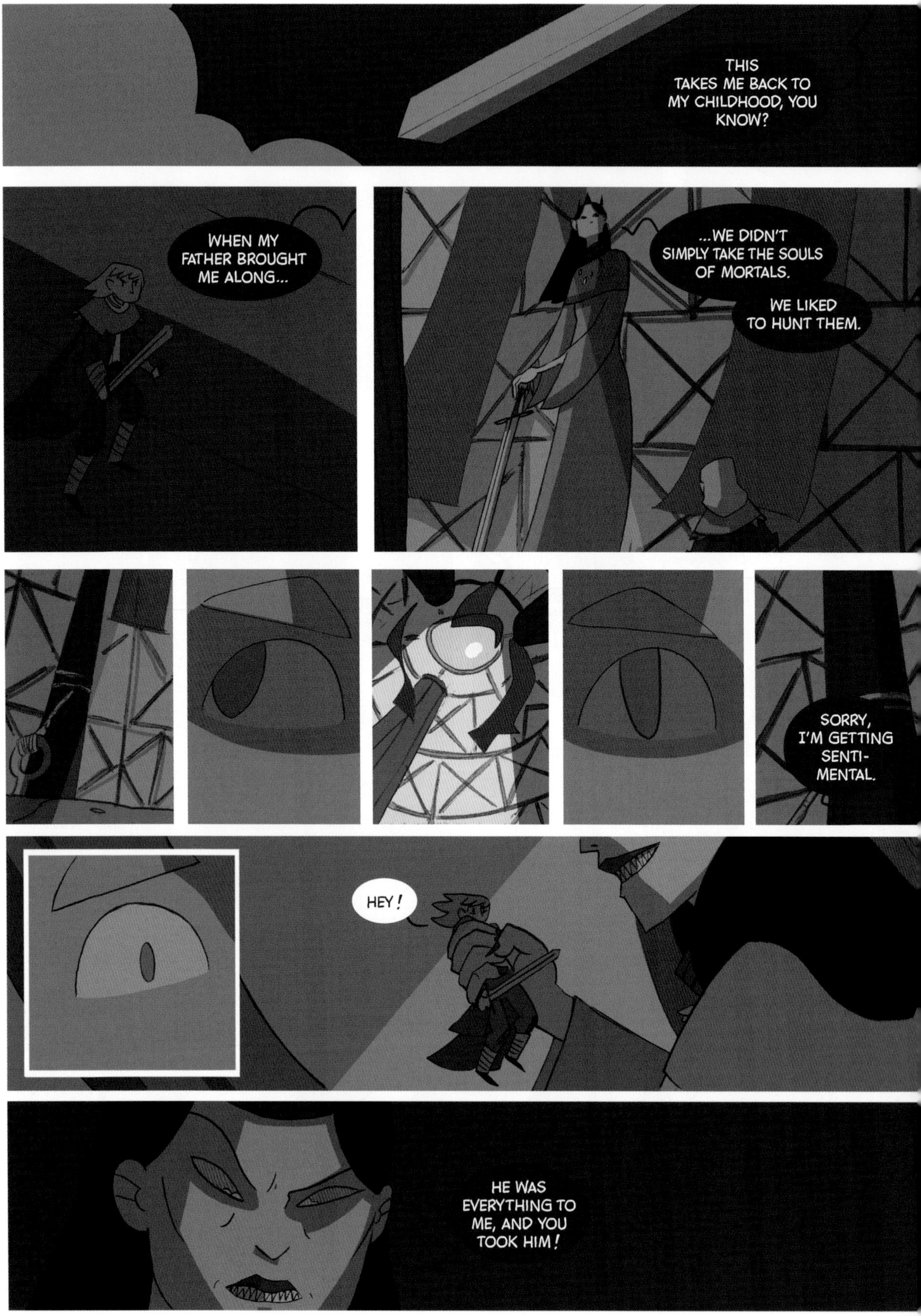
THIS TAKES ME BACK TO MY CHILDHOOD, YOU KNOW?
WHEN MY FATHER BROUGHT ME ALONG...
...WE DIDN'T SIMPLY TAKE THE SOULS OF MORTALS.
WE LIKED TO HUNT THEM.
SORRY, I'M GETTING SENTI- MENTAL.
HEY!
HE WAS EVERYTHING TO ME, AND YOU TOOK HIM!

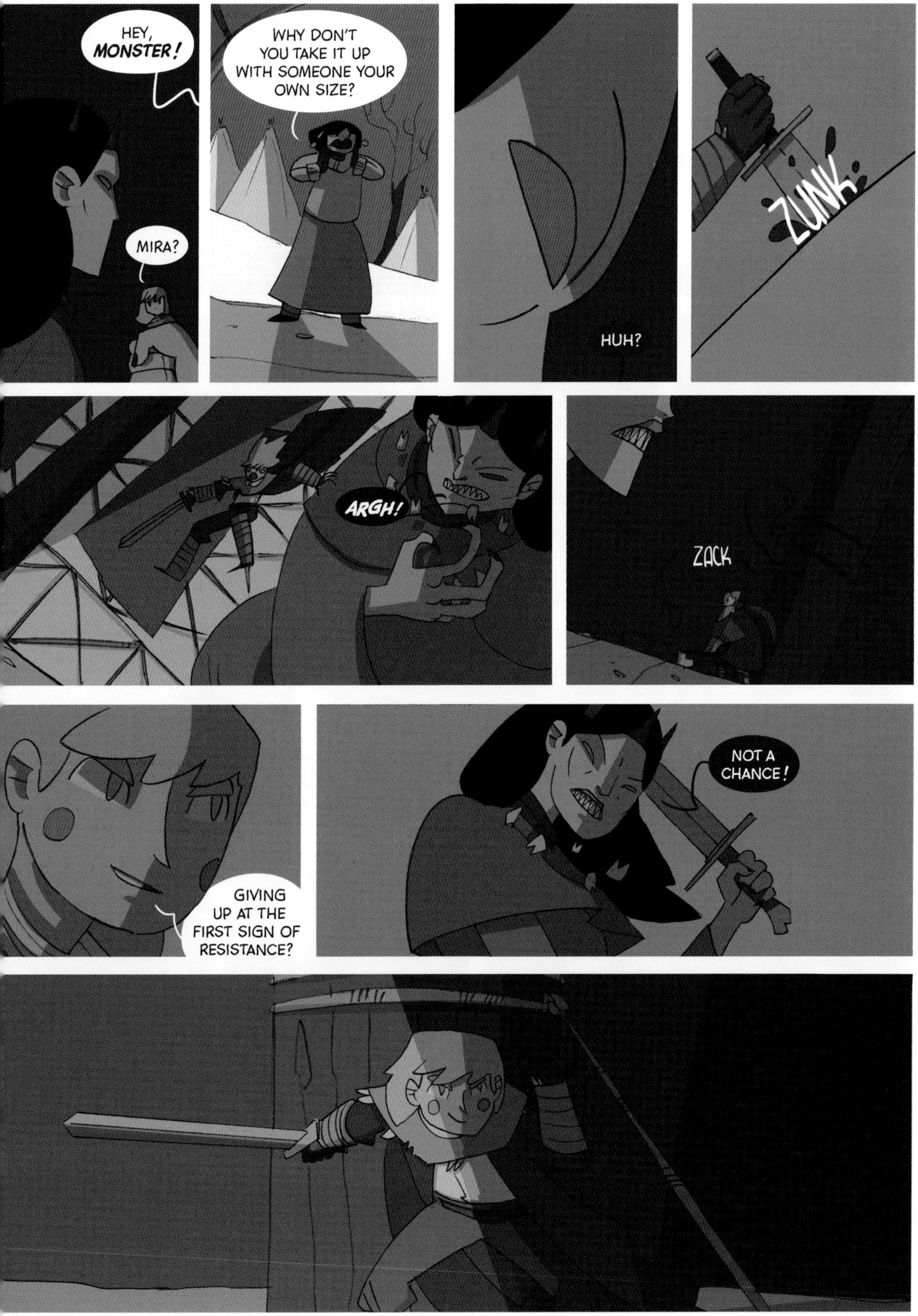
HEY, MONSTER!
WHY DON'T YOU TAKE IT UP WITH SOMEONE YOUR OWN SIZE?
MIRA?
HUH?
ZUNK
ARGH!
ZACK
GIVING UP AT THE FIRST SIGN OF RESISTANCE?
NOT A CHANCE!

MISSED!

HURRY, PAPA!

GOT IT!

NOW THE SUPPORTS SHOULD START TO WOBBLE.

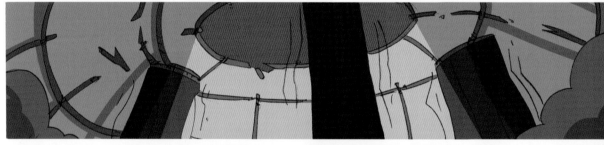

IT WORKED!

HURRY UP, TAMI!

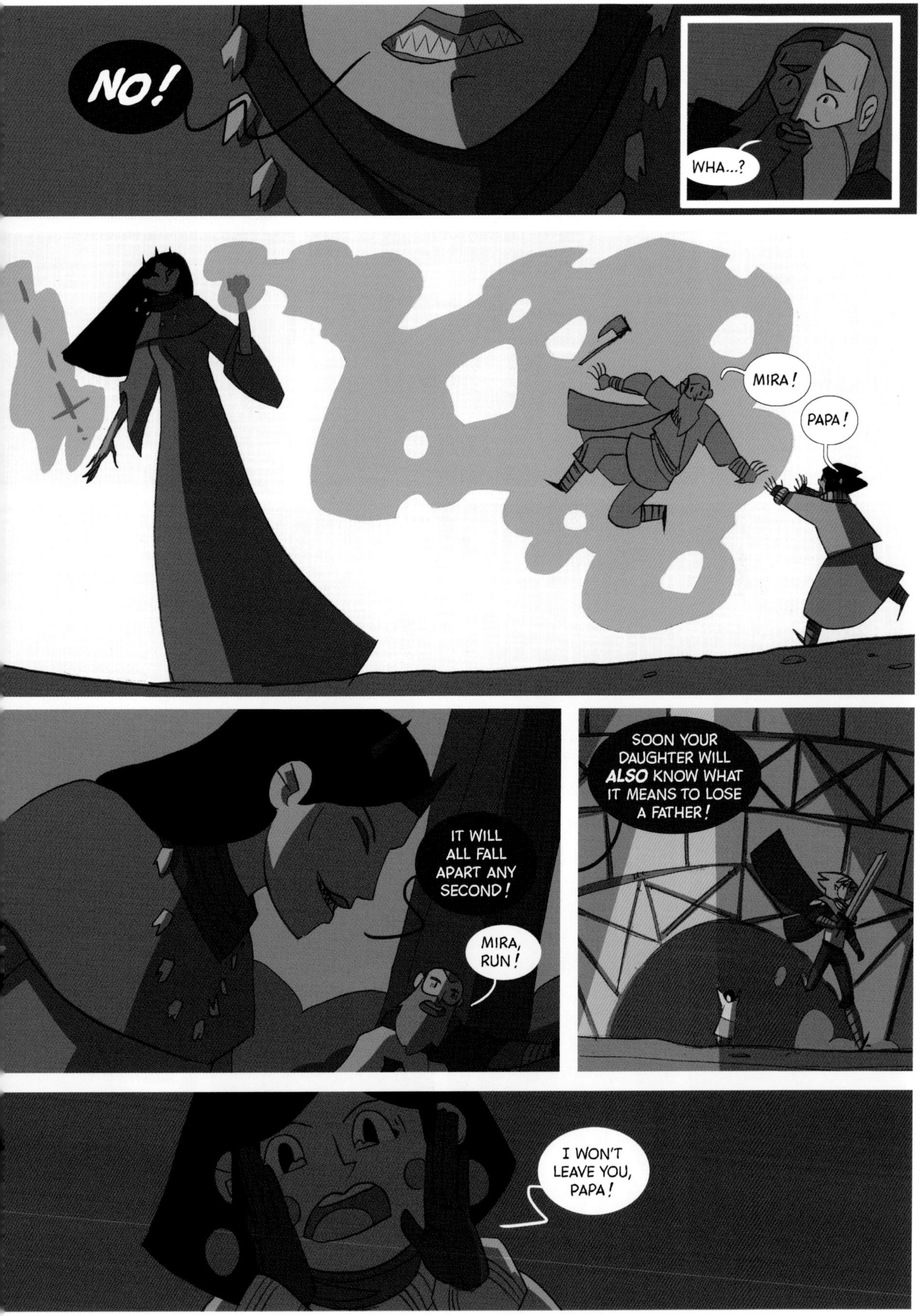
NO!
WHA...?
MIRA!
PAPA!
IT WILL ALL FALL APART ANY SECOND!
MIRA, RUN!
SOON YOUR DAUGHTER WILL ALSO KNOW WHAT IT MEANS TO LOSE A FATHER!
I WON'T LEAVE YOU, PAPA!

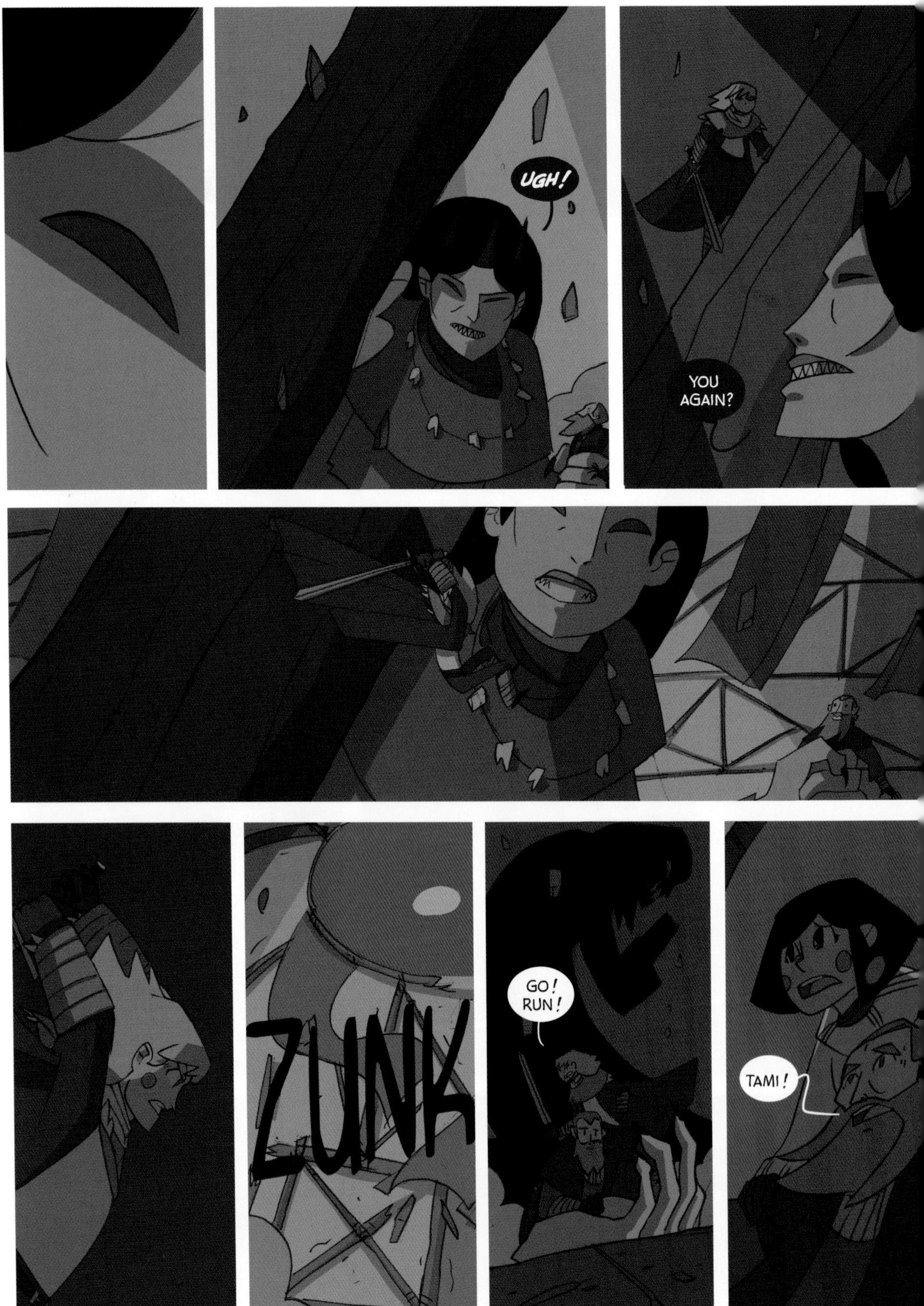
UGH!
YOU AGAIN?
ZUNK
GO! RUN!
TAMI!

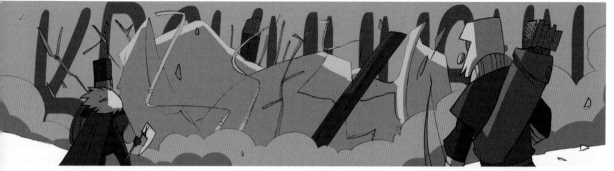

EEMIL!

MIRA!

ARE YOU OKAY?

IS ANYONE HURT?

TAMI IS...

TAMI IS BACK THERE WITH YABRA!

SFSSSHHHH

LOOK, OVER THERE!

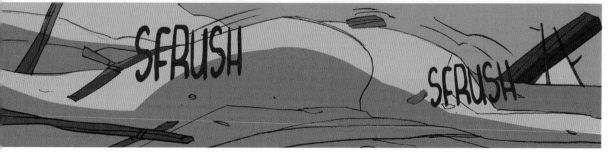

SFRUSH

SFRUSH

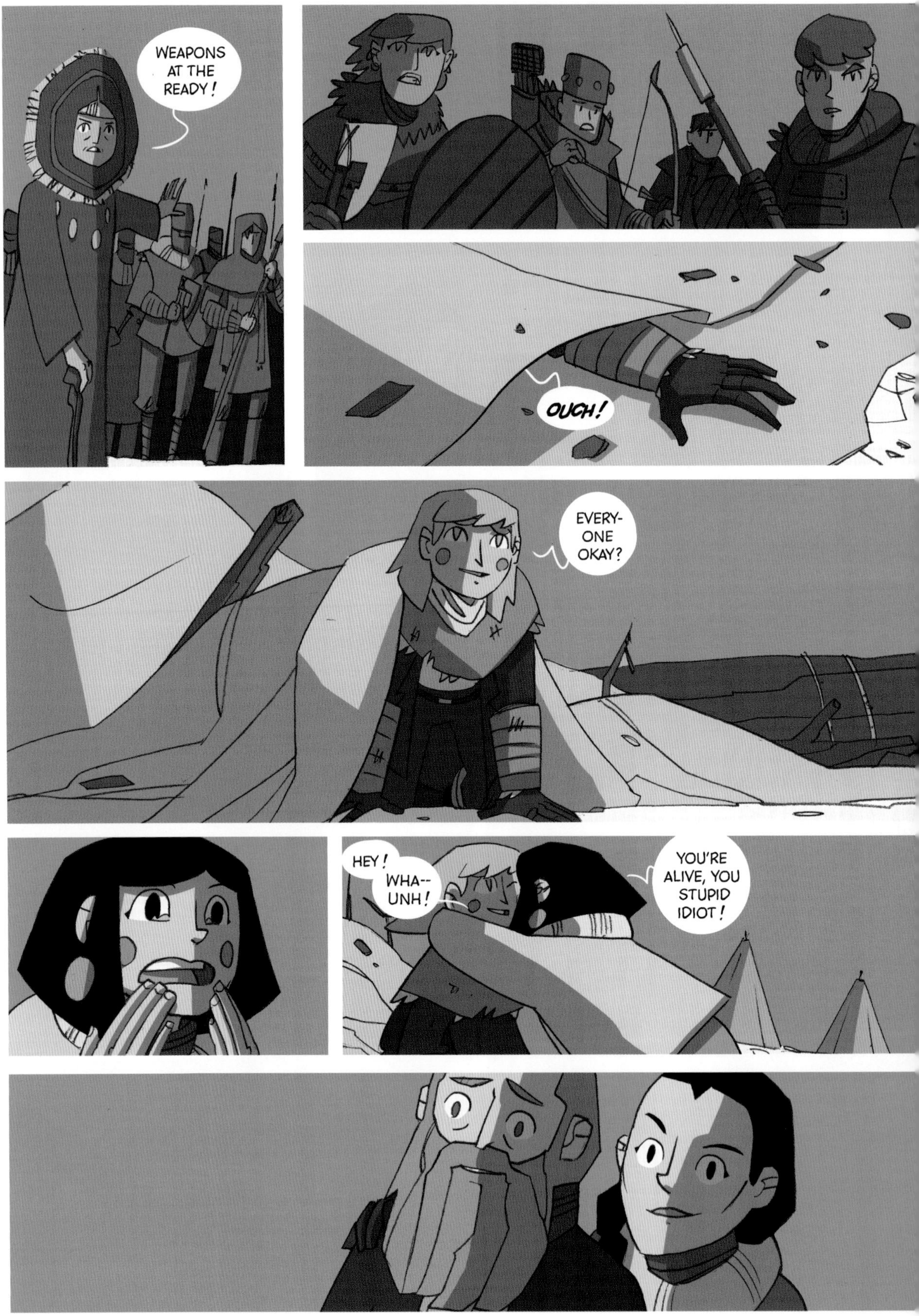
WEAPONS AT THE READY!
OUCH!
EVERY-ONE OKAY?
HEY!
WHA--UNH!
YOU'RE ALIVE, YOU STUPID IDIOT!

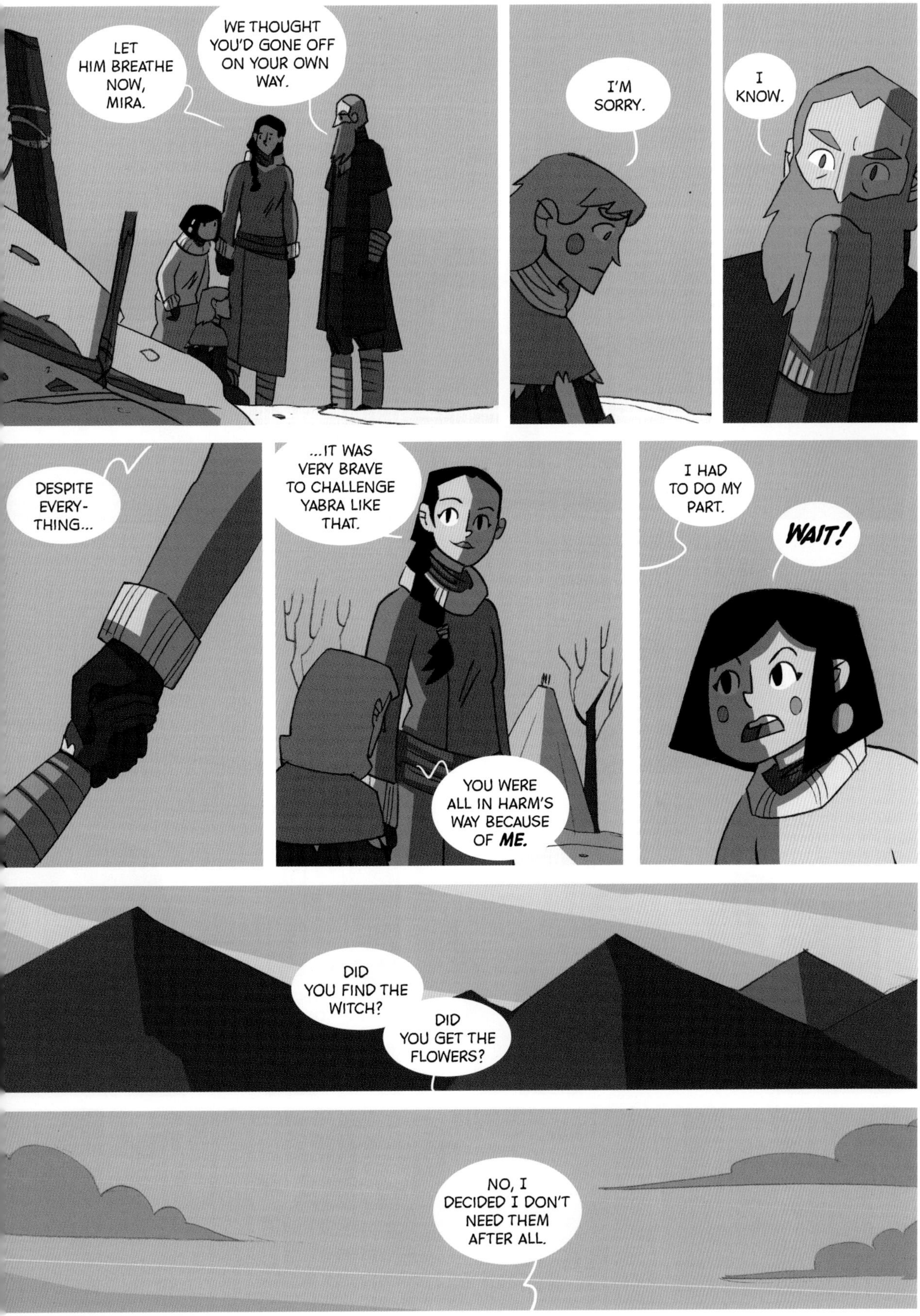
LET HIM BREATHE NOW, MIRA.
WE THOUGHT YOU'D GONE OFF ON YOUR OWN WAY.
I'M SORRY.
I KNOW.
DESPITE EVERY-THING...
...IT WAS VERY BRAVE TO CHALLENGE YABRA LIKE THAT.
YOU WERE ALL IN HARM'S WAY BECAUSE OF ME.
I HAD TO DO MY PART.
WAIT!
DID YOU FIND THE WITCH?
DID YOU GET THE FLOWERS?
NO, I DECIDED I DON'T NEED THEM AFTER ALL.

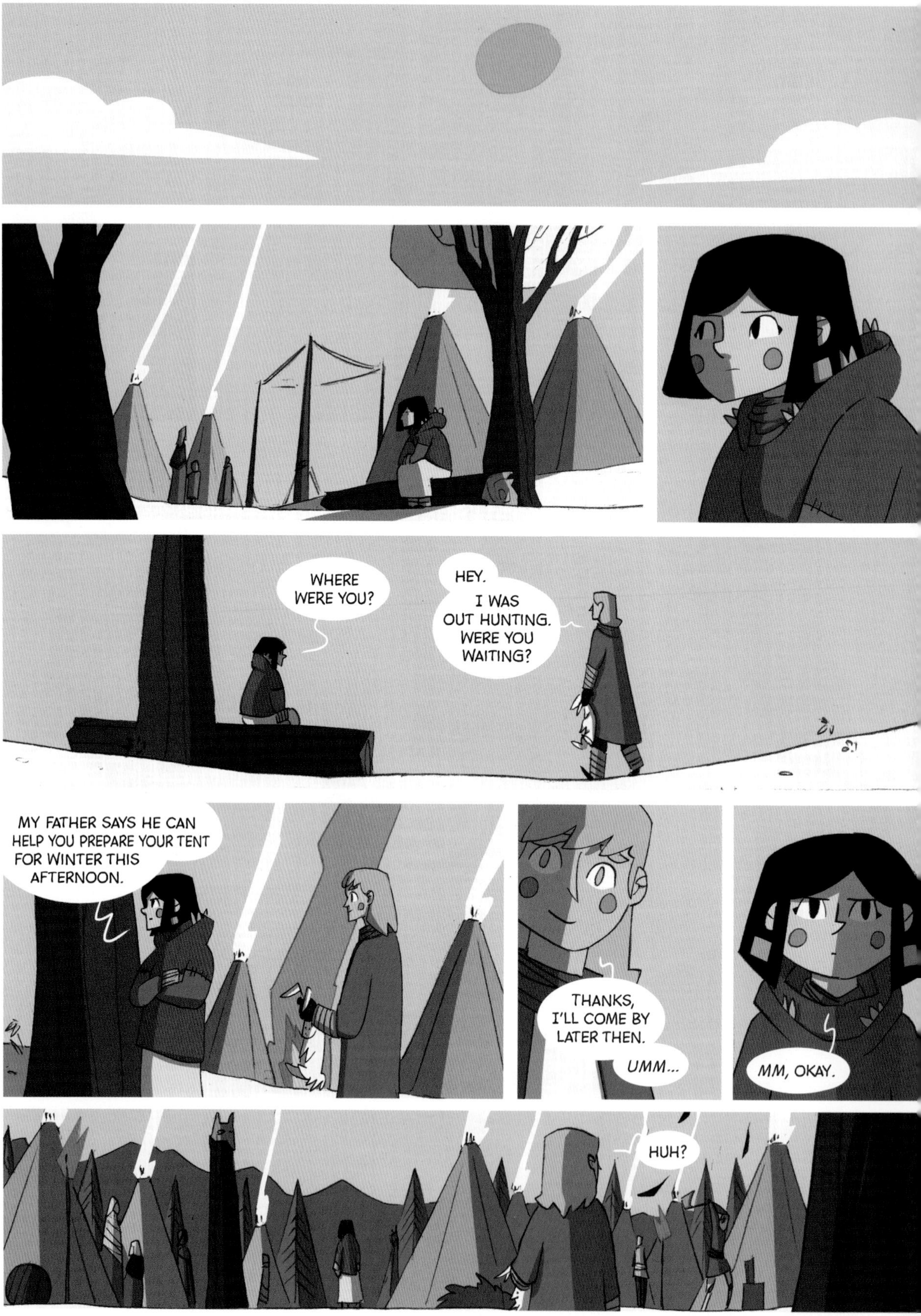
WHERE WERE YOU?
HEY.
I WAS OUT HUNTING. WERE YOU WAITING?
MY FATHER SAYS HE CAN HELP YOU PREPARE YOUR TENT FOR WINTER THIS AFTERNOON.
THANKS, I'LL COME BY LATER THEN.
UMM...
MM, OKAY.
HUH?

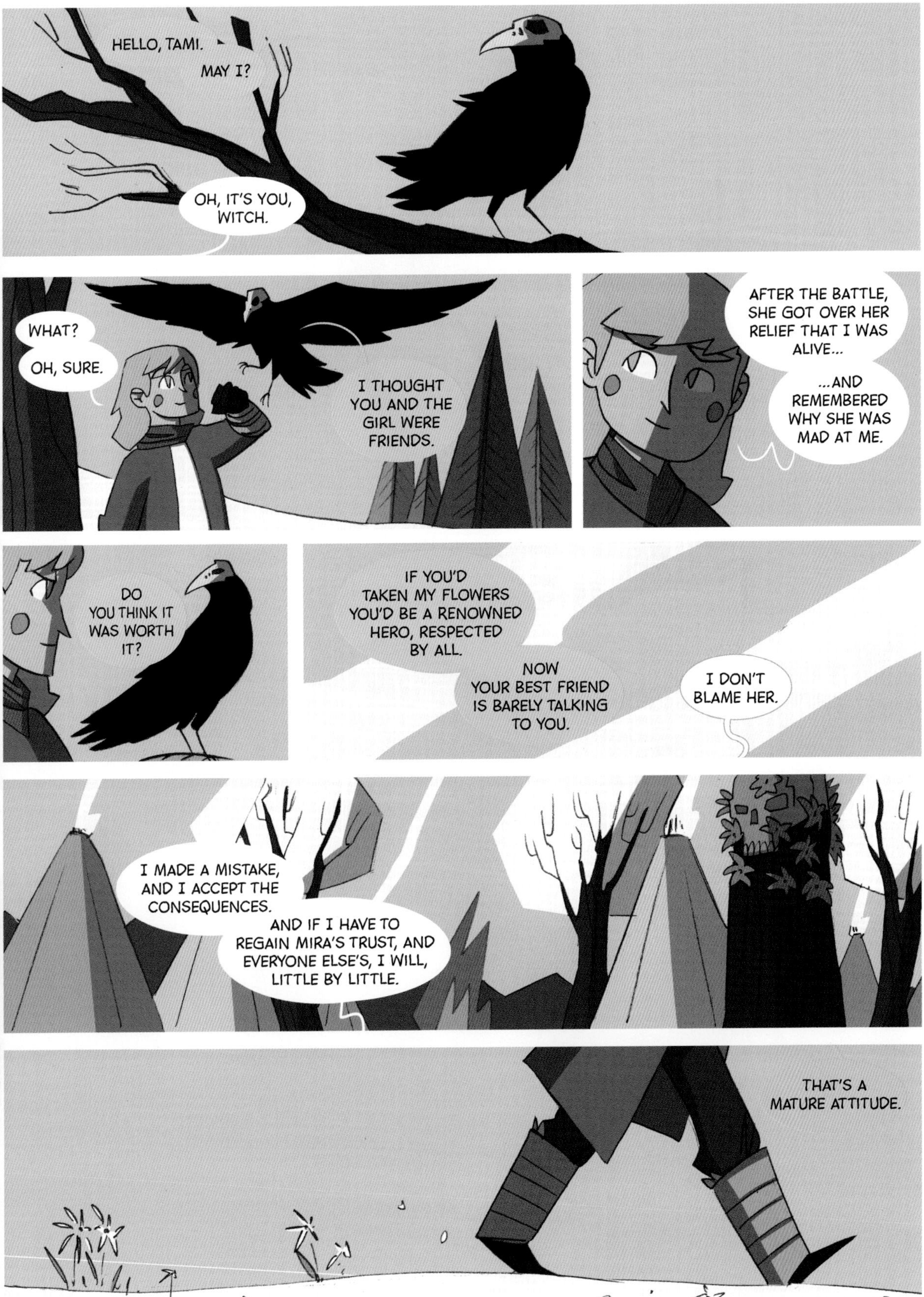
HELLO, TAMI.
MAY I?
OH, IT'S YOU, WITCH.
WHAT?
OH, SURE.
I THOUGHT YOU AND THE GIRL WERE FRIENDS.
AFTER THE BATTLE, SHE GOT OVER HER RELIEF THAT I WAS ALIVE...
...AND REMEMBERED WHY SHE WAS MAD AT ME.
DO YOU THINK IT WAS WORTH IT?
IF YOU'D TAKEN MY FLOWERS YOU'D BE A RENOWNED HERO, RESPECTED BY ALL.
NOW YOUR BEST FRIEND IS BARELY TALKING TO YOU.
I DON'T BLAME HER.
I MADE A MISTAKE, AND I ACCEPT THE CONSEQUENCES.
AND IF I HAVE TO REGAIN MIRA'S TRUST, AND EVERYONE ELSE'S, I WILL, LITTLE BY LITTLE.
THAT'S A MATURE ATTITUDE.

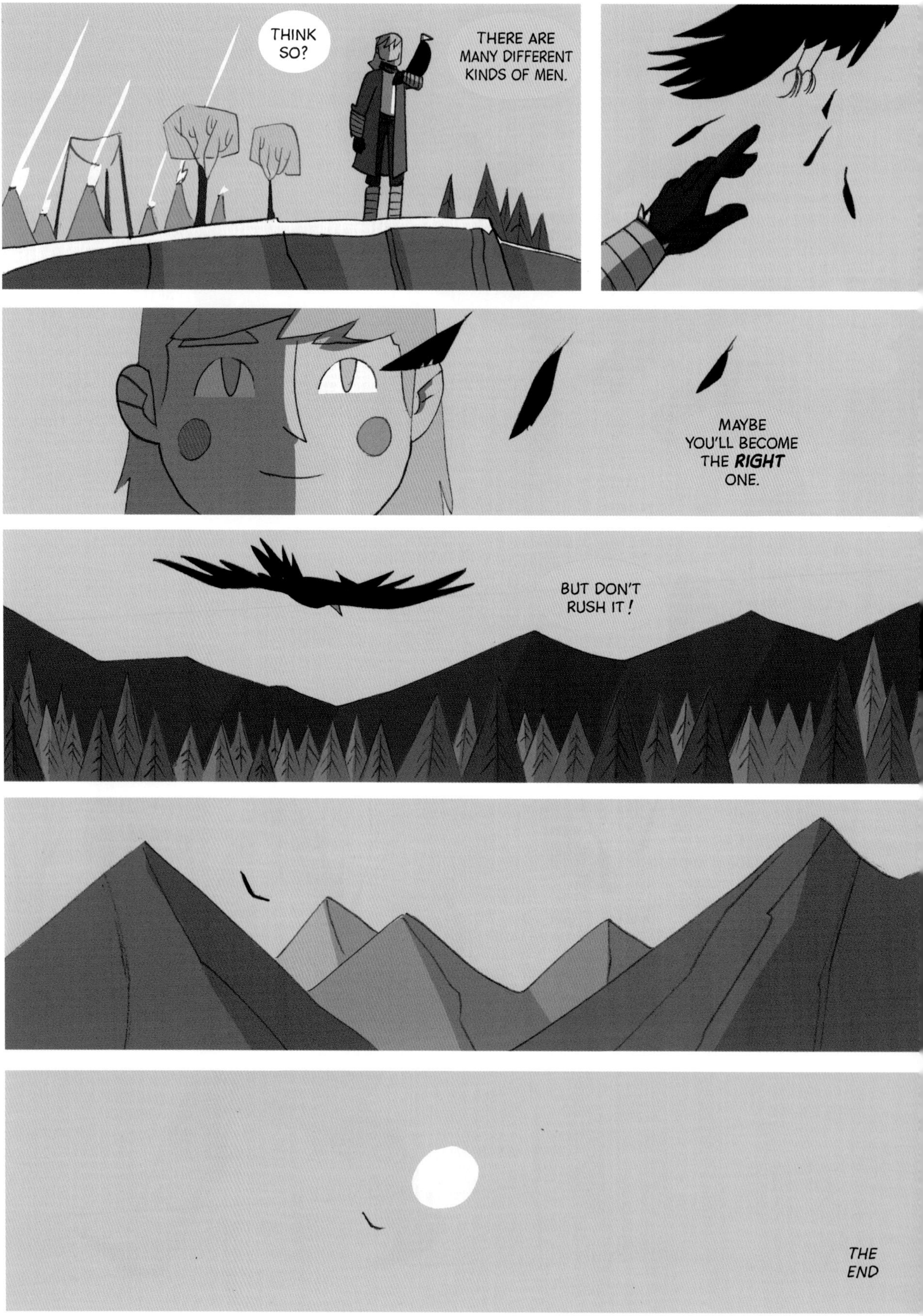
THERE ARE MANY DIFFERENT KINDS OF MEN.
THINK SO?
MAYBE YOU'LL BECOME THE **RIGHT** ONE.
BUT DON'T RUSH IT!
THE END

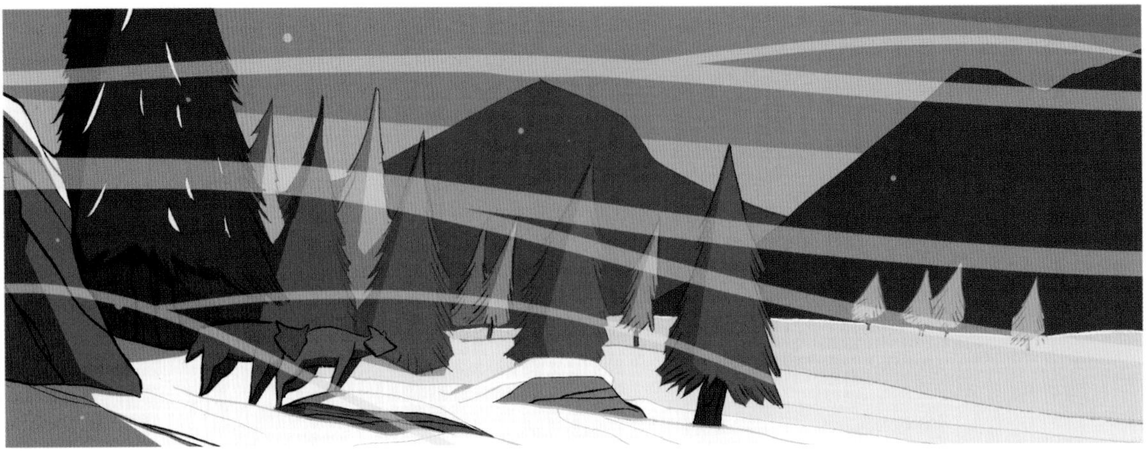

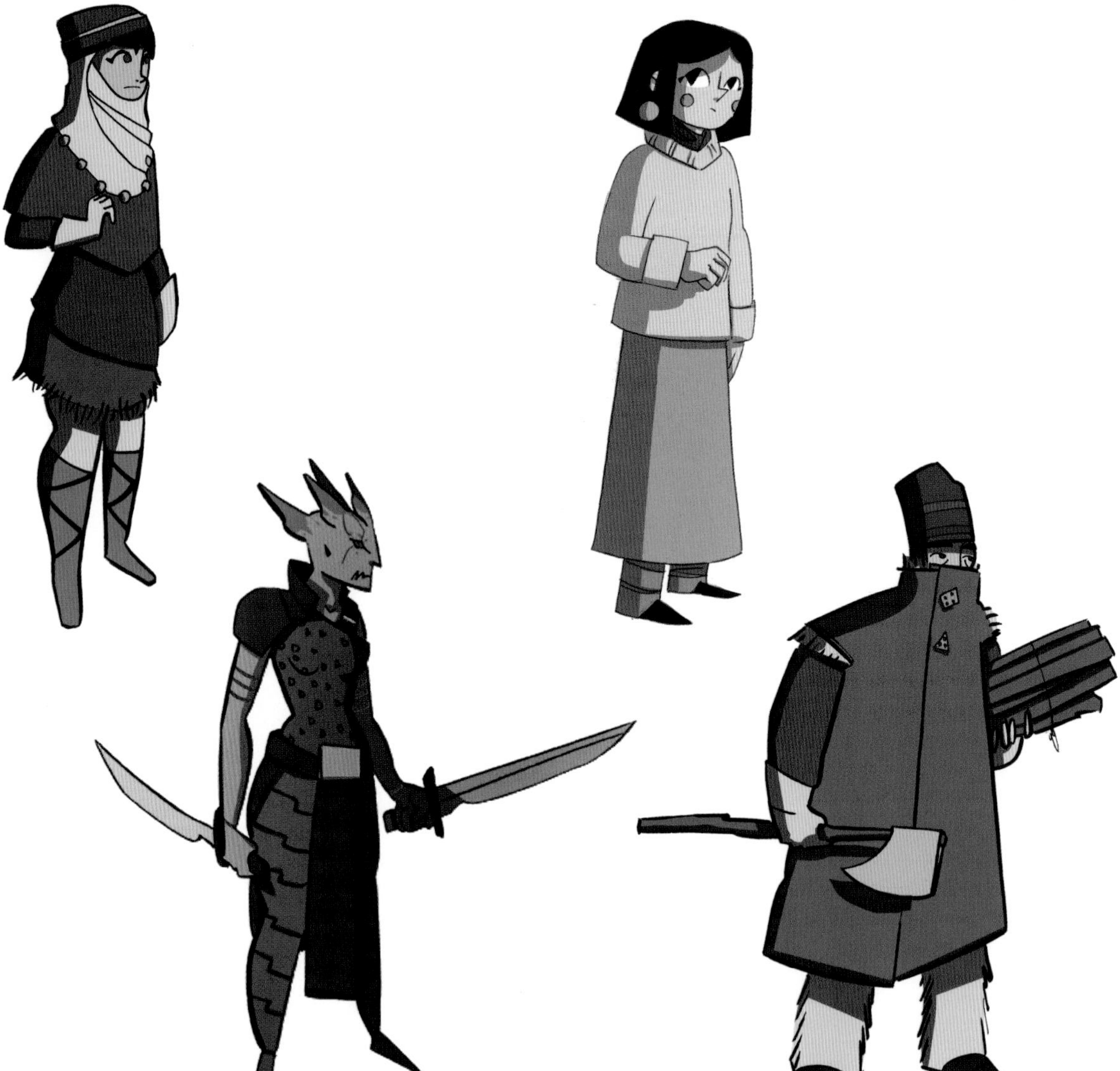

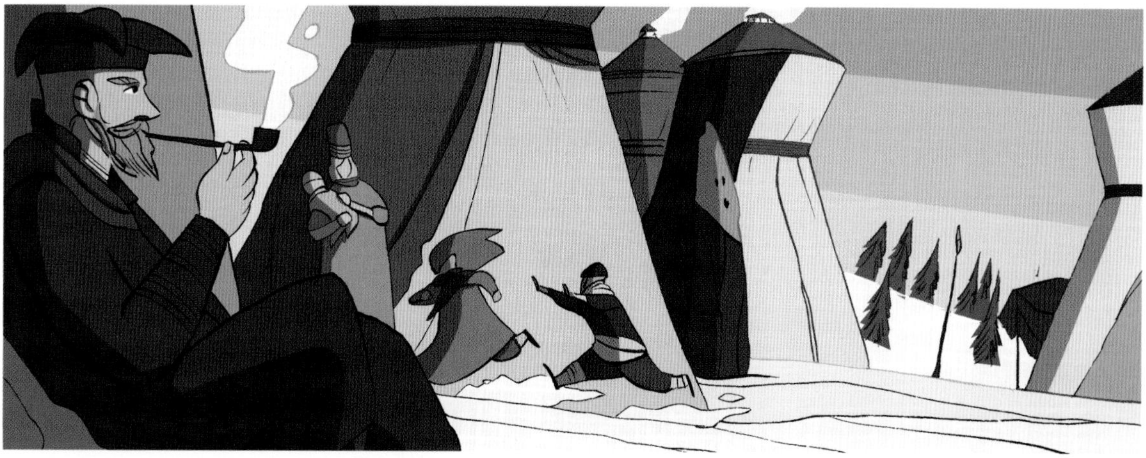

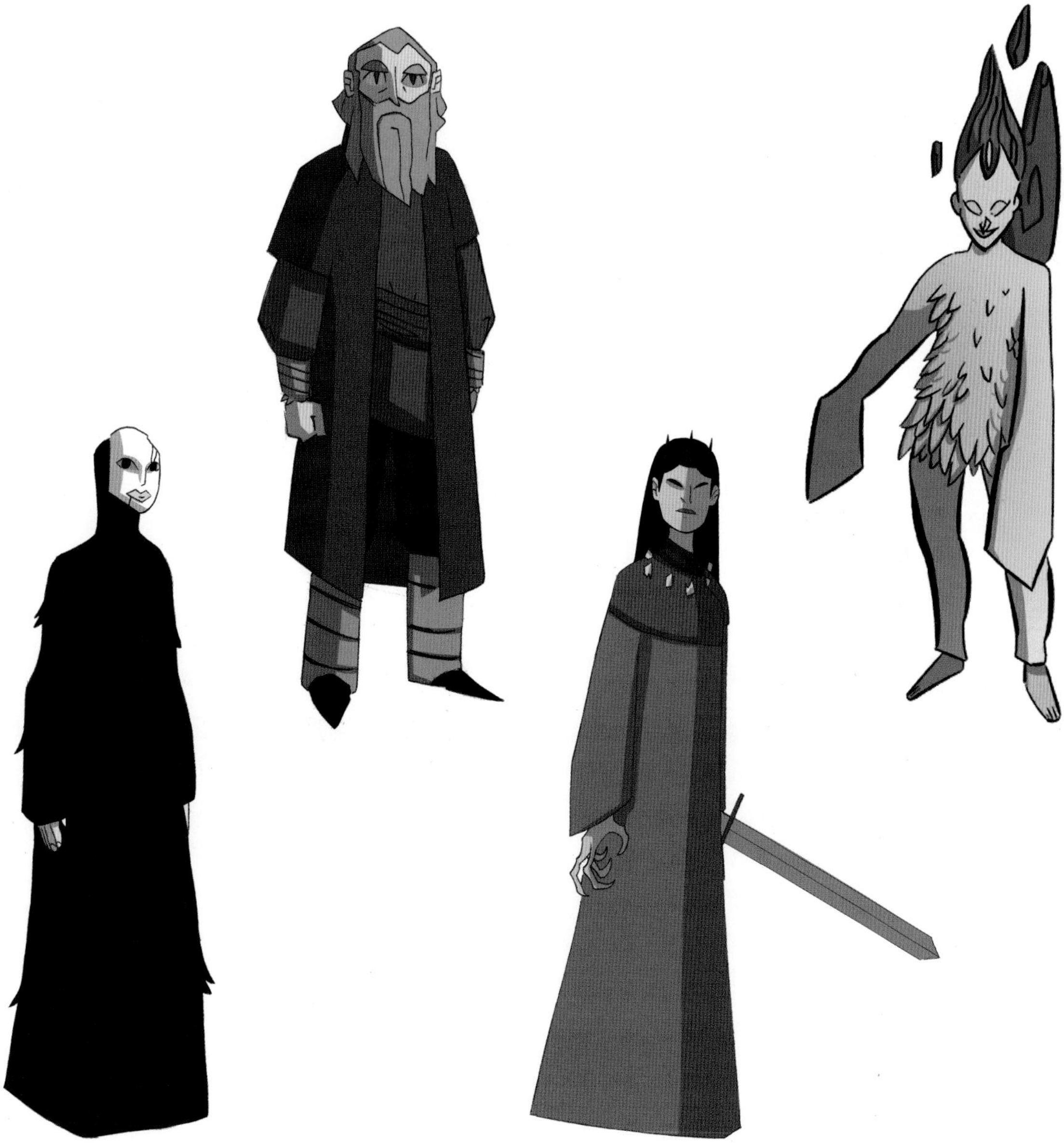

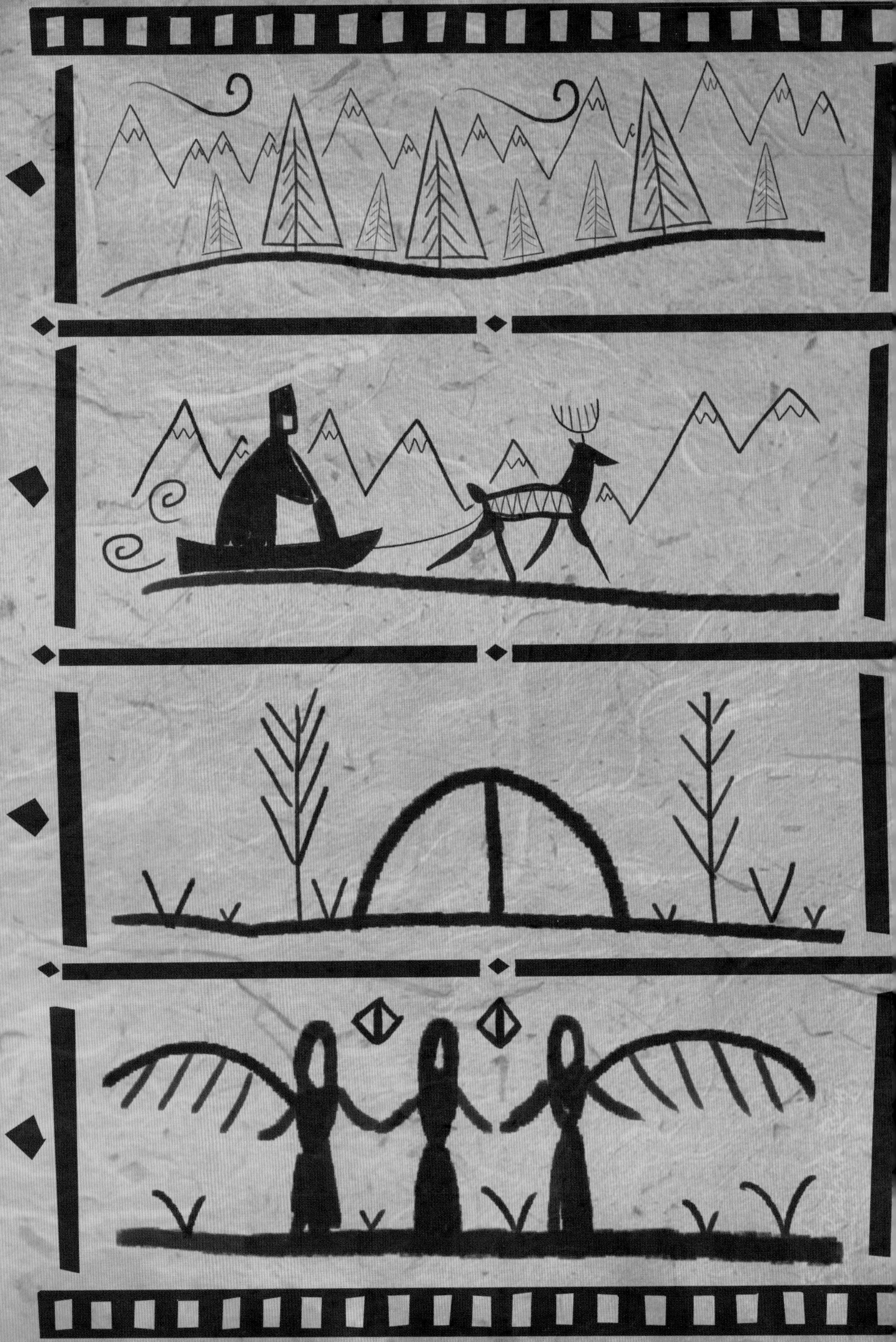